TRIPPING THROUGH

BY MICHELLE LARA MORGAN

For Peter, Kiara, Leilani & Kai

VALENTINE'S DAY

"What the hell is going on, Karly?" he demanded as he stormed in, slamming the front door of our small walk-up apartment behind him.

"Pardon?" I yelled back across the kitchen through the smoke, wondering if I'd heard him right. It wasn't the response I'd expected to the cheery "Happy Valentine's Day, sweetie" I'd called out when I'd heard the key in the lock, especially after all my efforts to make this a special night for us. I'd probably misheard him over the nerve-rattling beep of the fire alarm.

My plan had been to surprise him with freshly baked, heart-shaped cookies upon his return from the video store. I'd bought what should have been an idiot-proof instant bake package; the wrapper even promised, "Baking fun for ages three and up, under an adult's supervision." Maybe I should have invited another adult over to supervise me.

The TV program I'd had on in the background had momentarily sidetracked me-World's Funniest Animal Videos, who wouldn't have been distracted by a monkey in a space helmet playing the banjo? -and I'd totally forgotten I had something in the oven. Until an ad for Weight Watchers came on and I'd thought, *Mmm, I would love something sweet right now. Oh crap.*

He'd walked in while I was trying to get the cookie sheet out of the oven using a dishrag and spatula.

Why did they make fire alarms so annoyingly loud? Maybe I should invent one with soothing, dulcet tones, for regular listeners like me. The burning sensation in my hand yanked me back to reality and I dropped the hot tray on a stack of papers on the kitchen table, and then turned to him. Was it my imagination, or did he look really pissed off? I ducked beneath the black cloud of smoke that filled the top third of our kitchenette to get a better look. He appeared to be furious. That didn't make any sense. If it hadn't been a regular occurrence, my latest botched kitchen efforts might have been the cause for this set off, but he'd gotten used to my culinary limitations almost two years ago, after our first couple of months together.

What could have happened in the twenty minutes since he'd taken my car to the video store? Had they been out of those large Kit Kats he so loved? Had they refused to let him get new DVDs out until he paid the two-dollar late charge he owed from four months ago?

The smoke was probably stinging his eyes and making him screw his face up like that, I decided as I leaned over the kitchen table to wrestle open the heavy window. And he was obviously just yelling so I could hear him over the fire alarm. I stepped up on a chair, reached up and yanked the battery out of it. Ahh, quiet. Glancing at the oven, I saw that the spatula had melted onto the rack. Sighing, I picked up a serving spoon to try and pry it off, before it solidified and became a permanent part of the oven.

"Who is this Sam Schaeffer?" he shouted.

Why was he still yelling? Had he temporarily lost his hearing from the fire alarm? Maybe Sam Schaeffer was an actor in one of the DVDs he'd rented.

"I don't know, honey," I answered as I leaned over and scraped at the spatula while taking cookie inventory in my head. There were six more in the package, although why set myself up for disappointment again? Why hadn't I gone with my first instinct and just bought a package of Oreos?

"I'm sick of you lying to me, Karly! I've had it! First it was Nik-"

"What?" I straightened up and looked at him. Nik was a childhood friend of mine that I hadn't seen for ages.

"Then you were screwing around with Bob—"

"But I told you there was nothing going on between us."

"Whatever."

The drama of the heart-shaped cookies didn't seem so important anymore.

"But…I explained it all to you and you said you understood."

"Well, I changed my mind."

"And now you think I'm cheating on you with someone named Sam?"

"Stop playing dumb, Karly. I know you've gone to a lawyer to protect your assets and get rid of me or something."

"What are you talking about? We're not even married."

He waved a business card in front of me.

"Stop your bullshit, Karly, I found this in your car."

I squinted at the card, trying to bring it into focus, my eyes still stinging from the smoke. Oh. No wonder he'd thought…he'd laugh after I explained, and then we could get back to our romantic Valentine's Day celebration.

"I knew it," he said, grabbing me by my shoulders and thrusting his face within two inches of mine so that I could smell his strong, black licorice breath. "You stupid, lying cow. You screwed around with Bob and Nik and lied right to my face about it. And now you've gone and got yourself a divorce lawyer, haven't you?"

I wanted the fire alarm back on so I didn't have to hear the horrible words he was screaming into my face. Why wasn't he giving me a chance to explain? Surely he knew I wasn't that kind of person.

Tears streamed down my face. Maybe it was because I was tired of him not trusting me, exhausted from reassuring him all the time, and right then, just wanted the yelling to stop. I'm not sure what came over me, but I closed my eyes and heard myself whisper, "Yes. I cheated on you."

ME, THE STRANGENESS ATTRACTER

You know how some girls just have that "special something?" The way they move, their contagious smiles, or dazzling eyes that brighten the whole room? That certain "je ne sais quoi" that, if they were in a TV movie of the week, would justify slow motion hair-tossing and mushy orchestra music in the background?

That was so not me. Or to be fair, maybe it was, but anyone observing me was likely to be distracted by the escalator ripping my skirt down to my knees to expose my cow print panties, the automatic doors to the supermarket bizarrely choosing not to open just for me, or the shadow of the seagull swooping over my head and choosing that very moment to…well, you get the picture.

These kinds of unfortunate events plagued me on a weekly basis, resulting in my friends nicknaming me the "Strangeness Attracter."

As a result, I tried to make a point of wearing underwear that was fit for public viewing and made sure I was up to date on my tetanus shots. Worse than the physical disasters I got myself into, I seemed to have a knack for saying the wrong thing at the wrong time to the wrong person.

Other than that, I, Karly Masterson, was your typical twenty-nine-year-old, living in a little apartment in North Vancouver and dealing with regular day-to-day challenges. Well, besides the fact that I'd just been dumped because of an affair I didn't actually have, of course. Oh, and there was also that little matter of destroying my career. And my best friend, Nik, wasn't talking to me.

But other than those trivial details, everything was fine. Yep, just fine.

THE NON-AFFAIR

What led up to the split? Well, that came about in a way that would only make sense in my world.

I'd been helping my friend Bob plan a surprise anniversary party for his wife, Shannon. Apparently the Ex had been eavesdropping when I'd phoned and told Bob to open up a new email account so his wife couldn't find out what we were up to.

Bob left a voice message for me: "Karly, I just invited my entire hockey team so we may have to move to a larger venue. Can you come check out the Hotel Georgia with me this afternoon? I keep inviting people. I'm outta control!"

I shot him an email - "Got your message. Aren't we sneaky? Shannon will never catch on. I'll meet you at the hotel at one o'clock. Try to control yourself in the meantime."

Bob wanted to surprise Shannon by being able to ballroom dance with her at the party and had begged me to take lessons with him. I warned him of the risk but it turned out Bob was almost as uncoordinated as I was, so we were a good match. Or a bad match, if you were Madame Chretien, our instructor.

Bob had enrolled us in dance lessons at an old community center in the West End. Our skinny octogenarian teacher, dressed almost obscenely in a black body suit and long tutu, walked around with a cane that she beat angrily in time to the music as if that might magically help us feel the rhythm. She frowned extra hard and stomped especially loud around tall, lanky Bob and I. One morning he sent me an apologetic email, after an aggressive twirl the night before that had resulted in me taking out the instructor and a stack of folding chairs.

SneakyBob@hotmail: "So sorry about your back last night. I'll be gentler next time."

Karly101@hotmail: "Don't apologize, Bob. It was fantastic."

Bob begged me to keep the party and the dance lessons a secret so I'd been telling everyone that I was working late on Tuesday nights. The Ex broke into my email account, read the correspondence between Bob and I, and assumed the worst. But it wasn't like Valentine's Day when he'd stormed in screaming. He waited until the Arnie movie he was watching ended, debated which sitcom re-run he should watch, and only then asked me what was going on. After I explained (during commercials of course), he seemed fine.

We'd been through a similar thing months earlier. I'd missed my childhood friend Nik terribly when he moved away after University and had been so excited when he'd been temporarily relocated to Vancouver. But the Ex had made hanging out with Nik unbearable, accusing me of having an affair and giving me the tenth degree every time I came home after hanging out with him. When I told Nik I'd have to stop hanging out with him, he got mad that I wasn't sticking up for myself and then went on with some psycho babble crap about why I put up with the Ex and had problems dealing with confrontation. I tuned out while he went on my inferiority complex stemming from being compared to my perfect older sister and deep-rooted psychological issues from my childhood because of my parents, blah blah blah. I suspect he'd watched Dr. Phil earlier that day.

I'd called Nik and apologized since the break up and in true Nik fashion, he'd made one sarcastic comment and then asked me to pick up Chinese food on the way over to watch COPS with him.

Ever since I was a teenager, whenever I'd fall down or say something I didn't mean to, I'd wish I had the power to rewind that little bit of my life and start over. I longed to go back in time to when the Ex had asked about Sam Schaeffer's card and come up with a better answer.

Yep, the business card. I'd been driving around in a panic, late for dance class one night and after three times around the block, had finally found a parking space beside an office block on Hastings Street. Okay, the sign had said "reserved" but *come on*, I'd thought, it was seven thirty at night. So I'd pulled in and scrambled to class. After, I'd trudged back to my car to discover that somebody had double-parked their Cadillac so that I couldn't get out. A tersely worded note and business card from one Sam Schaeffer had been left on my windshield.

I'd tossed the card and my gym bag in the car and headed off to find Suite 201 where I'd apologized profusely to Mr. Schaeffer, who, other than using the word "Goddamn" a lot, reminded me of a TV evangelist, with his commanding presence, southern accent and constant theatrical movement. He'd moved his car and afterwards, had stood there, coffee cup in hand, yelling instructions at me and jumping about while I backed out. "More to the left! Stop! Goddamn! Now back right again! That's it, that's it, yes! Hallelujah! Praise the Lord!" (Okay, I might have imagined those last bits.)

I'd completely forgot about the card that I'd left on the passenger seat. And that was the start of the end.

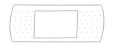

MEETING THE MAN OF YOUR DREAMS…

My stomach butterflies jumped into warp speed, accompanying my nervous-because-it-could-go-horribly-wrong but excited-because-it-could-go-wonderfully-right kind of feeling. But I wasn't going on a date. I was on my way to a university study group that Nik had signed me up for.

Nik had seen a poster for the study on accident-prone individuals when he'd taken me to emergency for a sprained wrist I'd gotten when we'd done groceries the week before. When the Ex and I had broken up, he'd yelled that the sight of me made him sick and told me to get the hell out. I was in such shock at what I'd done that I'd gotten all the way out the door before remembering that the lease was in my name and that I paid the rent. He'd finally stormed out, grabbing a knapsack of clothes and a bunch of food from the kitchen, including the icing pack for the burnt cookies. I'd holed up in my apartment for three days. I'd been eating creamed corn, artichokes and sardines straight out of the cans until Nik insisted he take me to the grocery store to load up on ice cream and gummy bears, so that I could deal with the break up like a normal woman.

I'd been so intent on shoving my shopping cart into the one in front of it to get my quarter back that I hadn't noticed one of my hands was still inside the cart.

"Next time I'll give you two quarters to leave the damn thing in the parking lot," was Nik's only deadpan comment as he drove me and my throbbing wrist to the hospital.

While waiting, he'd signed me up for the study as a joke. But when the doctor running the program phoned to set up an appointment, there was something about his voice that I just couldn't say "no" to.

I sloshed through the puddles of my old campus in my favorite bright yellow rain boots, thinking. Nik would tell me not to get my hopes up but I really hoped the study could cure me of my mishaps. It would be so nice not to have to travel with a fully stocked first aid kit or waste so much time in the emergency room. I imagined a world where I didn't feel the "You break it, you buy it" signs were written for me personally, a world where I didn't buy stain remover in bulk, a world where...Crap. Where was I?

North and South had perplexed me once again and I had to run back the way I came from. This campus was so confusing. I'd been lugging the new Sophia Kinsella hardcover with me because I thought I'd get here early and have time to read and I swear it'd grown heavier since I first stuck it in my messenger bag. Exhausted and out of breath, I arrived and almost fell onto the reception desk.

"Hi. Karly Masterson. Sorry I'm so late. Did I miss my appointment?" I huffed out.

The receptionist laughed. "No, Karly. Dr. Weiss left a half hour window in between appointments in case any of the participants showed up late. I didn't really understand why until we had one participant cancel due to a raccoon attack, and another who showed up late in a neck brace because she pulled a muscle trying to get a knot out of her hair."

Wow. My people.

A tall man walked in and was standing there, watching me talk to the receptionist. He wasn't model, chiselled face, fantasy cabana boy gorgeous, but the quiet kind of attractive you'd notice if you took the time to look past the somewhat old fashioned blue sweater and grandfather type reading glasses on a mid thirties face. The fact that I could make out at least three pens stuck in his chest pocket underneath his sweater made him more endearing. It sounds corny but I honestly thought we had one of those movie of the week, boy sees girl for the first time and birds chirp in the background moments. I got the most incredible feeling from him, like he was totally mesmerized and wanted to know all about me. It took my breath away. Until I noticed the receptionist staring down at my messenger bag. I looked down at it. No, there wasn't anything unusual about my satchel. Oh. Well, except for the fact that the left side of my skirt had ridden up in between it and my hip and half my underwear was on display. Oh God. I quickly rearranged my clothing back to where it was supposed to be.

"Hi, I'm Dr. Weiss," the man said once I'd sorted myself out.

I felt like such an idiot as he led me to a small office while making small talk. Sure I'd gotten the feeling that he was looking at me. Half my skirt had been hiked up the side of my body. And of course I'd gotten the feeling he was interested in me. He was, but just as a subject for his klutziness study.

"So, Karly, I'm doing a study on how certain people attract particular situations with the overall goal being to determine any common denominators. It's my theory that certain people have a higher statistical average of physical disaster."

"Well, I'm definitely your girl. I mean, I'm not your girl. Not that I wouldn't want to be. I'm sure you'd be an amazing boyfriend. Not that I really know you. Yet. I mean, not that I'm looking. But if I was, I'm sure you'd be-" God, what was wrong with me? I remembered Nik's advice when I started to babble: take a deep breath and get to the point. "I fall down a lot."

"Uh, okay. Well, that's great. I mean, that's not great for you, but for me. I mean, it's not great for me because I want you to fall down, but if you have to anyway, I'm glad that you're here. I mean-"

He stopped talking, looking confused at what was coming out of his own mouth, as I had been earlier. We looked at each other, shocked, for a second. And then cracked up.

"Why don't we rewind that bit," he said with a smile on his face. Oh my God. He did the rewind thing. Just like I did.

"So," he continued, "as part of the study I'd ask you to keep a journal and submit it for my review. I have a sample that you can pick up from the receptionist on the way out, if you're still interested." He smiled his dazzling smile that would have had me donating my organs if he'd asked, even the ones I was still using.

"We'll also meet every two weeks as a group," he went on. "I'm hoping to provide some insight on why these things happen more frequently to certain people and maybe even discover how to minimize accidents."

He continued and I nodded my understanding while subtly

checking out his athletic build underneath his loose fitting sweater and well-ironed khakis. He had long legs. They looked strong. I wondered if they were hairy. Gosh, what was wrong with me? I wasn't normally like this. Less than a month of single-dom and here I was practically undressing this stranger with my eyes. Or at least picturing him in shorts. In his cramped office, our chairs were only two feet away from each other. We were so close. I could reach right out and touch his thigh if I wanted to. Hold on, was that a stain on the knee of his pants? And in his, uh, winkle zone? Could he also be a Strangeness Attracter? He stopped mid sentence and gave me an alarmed look when he caught me staring at his crotch.

"Oh. Um. Your knee?" I stuttered. "I was looking at your knee. I mean, not your actual knee because it's hidden under your pants. Not hidden. I just mean your pants are there. As they should be. I mean… there's a stain. That I was looking at. On er…your knee and maybe other places?"

Blushing, he explained that his morning appointment had swung her purse about while sitting down, upsetting his full coffee from his desk, and his afternoon interviewee had tripped and landed on his lap along with her jam sandwich. I wondered what our group sessions would be like. Would the room just spontaneously combust when we walked into it?

Dr. Weiss went through a questionnaire with me while I recovered from my embarrassment and tried to contain my excitement at both the discovery of people like me, and the fact that this God of a man was running the study. I answered all his questions, explaining that my injuries were never very serious and that others didn't get hurt. In addition to the physical disasters, I added, a lot of my embarrassing moments were non-physical. Like the time Nik needed a date for an important work dinner with potential Japanese investors and had, against his better judgment, asked me to go. After drinking a harmless looking thimble of sake and eating a piece of octopus sushi, I'd confused "tentacles" with "testicles" and went on and on about how odd they felt in my mouth. I wouldn't normally have given a stranger this somewhat X-rated example but hey, I'd just been caught staring at his groin. He listened with a serious expression, while nodding and taking notes, as if I were giving him driving directions.

"I'm actually studying both physical and situational

embarrassing situations," Dr. Weiss said with a proud but shy smile. "I think I can help a lot of people if I study both. It's something I've wanted to do for a while. The insurance company will only fund the physical research, though, so I'm using my own resources to fund the rest."

"That is so nice of-"

"So are you single?" he blurted out suddenly. He <u>was</u> interested in me. I knew it. Quickly, I raised one eyebrow in a "come hither" look that I'd read about in Cosmo last month.

"Why yes, I am." I smiled in what I hoped was a seductive manner. Oh. He reached over and jotted on his notepad. Crap. My seductive smiled turned into a forced one and I quickly filled up the silence babbling about my "Even Steven" theory to him, explaining how every time a bad Strangeness Attracter event happened to me, something great soon followed.

Dr. Weiss seemed genuinely interested in hearing more so I continued, telling him about the time I'd walked through a hotel lobby looking for the bathroom. One of the employees had dripped soap all over the floor and I'd slipped and briefly knocked myself out. I hadn't had any intention of suing and had kept dazily saying "no, no" to their lawyer who had sprinted over from his office and started spouting numbers at me as I lay flat out in the lobby. He'd interpreted this as me saying it wasn't enough so before I'd even stood up, I'd signed a piece of paper accepting a generous settlement.

The Ex had loved this story that I'd told him on our first date. He'd thought it was great that I'd popped into the hotel to wash off the seagull poop that had landed on my jacket and ended up with the equivalent of one year's salary.

Nik often teased me that what I considered the "good leg" of the Even Steven factor stemmed from companies not wanting to be sued. I chose to think about it my way. And it wasn't just the settlement that I felt had "Even Stevened" me though, I explained further, smiling with the memory. The very next day I found the most amazing cow print slipcover that fit perfectly over my loveseat plus I got the job I wanted at an accounting firm. Dr. Weiss, or Alex as he asked me to call him, smiled and said he wished more people had my positive attitude.

"So Karly," he continued, "Now that you know all that's involved, will you have the time to dedicate to the study? It's a ten-month commitment. If you do sign up, I'll need to know I can rely on you for the entire study."

I hesitated and then explained why I had so much free time on my hands. The disaster had happened two weeks before the Ex dumped me and I'd avoided thinking about it since.

DISORIENTED WHILE CAREER ORIENTED

I liked numbers. They couldn't spill on me or trip me or be offended by my big mouth. As an auditor with KLDP, I just took a look at what had already been done financially so there was never any danger of screwing up the outcome. I loved to sit at a desk, surrounded by ledgers and reports, and immerse myself in the safety and predictability of it.

That week's assignment had been the audit of a small emerging markets investment firm.

I lugged my heavy audit bags and laptop into the office tower elevator and then realized I'd forgotten to find out what floor they were on.

"Morning, does anyone know what floor Smith, Goldstein and Kramer are on?" I called out to the people in the elevator. Talking to people in an elevator kind of freaks them out but they were helpful after they got over their initial shock.

"Maybe the twelfth?" someone suggested.

A bike courier stopping on the same floor helped me with my bags.

"SKG, how may I direct your call?" the receptionist sing-songed into her headset as we approached. "Sorry, Mr. Smith's not in yet, may I transfer you to voicemail? Thank you." She pressed another button. "No, sorry, Mr. Goldberg's still not available. May I transfer you to his secretary to reschedule?"

She finally got a break from the ringing and talked to the courier while signing for a package, "God Zeke, what a start to the day. There was a big accident on Lions Gate Bridge. Half the office isn't here yet. Doug was supposed to take Muffy to the day spa but can't get there. You know he'll be in a mood for the rest of the day."

They both laughed.

"Muffy is his wife's Pomeranian," Zeke explained in answer to my confused look. "She's got them both on a tight leash."

"I'm delivering an auditor for you too, Deb," he directed towards the receptionist.

"Hi, Karly Masterson," I said.

"Oh hi. I wasn't expecting you. Why don't you set up in the boardroom while I see who's available?"

I lugged my bags to the boardroom and set up. Then I sharpened my pencils. Twice. I re-read last year's files. Darryl, my manager who was supposed to be there getting me started, was probably caught in the traffic jam.

"Hi, I'm Ali, the summer intern," a freckly twelve-year-old in a suit popped his head in. "Deb said you were the auditor?"

I nodded and introduced myself.

"We didn't think you were in until next week but we're pretty much ready anyway. I'll grab the reports you need and you can also log onto SKG.com to access information from our network on that computer in the corner there. I'll get you a password. Help yourself to coffee in the meantime."

I made my way to the lunchroom where the employees were gathered, catching up on each other's weekends.

"Hi, you must be the auditor. Come to test our doughnuts?" the chubby guy who must have been the office clown said. "Aw, just teasing, help yourself. We had them brought in for Old Smittie's birthday."

Mmm. Plain was always the safest bet but I was wearing a dark suit over a red blouse. I reached for the last jelly and wrapped it lovingly in a napkin.

"So do you know Ingrid Ward?" the office clown asked.

"I don't think so."

"You don't? Really? We were in Commerce together. She's a manager at PWC."

"I'm with KLDP."

"Oh? I thought you were PWC but they all sound the same, don't they?"

***

There was a stack of reports waiting for me back in the boardroom and I tucked into them. The revenue pattern was totally different than prior years with fewer transactions and much higher dollar values.

Ali still hadn't returned with a password but I turned on the computer in the corner of the room and saw that Douglas Smith had left his username up. Testing information security was part of my job so I typed in a couple of guesses - "Doug" - "Dsmith" - "Smith."

The image of a grumpy man in a suit carrying around a Pomeranian with a pink bow popped into my mind and I typed in "Muffy" and was logged in. Information about a potential sale of the company popped up. That was a surprise. Most clients would have asked us to advise them on such a transaction. I read through their reports, noting that they also seemed to have changed their key business strategies.

Half an hour later I called Darryl to give him a status update, pretty damn proud of myself. Maybe I'd finally get the promotion I'd been hoping for. My older sister Desiree kept telling me I should take the initiative and ask but…what if they said "no?" I just wanted to prove myself a bit more before asking. Yes, many of my peers had been moved up the ranks but I just hadn't found the right time to bring it up. The managing partner always seemed busy, or not in the most receptive of moods. Hopefully my work on this job would finally show them I was executive material.

"Karly, where the Hell are you?" Darryl asked.

Poor guy, he must still be stuck in the bridge traffic, worried about me being able to cope without him. Well, he was about to be dazzled.

"Don't worry Darryl, I'm already at SGK. I've completed the revenue stream and am about halfway through the balance sheet," I reported proudly, fantasizing about moving from my small, dark cubicle to an ocean view office.

"What?"

I started to repeat myself but he interrupted, "No. Where are you exactly?"

"In the boardroom at SGK."

"Really? Because that's where I am and I don't see you."

"You are?"

"Yes, I'm sitting here with my second coffee on the fourth floor of the Guinness Building, running out of excuses to the client as to why you haven't arrived yet."

"Fourth floor?" I repeated as I experienced flashbacks to earlier that morning:

"might be on the twelfth...wasn't expecting you...didn't think you were in until next week ...thought you were PWC..."

I looked at the client name from last year's files: Smith, Goldstein and Kramer.

In a panic, I grabbed an annual report from the boardroom table and read: Smith, Kessler, and Goldberg. Oh crap.

"Karly!" I finally heard the yelling from the phone through the panic bells in my head.

"Oh my God, Darryl, I'm at the wrong company. I'm on the twelfth floor at Smith, Kessler and Goldberg."

"You're what?"

And then, thanks to Murphy's Law, I heard from down the hallway, ""Happy Birthday, Mr. Smith."

There was undecipherable grumbling in response and then,

"Who ate all the damn jelly doughnuts?"

A voice responded that sounded like it might be Ali's, although it was even higher-pitched and faster than it had been earlier. And then the grumpy voice again, "PWC showed up early? God Damn it. That's all I need today. Get me a stack of newspapers and put them in the corner of my office, will you? Muffy, get the Hell out of there. Damn dog."

A grey-haired man stormed into the boardroom holding whom I assumed was Muffy, and I froze. Well, other than sliding my by-then trembling hand over the huge KLDP logo on one of our files.

"You're early," he barked at me. I could only nod in response.

He stared at something on the desk. Had I missed covering up one of our logos?

"Is that-" He was so mad he couldn't speak and had to stop and clear his throat, "-a jelly donut?"

"Help yourself," I squeaked. And then he, the dog and the donut were gone.

Darryl burst in then, panting like he'd sprinted up all eight flights of stairs.

"OhmyGodKarly, how did you do this? These guys are complete freaks about their privacy. They sued an ex-employee last year for just referring to one of their deals while working at his next job." He looked at the computer screen that I'd previously been so proud of myself for accessing and his voice went up an octave, "Highly Confidential? They gave you access to all their private files?"

"Uh, not exactly. I might have broken in?"

He stared at me for a while as I babbled on in a panic about Muffy the Pomeranian and jelly donuts and then interrupted, "Karly, just get out before you make it worse."

I stood there frozen, trying to get my breathing under control until he turned me around by the shoulders and pushed me in the direction of the door as he pulled out his cell phone.

"It's Darryl, put me through to legal. It's an emergency." I heard as I zombie-walked away.

He phoned me the next day and told me to take some time off while they had their lawyers figure things out and I hadn't heard from them since.

***

Alex had been listening attentively. Or maybe he was just in such shock that anyone could be so bumbling that he didn't know what to say. In the end, he asked why I didn't phone and find out what was going on. I didn't have an answer and he didn't press me.

"So, did you have a positive Even Steven event after that?" he politely changed the subject for me.

"Oh yes, I found a real working lava lamp at a garage sale."

He smiled.

"Have you always wanted to be an accountant?"

I didn't usually talk about my earlier, abandoned career path but I felt like I could tell Alex anything and he wouldn't judge me.

"You wanted to be a social worker? Why?" he asked after I told him.

"To help people," I answered, thinking it was an odd question. What other reason would there be?

"Really?" he asked and his expression changed completely, as if he were talking to me as a friend, instead of a University study subject. "That's why I went into Psychology. I tried social work too for a while but I just couldn't handle it. I don't admit this to many people but it was just so tough. I had such high hopes of making a difference and instead-"

"You felt useless and frustrated?" I finished for him.

We looked into each other's eyes as if we'd just discovered each other. I felt this incredible attraction to him. He understood me. None of my friends or family could fathom why I wanted to be a social worker in the first place. And when I quit, no matter how many times I tried to explain it, none of them could relate to how torn I was.

"Exactly," he answered.

"That's how I felt. And when I quit, I felt like I was giving up on helping people."

"Yes, me too."

"Did you ever get over the guilt?" I asked.

He was silent for a while, looking like he was wrestling with what to say.

"No one's ever asked me that but if I'm being entirely honest with myself, not really. I mean, I tell myself I help people now with my research and the lecturing and counselling I do. But helping a bored trophy wife come to terms with aging doesn't feel as important as helping get a kid off the streets."

"I had all these dreams of changing the world," I said, "but when I did my practicum, instead of coming home feeling like I'd made a difference, I was totally depressed. My career counsellor told me I didn't have the right personality for it from the beginning. I guess I should have listened."

"No, I disagree. It's something you had to find out for yourself. And it's an important part of who you are now."

I listened to the first genuine understanding I'd had for my social work, coming from a complete stranger. One that I felt like I'd known my whole life. We just stared at each other until the receptionist announced that his next appointment had arrived.

"Did a whole hour go by already? It feels like we just started talking," he said, looking at his watch. "Well, Karly, I look forward to seeing you in two weeks."

I tried to control the ridiculously huge smile that was trying to take over my entire face.

We walked out to the reception area where I floated out and a stocky, Asian guy wearing one shoe limped in.

INCONVENIENCE AT THE CONVENIENCE STORE

Was it already five o'clock? I'd spent all day at home looking online for a new place to live. I'd told Nik it was because I wanted a cheaper apartment while I didn't know what was going on with my career but I also couldn't stand being reminded of the Ex every day.

I hadn't eaten since my breakfast ice cream and was starving. The sight of the half empty bag of gummy bears made my stomach turn so I stepped into my yellow gumboots and walked to the convenience store at the end of the block.

"Hi, Mr. Cho," I greeted the owner as I strolled in past the crowded flower display and candy section.

"Karly, how you doing after break up?"

Amazing. How did he get his information?

"Fine, thanks."

"He no right for you anyway. Fat and lazy. Buy too many chip and chocolate bar. And pay with dime and nickel. No good." His opinion giving done for the time being, he turned back to watch the Chinese soap opera on the little TV he had on the counter. So that's where all my change had disappeared to. I'd been emptying it into a jar so I'd have lots to put in the kid's Unicef boxes at Halloween and thought it was taking a long time to fill up.

Five pre-teen neighborhood boys walked in, loud and excited, acting cool for each other. They kept handling all the loose candy-the five-cent sours and gummy coke bottles-and then talking about not having enough money to pay for them.

"Hey Jimmy," Mr. Cho said without even looking up from his program. "You don't have money? No problem. I ask you mother when I see her. What she buy this morning? I try to remember. Oh, I know. Stain remover. I try to remember why she say she need stain remover-"

"No, I have money." Jimmy quickly dug into his pocket and paid.

Mr. Cho rang up the next boy's loot, "Five licorice at ten cent and two gummy at five cent you already eat that you don't think I see. Plus five dollar for the flower you buy to take home to you granny."

"What? No way."

"That okay. I explain and collect from your dad when he come in Saturday for newspaper. He a cop, right?"

The boy paid.

"Don't forget flowers, hey, you pay for them!" Mr. Cho called out as the group of boys quickly exited, considerably quieter than they had been on their way in.

"That was awesome," I said.

"Huh, that nothing. You should see how I scare off robber six month ago."

Chuckling to myself, I shuffled over to the fridge to grab some eggs and cheese for an omelet. Ugh, one of those idiot kids had spat out their gum on the floor and I'd stepped right in it. This had to be the most humongous wad of gum known to man and it had become one with the bottom of my plastic boot. Trying not to lose my balance, I raised my foot up as high as I could.

"What you doing?" Mr. Cho looked up from his TV.

"I stepped in gum," I answered as I tried hopping away while raising my leg in can-can fashion.

"Watch out!" cried Mr. Cho as I lost my balance and fell backwards, knocking down not the toilet paper stack or the display of plastic storage containers, of course, but the baking goods shelf. Three bags of flour crashed to the floor, split open, and sent a cloud of white onto me and throughout the store.

"Sorry," I coughed out as Mr. Cho ran over.

"No breathe," he said as he led me away from the flour

avalanche.

We stood back and assessed the damage. Mr. Cho sighed, "I go get mop."

"Wouldn't a vacuum cleaner be better?"

"Yes, but don't have one."

"I'll get mine."

I ran home, used my Superjet 8000 to clean myself up first (I'd freaked out some little kids in the parking lot with my ghostlike appearance), and then wheeled it down to Mr. Cho's for the unintended entertainment of the passing motorists.

"Hey, taking your vacuum cleaner for a walk?" asked a middle-aged woman in a Prius with a loud, snorting laugh.

"Better check that your dog's not plugged into the wall!" shouted out an elderly man in a Lexus who actually stopped traffic to unroll his window and crack his joke.

Mr. Cho was busy with some customers when I returned so I set up the vacuum cleaner, unplugging what I guessed was the unused fan standing nearby. I got to work and everything was back to normal by the time the customers had left. The phone rang and from what I could hear, it was Mr. Cho's wife, nagging that he kept putting off the holiday he'd promised her.

I still needed to pay. My attention was drawn to the lottery ticket stand while I waited for Mr. Cho to get off the phone. Well, why not? I'd had such bad luck recently. If my "Even Steven" theory really worked, I should end up a zillionaire.

Mr. Cho was now yelling in Chinese so I couldn't tell what he was saying, but it seemed like I had some time. I grabbed a blank lottery ticket form and thought of figures that represented bad luck to me – from the hospital phone number, from my medical insurance policy, my soon-to-be ex apartment address, the floor that SGK was located on, and finally, the floor that SGK wasn't located on.

ASS GROOVE REFLECTION

A smile crept slowly across my face while I read over my new rental contract. Nik had come apartment searching with me and thought the one bedroom near the hospital I'd fallen in love with was old and dingy, but I thought it had a lot of character.

I needed to make a change, to erase every trace of evidence of the Ex and move on.

He was supposed to have had all his out stuff by now. I'd emailed him that I was moving this weekend and that he needed to collect the rest of his things while I was out. The lazy jerk had dropped by but packed up only some of his clothes, and in my suitcase. He'd raided the fridge again (only the vegetables remained safe) and my prized cow print attaché didn't seem to be around either. When I went to use the toilet, I also noticed he'd taken the full package of Charmin I had in the cupboard underneath the sink. Had I really wasted two years of my life on the kind of guy that stole toilet paper?

I dragged myself back to the kitchen hoping he'd left me some paper towels and saw that the ledger that had been stuck on the side of the fridge was also missing. Because I had a regular job and he explained that he wouldn't have any cash until he published his novel, I'd been paying for, well…everything. It had started off with me paying for a couple of dinners out. He'd insisted on keeping track of how much he owed for his share and "The Ledger" was born. After a while, it just seemed easier for me to pick up all the bills. I mean, I had extra cash from the accident settlement plus a paying job and it was better if he could just concentrate on his writing and not have to worry about things like groceries or rent. Once his novel was published, he'd promised, not only was he going to pay me back, he was also going to take me on a trip to Italy. Picking up and looking longingly at a postcard of the Leaning Tower of Pisa that he'd stuck on the fridge, I realized that was never going to happen. I sighed and fought back tears.

Wanting to focus on something else, I sorted through the pile of papers on the kitchen table to see if any of it was his that he'd want to keep. Most of it was garbage-used napkins, take out menus, fast food coupons, old TV guides. He was such a slob yet it suddenly dawned on me that I never saw any notes or rough drafts of his novel. With a sick feeling, I wondered if he'd been doing any writing at all. He never seemed to want to talk about it. When I offered to help proof read, he always declined, saying the relationship between an artist and his craft was very private. And when he told other people he was an author, the genre seemed to change all the time-science fiction after he watched Star Trek, mystery after CSI, and comedy after a Seinfeld rerun weekend marathon.

I threw the pile of papers and the postcard into the recycle bin and looked around the apartment. Crap. I had a lot to do before Nik's friend's moving company arrived tomorrow morning.

I put some dishes away and surveyed my kitchen cupboards, amazed at the sheer volume of stuff in them for someone who didn't cook. Depending on how you looked at it, I had four partial sets of dishes or one big mismatched set. It drove my sister Desiree crazy but I liked it this way. In fact, when the Ex's friends came over on Thursday nights to game, it was easier for them to keep track of which pizza slice was theirs if they all had different plates. Although, I guessed they wouldn't be coming over any more.

Feeling very alone, I sat down cross-legged on the floor. I wanted to curl up into a ball until my life magically sorted itself out. What had I done? Was it too late to phone the Ex and explain that the divorce lawyer was just a stupid misunderstanding? I could tell him I'd lied about cheating and then explain why. Although, I wasn't entirely sure myself.

Then, I remembered how I usually ended up paying for the pizzas and how he always took the credit. Maybe I was better off without him. I just had to focus on my great, new, independent life. Standing back up, I started tidying, starting with his dirty socks I'd seen under the couch while sitting on the floor.

Come on, Karly, you were happy before you met him and you can be happy now, I told myself. *What did you do before he came along?*

Actually, I used to do a lot. I loved learning new things and used to sign up for everything. The Ex, on the other hand, was content watching re-runs on TV. Sometimes he'd even tape those re-runs and re-watch them. Before I knew it was a repeat, I thought he was an absolute genius after he came up with all the questions in Jeopardy.

Getting him to try new activities with me was like pulling teeth. It always conflicted with Sitcom Wednesday, or Jackie Chan movie marathon weekend. Eventually I stopped signing up for things myself and joined him on my leather sectional where, after our first six months together, he'd carved out a permanent sag in the corner with his extra-large body in its regular quasi-horizontal position. I'd first noticed the deformity when he'd got up to let the pizza delivery guy in after an all day Sunday Simpsons marathon. It wasn't quite to the point where I had my own dent-or was it? I ran over to check and oh God, there it was, the beginnings of my very own ass groove.

I stood there in front of my butt imprint, horrified yet now motivated about starting with a clean slate. Darn it, I was going to join everything I'd always wanted to but didn't have time for before. Yes, I was going to learn-I looked at the furniture again-upholstery, and karate, and tap dancing, and...I was never going to date a good-for-nothing TV zombie ever again!

I felt like roaring as I shoved the dirty socks into the garbage bag already full of the Ex's clothes and hauled it towards the front door. Hold on. This was the new Karly. If I felt like yelling, I would. There was no around to shush me if I happened to be making noise during the crucial part of a murder mystery. I took a deep breath and hollered out, "Girl Power!" as I flung open the door and threw the bag out.

"Jesus freaking Christ!" cursed the man who happened to be about to knock on the door as I hit him in the torso with the bag, knocking him backwards.

"Sorry," I called out as he scrambled to his feet and stormed away. "Hey, you dropped your pamphlets."

"You okay, Karly?" My neighbor, Jim, had opened his door to see what the noise was about

"Yeah, I accidentally wiped that guy out with a bag of clothes."

"Well, that's one way to get rid of a Jehovah's Witness," Jim smiled as we watched the bible thumper storm away, still muttering obscenities.

I did one final check of the apartment for the Ex's things then turned on my computer and started researching the community centers and karate schools. Tomorrow morning I'd wake up early and finish organizing before the movers arrived.

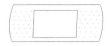

OUT OF THE OLD

Oh come on. Who was ringing the doorbell so early?

I pried my eyes open and looked at the clock. Ten already? Crap. I'd slept in. That must be the movers. I threw an old sweatshirt over my somewhat flimsy old white cotton nightie, jumped into my bunny slippers, and stumbled to open the front door.

A crew of eight burly men stormed in. It was like watching a military operation. Or ants at a picnic. (Okay, so I'd never seen either of these things but this was what I imagined they'd look like.) Within seconds, boxes were being assembled, dishes were being bubble-wrapped and the zinging sound of tape peeling off the roll echoed through the apartment.

"Nice to meet you in person," the owner, Ron, introduced himself and started going over some of the details.

I moved to allow two of the men to maneuver my kitchen table out the front door. Unfortunately, I stepped onto a dolly which already held my glass coffee table propped up on its side and lost my balance as my foot went sliding out from under me. One mover put his foot out to stop the wheels, the other rebalanced the coffee table with his spare hand, and Ron grabbed me by the waist like a rag doll and propped me back up on my feet. Not missing a beat, coffee-table-saver and dolly-steadier continued in the same motion, negotiating the table through the door frame.

"Wow, thanks," I said to Ron as I regained my balance. "You guys are like ninjas. I should have you follow me around and catch me all the time."

"Oh, that's right. You're Nik's accountant friend that always drops things or lights stuff on fire."

Obviously Nik was having problems letting go of the birthday cake-burnt curtain fiasco.

"No wonder you wanted us to pack for you," he laughed, "Now, did you pack your toiletries and some clothes for the next couple of days?"

"Don't you guys do that?"

"We can, but you might want to pack your essentials so you know where they are."

"That's okay, I'll be unpacking right away."

"You sure?" he asked. "There's usually a lot more than people expect. It can take a long time to get settled."

"I'll be fine," I answered, not wanting go into detail about all the free time I had due to my recent career flub and dumping. "Is there anything I can do to help?" I stepped, carefully this time, out of the way of movers carrying out my TV.

"Do you want to label the boxes as we pack them, starting in the bedroom?"

"Sure."

I walked into my room. It was a little disconcerting really, to see two burly men at my closet, taking my clothes out and putting them in boxes.

"You sure got a lot of stuff," one of them said.

I guess I was a bit of a packrat. Well, you never knew when certain fashions would return. Parachute pants were definitely going to come back in style sometime and when they did, I'd be ready. My closet also contained all the Halloween costumes I'd ever owned. Every textbook I'd used in University was scattered throughout my apartment. A decade of magazines with the corners folded down, and cards from friends littered every available surface area. My cow print collection was displayed in every room. Except my cow print underwear, of course.

Oh my God, my panties. The moving men would be in my drawers next. I didn't want strange men handling my undies and bras and the two pathetic pieces of lingerie I owned. My face turned red thinking about it.

"Hey, you wanna label these and I'll take them out?" Ninja Mover One asked about the two boxes he'd filled up.

"Sure," I answered while wondering what to do.

"These are ready too," Ninja Mover Two said.

I needed these men out of my room so I could shove my unmentionables out of sight. Quickly, I whipped the top off the black marker Ron had given me and scribbled a consecutive number, "1", "2", "3", on the top of each box.

"That's all you wanna put?"

"Yeah."

"You don't want to write what's in it and label it on the sides or anything?"

"No, this'll be fine. I have a system."

They looked at each other and shrugged. Then Ninja Mover One loaded up a dolly with all four boxes and left Ninja Mover Two in the room with me. Crap. Five seconds alone in my room was all I needed. What could I do?

"Do you mind packing up my books from the living room next? It'll mess up my system if we don't do it in order. Here." I shoved an empty box at him, labeling it "12." He gave me a weird look and walked out with the box.

I sprinted to my underwear drawer. Crap. Annoyingly efficient Ninja Mover One was back already with four more empty boxes.

"Could you get my DVDs in the living room?" I asked as I wrote "A" on the top of the box, and to buy some more time, added, "and make sure they're in alphabetical order?"

He looked annoyed but took the box and walked out. Within seconds I'd grabbed the entire contents of my drawer, and shoved them into a box.

"Karly?" interrupted Ron, causing me to jerk away from my bra drawer as if I'd burned my fingers on the drawer knob. These movers were surprisingly stealthy considering their hefty body mass.

"Yes?"

"Do you really want us to spend time putting your DVDs in alphabetical order? Maybe it'd be better if you did that while unpacking."

"Oh, sure."

"And the guys were saying you have some kind of numeric labeling system?"

"Actually more like a numeric, alphabetic sort of thing?"

"You accountants," Ron teased. "Okay, but I really think you should label the sides of the boxes. You won't be able to see the tops if you have other boxes stacked on top of them."

"I'll do that," I lied, figuring I'd unpack everything tonight and be sorted by tomorrow anyway.

"Are you done with that box or can we fit some more stuff in it?" he asked, approaching my underwear box.

"Oh no, it's full." I grabbed whatever was within reach, my cell phone and recharger, clock radio, and pillow, shoved them on top of my undies, and shut the lid. Ron had it taped up in two seconds and carried it out after I labeled it "C."

Operation "Hidden Panties" had been completed successfully and Mission "Covert Brassieres" was underway. I grabbed a box, threw all my bras and lingerie into it, and had it covered with my sweaters before Ninja Mover Two came in and taped it up. I let out a long breath I hadn't realized I'd been holding in and silently congratulated myself.

I sauntered out to the kitchen and took my time with my non-sensical labeling, now that all my unmentionables were boxed up, safely out of reach of any moving men.

I'd finished labeling one of the kitchen boxes "2468LMNOP" and was pretending to study the contents of the next box-tin foil, sandwich bags, and saran wrap-to label it "correctly" as "3.14." Why did I have this feeling I was forgetting something? Oh crap. Condoms!

In the bedside table, in my sex drawer! Okay, maybe some people have more in their sex drawer than just rubbers but that's all I had. Maybe it didn't even warrant being called a sex drawer. In fact, I-Okay focus, Karly. The point was that I didn't want these guys packing my birth control up for me. Plus, they were in fun, colorful wrappers. I didn't want these guys thinking about me having any sex, never mind *fun* sex.

I had to get back there and protect my virtue before the ninja movers discovered my dirty little secret. Okay, not that *I* thought that *they* thought I was a twenty-nine-year-old virgin that didn't wear any underclothes, but I just didn't want their large man hands handling any evidence to the contrary.

"We're all done packing up in the living room," Ron announced. "Once you're done we can tape 'em up and get 'em in the truck. Or, if that'll take a while, we'll finish packing up your room."

I needed to keep them out of there.

"Oh no, it'll take me two seconds."

I attacked the boxes with the marker. A diagonal line here, vertical line there, horizontal line, squiggle, underlined squiggle, dot, happy face, more undecipherable slashes of marker, and I was done.

"Wow. That's some complex system. How'd you come up with that?" Ninja Mover Three asked.

"Internet," I called out as I dashed to my room.

Ninja Mover Four was on his way out with five boxes so I was in the room alone but it wouldn't be for long. With speed and dexterity that would have impressed the CIA, I ran to the bedside table, threw open the drawer and grabbed the three condoms that were there. Phew! I had them. Now, to stash them somewhere. Crap. Why was this room almost completely empty?

"That's it in here, then, boys. Let's get the rest of the bedroom done," I heard Ron say.

Oh God. I'd thought it would be embarrassing having the movers pack up my condoms but now, I thought it would worse to be caught panicked and frozen in the middle of my empty room with them clutched tightly in my sweaty hand.

Footsteps approached.

In an act of both inspiration and desperation, I yanked up my nightie and shoved the little packages in the back of my panties. My sweatshirt was just long enough to cover any weird lumps that might be poking out of me.

The crew arrived and finished packing up the room while I stood there, in a casual, I-don't-have-prophylactics-up-my-derriere pose.

"I'm sure we've got everything but we should do an overall check together to make sure," Ron said to me.

"Sure." I went to walk towards him, moving a little funny as the edges of the wrappers poked around uncomfortably. Oh God. Ouch. And did anyone else notice the crinkling sound coming from my hiney that happened only when I walked?

"You know, I'm happy skipping that part," I said as I halted to a stop.

"It's actually company policy, to do a walk through with you so we can't get in trouble for leaving anything behind."

"Right."

I had to block out the noise.

"HERE-WE-GO-INSPECTING-THE CLOSET-AND-HERE-I-SEE-THAT-IT-IS-INDEED-EMPTY!" I yelled in one stream of sound as I speed walked across the bedroom to the closet.

"Okay then." Ron was understandably looking at me like I was crazy.

"AND-HERE-I-AM-GOING-TO-INSPECT-THE BATHROOM-WHICH-I-SUSPECT-IS-ALSO-GOING-TO-BE-EMPTY-LIKE-THE-BEDROOM-JUST-WAS-AND-YES-YES-YES-IT-IS-IT-IS-INDEED!"

We inspected the rest of the apartment with me babble-yelling every time I had to walk. On the bright side, the sudden loss of control over my voice's decibel level seemed to distract Ron from my funny walking, or from the fact that I still had my bunny slippers on as I stepped out of my empty apartment.

There was no time to get emotional as I locked up for the last time and loudly speed-rapped the first thing that came to my mind ("I'm a Little Tea Pot" – my niece's request the last time I visited), as I passed the movers and got into my car.

Then I drove to my new apartment and the beginning of the next stage of my life.

INTO THE NEW

Shoot. It was taking a long time to get to my new apartment. The movers would be sitting around waiting for me to let them in.

After a lot of grabbing, pulling, stretching and shifting around my crotch and bum area at a red light, I'd retrieved the condoms, providing a high level of entertainment for the three young kids in the minivan beside me and an equal amount of mortification for their parents. I'd tossed the small packages in the glove box, smiled sheepishly at the family, and hit the gas when the light finally turned green. Unfortunately, that peel out should have been a right turn and it took a while for me to get my bearings again.

Then I'd gotten caught in a traffic jam a couple blocks away from the apartment. It looked like there had been a fire or explosion at one of the businesses on Lonsdale Avenue. Fire trucks, ambulances, police and reporters were everywhere. I thought of parking and walking but didn't want to make a spectacle of myself in my nightie, sweatshirt and bunny slippers.

By the time I finally got to my new apartment, Ron's crew was done unloading and had everything piled up in the building hallway. I stood at the doorway and pretended to look at each box's hieroglyphics in order to direct the movers to the right room.

After they left, I took a deep breath and looked around my new residence. Everything had happened so fast that I hadn't thought about living all by myself. I'd moved from my parents' place straight into University residence for seven years, back to my parents' for a while, and then into my old apartment which I wasn't in for very long before the Ex showed up. He'd just stayed over one night and never left.

Walking around, I imagined what my apartment would look like once I'd unpacked. My very own place. I wouldn't have to share bathroom counter space. Or watch what the Ex wanted on TV. The damn thing didn't even have to be on at all. I giggled and did a tentative

Sound-of-Music twirl in the middle of the living room. And then did a more committed series of spins, laughing out loud, until I collapsed, dizzy, in the middle of the mustard shag rug.

I looked across the aging carpet at the large stack of boxes. Well, no time like the present. Less twirling, more unpacking, I told myself. I'd get started right away. Okay, how was I supposed to open these? Ah-I'd just get a knife from the kitchen and-oh, right.

Well, then there was no time like the present to start my meeting and greeting and borrowing from my new neighbors. Although…I ran to the bathroom mirror to assess myself and decided I wasn't fit for public viewing. Maybe I'd wait until I'd cleaned myself up a bit.

Returning to the boxes, I picked at a tape corner and slowly peeled it back. This was going to be terrible for my already awful nails and take forever. Maybe the first box I'd unpack would be the kitchen knives. Nope. Clothes and my manicure kit. That was okay. I could change, use my file to open boxes, and fix my nails up afterward. Darn, these clothes were from the very back of my closet, old pieces that I'd been meaning to give to charity and all my Halloween costumes. At least they were clean. I changed into a pair of hot pink spandex exercise tights, an Expo '86 Tee shirt, and a shiny purple and gold vest that was part of a Halloween pimp outfit. It was definitely not any look that was currently being featured in Vogue unless "retro bag lady" was in, but at least I was comfortable.

It was stuffy so I slid open the porch door. The fresh air was invigorating but there was a bit of a chill in the air. I added a white fingerless Michael Jackson glove and an oversized pink boa to my ensemble. Perfect.

An hour later I took a break and was sitting on the couch wishing I knew which box my milk and cereal were in when I heard voices yelling.

"They shot Bob! They shot him in the head!"

What? Was that the TV? It must be. But it sounded so real. Curious, I followed the sound out to my tiny back porch where I could see through my neighbor's balcony door. Four men were standing in a circle, huddled around-aack, was that a body on the floor that they were all bent over? It was. A really big, fat one. And it wasn't moving. I ducked down before anyone could see me. Their yelling continued.

"We got to get rid of the evidence!"

"We have to get rid of this body!"

"Bury him."

"What?"

"The garden. Take him there. Move, people. Let's do this!"

"Get your hands off him! Get off!"

"What the Hell do you think you're doing? This is a man! You killed him!"

"He was killed in action."

"No! Look at you! You're...you're running around in ski masks, exploding things-"

"He was killed serving Project Mayhem."

How did these things happen to me? I'd moved in next door to terrorists. One of them had been shot and his big fat corpse was lying in the apartment right next to mine! Were they the ones responsible for the explosion on Lonsdale Avenue? Was it part of their Project Mayhem? Heart pounding, I crawled back into my apartment to phone the police. Where was my cell? I threw the contents of my purse onto the floor. Oh crap, I'd dumped the phone and recharger into a box this morning in my panty-hiding panic. There was no way I was going to hang out and unpack forty boxes looking for my phone with a group of murderers next door. I'd have to run for it.

What was that I'd learned from watching the Ex's detective shows? Oh yes, "serpentine." It was harder to aim at a moving target so I started weaving back and forth in my living room in case anybody was aiming for me. Or was it better to crawl? On Law & Order, people always got down on the floor when there was gunfire. I was so panicked I wasn't thinking straight. Opting to do both, I weaved back and forth slalom style on my hands and knees towards the front door across the shag mustard carpeting, almost strangling myself when my boa got tangled around one of my pink spandex-covered legs.

I was almost there when I noticed it-an old phone lying on the floor, plugged into the wall. Please let there be a dial tone, I prayed as I serpentine-crawled towards the phone. I could still hear the criminals next door, talking about the body and what to do with it. They were really stuck on whether or not they'd bury it in the garden. Actually, it wasn't a bad idea. The overgrown area in the back of the apartment was a perfect place. They could wait until it got dark and then dump the corpse over the side so they didn't have to carry it down the hallway. The guy was so massive I'm not sure how they had gotten him there to begin with. Especially without anyone noticing. Oh my God, what was I thinking? Focus, Karly. I grabbed the phone and wept with relief when I heard the dial tone.

"Police, what's your emergency?"

"There's a dead body in my neighbor's apartment. A fat one. And terrorists, with ski masks. They blew up a building."

"Ma'am, are you in any immediate danger?"

I listened. It had gone silent next door. If I could hear them, they must be able to hear me. I'd finally convinced myself it was a good thing I'd gotten rid of my leech of an ex boyfriend and was about to start my new life. There were prepaid karate lessons to start, reupholstering courses to take, cavities to be filled, a ruined career to recover from. I wasn't ready to die.

"Save me," I begged for my life before running to the bathroom and climbing into the tub. Something about covering myself with a mattress tweaked in my memory but there was no way I could have lifted it all the way there. Who on earth kept mattresses in the bathroom? No wait, that was for a hurricane. My mind couldn't settle down and think straight. I should hide. But where?

All I saw were boxes as I crawled back into the living room. The adrenaline from fearing for my life gave me the strength to rearrange them into a fort around me before I heard the men next door talking again, still arguing about whether or not to hide the body in the garden. God, they were the most inefficient terrorists around. They really needed to just make a plan and get on with it.

Suddenly I heard a lot of shouting from the hall, the door being kicked down, and then more yelling.

"Police! Everybody down!"

It sounded like they were going down without a fight. Thank goodness, I was safe. And then I heard…laughter? There was a knock at my door.

"Miss Masterson? Constables Harquail and Jackson here. Open the door, please."

"Coming," I called out as I shoved my way out of my fort and ran to my saviors, ignoring the breaking sounds from the falling boxes.

"Did you get them?" I asked in one breath as I flung the door open.

"Um, yes, you're quite safe," the younger of the two officers answered. A huge sigh of relief escaped and my shoulders lowered to their original position from up around my ears.

Now that I wasn't in any danger, I wondered if there was any kind of reward for helping catch terrorists. Just in case my career was ruined, it wouldn't hurt to start being careful about money. Probably best to inquire later, after I did my interviews. Although, was it the best idea to be on TV for catching terrorists? What if other members of their faction made it their life commitment to exact revenge on me? It was definitely a trade off that required some careful analysis. Doing the Larry King, Barbara Walters circuit versus living my life in fear. Maybe I'd do an anonymous interview in the paper instead. That would still be cool. I had a brief flashback to the time I'd been in my high school paper.

The concert band (that I was lead tuba in) had accompanied the cheerleading team (that my sister Desiree was captain of) to a provincial competition. Daylight Savings had messed me up and when I finally realized what time it was, my band was already on the field. As I rushed to join them, my oversized uniform hat had slipped over my eyes and I hadn't been able to adjust it because I needed both hands to carry my tuba and sheet music. In my defence, the path from the changing room to the band was clear when I'd first started running. Anyway, our school reporter had got a picture of me taking out the cheerleading squad that had made the front page.

High school in general had been torturous for me. I was always being compared to beautiful, popular Desiree. I arrived in grade eight with glasses, braces and headgear and had sealed my fate by joining the concert band, Chess Master and Scrabble club. The kids in the older grades and even the teachers were always asking "You're Desiree's sister? But you don't seem anything like her."

My older sibling was always looking out for me. She'd defend me, saying that no, we weren't the same at all, that I was way smarter and would be the one voted "Most Likely to Succeed" at graduation. Instead, I'd been voted "Most Likely to take out the Cheerleading Squad with a Tuba."

"Miss?" one of the policemen was saying something to me, "Could you come next door with us please?"

"But...but...I don't want them to see me. What if they escape from prison and come after me? Or describe me to their terrorist friends? I don't want to go into the witness protection program. I-"

"Just follow us, please" the older cop cut me off with what looked like restrained patience.

I stepped out. Many of the neighbors had come into the hall to see what the commotion was and were staring at me. I'd forgotten about my outfit. Maybe it was good I'd decided against a TV interview. But then again, why should I be embarrassed? If anyone should be red-faced, it should be the very unorganized and loud terrorists who just got caught shouting about a dead body in their apartment. Standing up straight in my spandex/pimp outfit, I cleared my throat and used my white-gloved hand to toss my pink feather boa over my shoulder. I was Karly Masterson, brave citizen who had sabotaged Project Mayhem.

"The corpse is covered up, right?" I asked when we got to my neighbor's door, which lay on the ground. I didn't want to see a dead body. My proud resolve from three steps ago had completely disappeared as this disturbing thought took hold. I started the non sensical babble I did when I was nervous.

"He was really fat. Huge. He probably wouldn't fit into a regular body bag. Do they come in different sizes? He'd need an extra large, at least. You might think about using a shower curtain."

"What?" Both officers gave me a confused look. For men whose lives depended on staying level headed in the most violent and chaotic of situations, they sure were easily perplexed.

"I saw it in a movie," I explained.

"Huh," said the older cop cynically.

"Have you seen the film 'Fight Club?'" the younger one asked, giving the other officer a knowing look. That was weird. Was he trying to distract me from my nervousness by naming random movies?

"Is that the one with Brad Pitt about the crazy guy who starts fight clubs and then forms a terrorist group and they run around..." I fell silent.

We'd arrived in the living room and there were my four terrorists, not handcuffed and lying on the floor, but sitting around the living room. And my fat corpse was no longer lifeless in the middle of the floor but on a reclining chair with a beer in hand. Their mood was festive, almost jovial. Until they got a good look at my outfit. Then they just looked confused.

"So," explained the senior policeman, "this is your neighbor Larry and members of his drama class, who were practicing a scene from Fight Club."

All five thespians cracked up.

My face burned hot from embarrassment and once again, I wished I could access life's rewind button. The actors were so nice, trying unsuccessfully to make me feel like less of an idiot, saying that it was a real compliment if I thought their scene was the real thing. Introductions were made, including one to "Mo, the fat corpse" which got them all laughing again.

Larry offered me a beer after the cops left. My original plan was to go back to my apartment to die of shame. But, I was thirsty and had also overheard talk of ordering pizza. There was a call out from the hallway. The two nurses who lived in 2B wanted to make sure everyone was okay and the Fight Club-Terrorists-Police story was told. Our laughter attracted the attention of the dental hygienists from 2A. More neighbors showed up, we ordered pizza, and it turned into a party.

What a great day, I thought as I wrote about it in my journal for Dr. Weiss later that night. It had started out a little bumpy but ended with a fantastic get together at which I got to meet all my wonderful new neighbors. I brushed my teeth with a sample kit the dental hygienists had brought me, changed into my flapper dress in lieu of pyjamas, and crawled into my sheetless bed using my big leopard print pimp jacket as a blanket.

MOOOOOOO

It had been over a week. I still hadn't managed to unpack any normal clothes and my abnormal ones needed a wash. Badly. I phoned and asked my sister if I could use her washing machine.

Desiree is married to Bill, a venture capitalist. They wouldn't have met if not for me. I'd been set up on a blind date in University. Doug had asked at the last minute if I had any single friends so we could make it a double date with his friend Bill. Desiree came out and the four of us had a great time. Or so I'd thought. I'd liked Doug. My twenty-year-old self thought it would be so cool if Bill married Desiree and Doug married me. We could have a double wedding and get pregnant at the same time and raise our kids together. So when I got home the next night and saw from the call display that he'd phoned, I was ecstatic. There were no messages for me but I called him back anyway. He seemed distant when we talked and didn't ask me out. I saw his number on the call display again later in the week and figured he'd just been shy or distracted before. But after an initially eager "Hello" when he first answered, I got the same uninterested response.

"Why would he keep calling and not leaving a message and then act so schizophrenic on the phone?" I complained to Desiree as we cleared the dinner dishes together. "Maybe I'll phone and ask him if he's okay."

"Sweetheart?" Desiree had looked ill.

"You don't think that's a good idea?"

"No. Look hon, Doug told Bill that he thought you were really nice but um, that the two of you didn't have much in common."

"What?" I froze with a casserole dish in my hands.

"Listen, he thought you were great, but that you just weren't his type."

"Oh."

"Are you okay?"

"Sure, I'm fine. I mean, he's probably right. We really didn't have anything in common, now that I think about it." I became entranced with the little flower pattern on the plates while trying not to appear too destroyed.

"Hey, let's go get some ice cream and see a movie."

"Isn't Bill on his way over to take you out to a party?"

"He can survive one night without me."

"Desiree, I'm fine. Really. I have a lot of studying to do, actually. You go out and have a great time. I'll finish up the washing."

"You sure?"

I looked at my sister and lied.

"Totally sure. You go ahead. Like I said, I've got a lot to do. I'm not sure why I even went out with Doug. I really have to concentrate on school if I want to get through this social worker program. I don't have time to date right now anyway."

"Oh. okay."

Yellow dish gloves on, I watched when Bill came to the door and saw how he looked at my beautiful, charismatic sister as she came down the stairs, dressed for the party. I suspected then why Doug had phoned the house. He hadn't been phoning to talk to me. It was Desiree he wanted.

Doug confirmed this four years later during a very inappropriate, tequila-inspired speech at Bill and Desiree's wedding. He slurred on about how both he and Bill had been after Desiree when they first met on a double date. Despite all his efforts and completely unfathomable to him, he garbled on while holding on to the mike stand for balance, Desiree had chosen Bill. Thankfully he seemed to forget who else had been on the double date and my name never came up. There was no point in everybody at the wedding knowing I was as much of a loser as I felt.

Bill was a nice enough guy. My Strangeness Attracter events

still flustered him but he always forgave me in the end. I found him a bit materialistic and image conscious but that probably made him more attractive to Desiree. I loved my sister but she had a huge chip on her shoulder about money.

We were born to the cheapest parents in the world. It wasn't that our family didn't have wealth. It's just that our parents didn't like to part with any of theirs if at all possible, which they soon became known for in the small community we lived in. We were the kids in the second hand clothes, the ones with the old Safeway bags instead of Holly Hobby lunch kits, the ones who had two friends over for casserole and crafts and Rice Krispie squares instead of a real birthday party with the whole class at McDonalds.

"How are things at home?" a high school counsellor had called Desiree in to chat once. "Is your family managing okay?"

"We're fine," Desiree had answered, confused. It turned out one of the teachers had put out an old suitcase with a broken zipper for garbage day and seen Mom, dressed in old painting clothes and wheeling home groceries from the nearby grocery store, haul it into her cart.

"How could you do that to me?" she had sobbed at them when she got home that day. "People think we're poor. They think I'm being raised by a bag lady. When I grow up, I'm never going to embarrass myself like that."

As an adult, Desiree wouldn't be caught dead even walking by a second hand store. She wouldn't consider buying things that were on clearance, even if they were from the high end designer stores she frequented. And she definitely wouldn't take anything that was free. Even the bonus packages at the department store makeup counters with all the miniature samples. God, I loved those. I'd go and spend $50 on makeup I had managed to live without so far, just to get a bonus of a plastic bag with two lipsticks in it. Often those lipsticks didn't suit me, but they were free.

Desiree and I still cringed thinking about the time Mom and Dad decided to renovate the house and do the contracting themselves. I couldn't tell you the number of times we were dragged into small claims court after they refused to pay a penny above what they thought was fair. They would deduct money if the job was delayed, or if the carpenter damaged other parts of the house while working, or if they thought the cost of the paint should have been included in the painter's quote. Desiree and I both had such dreadful childhood memories of being in court with our parents. Being lawyers, they usually won but still, it was awful. Especially when some kids started rumours at school that our family was too poor to pay our bills.

A lot of those same kids, now grown up, had been invited to my niece Siri's first birthday party. Desiree had it at a golf club with pony rides, two bouncy castles, a face painter, a clown, a magician and a videographer to capture the magic of it all. The loot bags had been contracted out to a professional shopper, lunch was a six-course sit down affair with a choice of steak tartar or salmon wellington, and the three-tier cake was photographed and featured in an edition of "Bon Appetit." Siri slept through most of it but did seem to enjoy the twenty minutes she was awake for.

Like I said, Desiree and Bill were a good match. When Bill gave a tour of their house, or mansion, he described everything in dollar terms.

"Here is the Jimmy Wright painting that we had commissioned for eight grand. And this little baby beside it was auctioned off at the Kensington's estate sale. Sweet deal. Picked it up a year ago for a mere eighteen thou and just saw a similar one on EBay for twenty four. That's a twenty five percent return. Touch it. Solid bronze."

Our parents were on a worldwide tour for a year (something they had been dreaming about their whole lives and had gotten a good deal on by flying stand by everywhere) so Desiree and Bill were all the family I had in town.

***

"Really, Karly? You want to come over on a Saturday night to do your laundry?"

"Is that what day it is? I'd kind of lost track."

"Hold on, hon. I want to ask Bill something."

I didn't know where my laundry basket was so looked for

something to carry my clothes in while waiting. I spotted some reusable grocery bags in the kitchen and started stuffing them full.

"Why don't you come over for dinner?" Desiree asked, back on the line. "We're having a little get together at seven."

"Really? Sure. That sounds great." I hadn't had a real meal in a week and was getting tired of eating cereal out of the box with my hand. I really had to finish unpacking. The only kitchen packing I remembered labelling was "2468LMNOP" but that wasn't helping me find it. Well, give it another couple days and I'd be able to smell out the food boxes.

"Why don't you see if Nik wants to come over too? It'll make the seating easier."

"Sure, what can I bring?"

"If you don't mind picking up a duck, that would save me from running out."

I giggled.

"Karly? what's funny?"

"Oh, I thought you were joking. Sure, I can pick one up. Is there a special place I should go? Like, a duck store or something?"

I could hear Bill yelling something to her in the background.

"Actually," Desiree said, "I have to run out to Whole Foods anyway. I'll just pick it up myself."

I knew Bill was nervous about me picking up the duck after I'd embarrassed him by buying no name brand canned olives instead of the imported olive tapenade he'd asked for the last time they'd invited me to a dinner party. Or maybe he was concerned because I'd made dinner for them once and used chilli peppers instead of red peppers. (In my defence, the recipe said red peppers and chilli peppers are red.)

"No, really, I can do it. I'll go to Whole Foods and make sure I pick out the best, most organic, expensive quail that they have."

"...it's duck, Karly. I'm making duck a l'orange."

"Right. No, seriously, I can do that."

"Well, okay." She still sounded doubtful and I could hear Bill objecting and her defending me yet again as we hung up.

I phoned Nik who said he'd come to dinner if he could drive my car, a charcoal gray, V6, 2010 Mitsubishi Eclipse. People who knew me were surprised I drove such a vehicle because it was a bit showy and I wasn't an image-conscious person. It was hard to be when you spent an unusually large amount of time walking into sliding doors that mysteriously didn't open or running around baggage carousels gathering your dirty clothes and feminine hygiene products after your suitcase ruptured on the conveyor belt. But one of my coworkers had always boasted about what good luck she'd had with it so when she got pregnant with twins after a crazy office Christmas party and bad judgment involving one of the senior partners in the back seat, I'd offered to buy it from her. So far, so good.

I walked to my car, discovered my laundry basket in the back seat, and emptied my clothes into it just as Nik pulled in.

We arrived at the store and he insisted that I wait in the car while he went in. Apparently I "dilly dally" when I'm shopping.

"I do not," I objected.

"Whatever. Back in five," he said and shut his door with finality.

I did love wandering around Whole Foods. Their selection of fair trade, organic, overpriced items was amazing. They had fruits and vegetables I'd never even heard of. And at prices that made my jaw drop. The price of a medium sized pack of locally grown, organic strawberries was enough to buy dinner for four at McDonalds, including apple turnovers for dessert. And it was really interesting checking out the lobster and crab tanks. Last time I was there they had an Alaskan King Crab in one of the tanks. I'd never seen one before. It was huge. And...

I was still reminiscing when Nik arrived back with the duck. Okay, maybe it was slightly more efficient to have me wait in the car. We arrived at my sister's and parked between a Jaguar and a Mercedes.

Desiree greeted us at the door and I could hear Bill already giving the "see how much this cost" tour of their fabulous house. She seemed concerned as we approached.

"Don't worry. We have the duck. Nik got it," I said in response to her look. He held up the bag as proof.

"Oh, it's not that, hon. I was just looking at your outfit."

I was wearing pants from my hobo costume and a hockey jersey from my hockey player outfit. I suppose I looked odd. Or even worse (in Bill's and Desiree's eyes), poor. I explained my unpacking predicament.

"Well why don't we go upstairs and find something of mine for you to wear?" Desiree offered.

"Thanks. I'll just stick a load in the washer first."

She looked panicked as she heard Bill's tour coming to an end and the guests coming up from the basement (where they would have been shown the twelve thousand dollar refurbished antique snooker table and forty thousand dollar media room).

"Let's just get you some more comfortable clothes first," she said and marched me up the stairs to her dressing room where I changed into one of her twenty LBDDs (Little Black Designer Dresses).

We joined the rest of the party in the kitchen where everyone was gathered around the large granite island drinking red wine and nibbling on bacon-wrapped scallops and caviar.

I was introduced to Emily, Darren, Lisa, Tom, Porsche and Craig. The women were all very attractive, well maintained, perfectly manicured and coiffed like Desiree always was. The men were carbon copies of each other in their khaki pants and golf shirts.

The women knew each other through the private Montessori school their kids went to and I left them gossiping while I excused myself to run to the playroom where Siri and Connor, my niece and nephew, were playing with their nanny. When I got back, there was silence instead of the laughter and chatter I'd left. Bill and Desiree looked uncomfortable and the rest of the group wore shocked expressions. I hoped Nik hadn't told them about the time I had forgotten to pack underwear to wear after my morning gym work out. I'd pulled a Marilyn Monroe on the way to my office walking over a grate and given the nearby construction workers a bit of a show. Nik thought it was pretty funny but not everybody had the same sense of humour.

"What's going on?" I asked.

They were all staring at something at the counter. I looked in the same direction. Bill had an empty recyclable grocery bag in his hand. It looked like the kind I used. And on the counter, that must have been the duck that Nik had picked up. But what was on top of it? It was something with cow print on it. Oh. My. God. Was that my underwear stuck to the top of the bird? And my sports bra hooked on one of its legs? And hanging from a wing and trailing all the way down to the floor, were those my control top pantyhose? Crap, my dirty laundry. And not just my regular dirty laundry, but my unmentionables. And not even my sexy unmentionables.

"Oh my God, I'm so sorry. I was using my recycle bags to carry my laundry in and I thought I'd emptied them out…and…and…Nik must have grabbed one not knowing when he ran out to buy the duck."

"Of course." Bill forced a smile.

"Why don't you all go finish your drinks in the living room while Karly and I figure out what else to make for dinner," Desiree said.

***

"I'm so sorry, Desiree."

"I know you didn't do it on purpose, Karly. I just…I don't know how you manage to do these things."

STRANGENESS ASSEMBLES

"Karly," Alex called out as I walked in five minutes late to our first group session. God, he was even better looking than the first time I'd seen him. And he looked thrilled to see me. It almost seemed like he was going to tackle hug me as his long legs carried him across the room but he slowed down at the last minute and awkwardly put out his hand to vigorously shake mine.

"Hi. Where is everyone?"

"They're probably just late. Hey, I was just going to run down to the vending machine and get a drink. Can I get you something?"

"I'd love a DC."

"What's that?"

"Oh sorry, a diet coke. I anagram things." Why did that sound so dorky?

"That's adorable." He looked embarrassed at what he'd said. "I mean...efficient. Uh, I'll be right back."

More of the group arrived while he was gone. Kal was the Chinese guy that had arrived limping and missing a shoe when I was leaving Dr. Weiss's office. He explained that he'd tripped over a storm drain and lost his shoe in the rushing water below.

A lanky guy with scratches all over his arms and legs walked in.

"Raccoon attack?" I asked.

"Yup," he answered and introduced himself as Nelson.

Kal, Nelson and I made small talk until I lost their attention to the next arrival. Jeanette sashayed in with beautiful, wild, long, auburn hair and a neck brace. She was wearing shiny, red, high heeled boots, tight black leather pants, a tight red top, and she had even taken a black chain necklace and put it on around her neck brace like a choker.

A plump, frizzy haired, freckled girl walked in next with tape holding her eyeglasses together.

"Hi, I'm Kathleen."

Alex returned with our two DCs. Patty, Matt, and Warren arrived, and our study group started. Jeanette took a seat and Kal and Nelson quickly grabbed the chairs on each side of her. We went around the room and introduced ourselves and then talked about our ability to attract disaster no matter what we did. When we took a break I asked Alex if I could get him a drink to return the favor, maybe an MD.

"Hold on, let me see if I can get this one. Hmm…Mountain Dew?"

"You're pretty good."

"Thanks. And yes, I'd love one."

After break, Alex has us do various mental exercises to test our concentration levels so he could compare them to average. Then we discussed my Even Steven theory, where something good happened after every bad event. Nobody had noticed a strong correlation the way I had but everyone promised to keep a look out for it and note anything in their journals. If my theory was right, Jeanette joked, she was going to start buying lottery tickets every time something bad happened to her. Kal and Nelson cracked up on each side of her like it was the funniest thing they'd ever heard. I shared how I'd bought a lottery ticket right after I'd flour-bombed Mr. Cho's and got everyone howling when I told them how I'd chosen my numbers based on disaster, like the telephone number for the hospital and my medical plan number. Kathleen offered to buy group lottery tickets based on all our medical plan numbers.

I couldn't stop smiling as I drove home.

Group was such a liberating experience. I mean, I was used to being the one who always found the bump in the carpet to trip over, the one to pick up the wine glass that spontaneously broke as soon as I put it to my lips. After all these years I expected it but part of me always felt like I was such a freak. It was reassuring knowing I wasn't alone.

And Alex. Wow. He'd walked me to my car and shared his frustration with one of his young patient's parents and actually asked for my opinion. The compassion in his voice fuelled my already-existing crush on him and I couldn't wait until next session.

SAMURAI KARLY TO THE RESCUE

"What's this? You're keeping a diary? You haven't done that since you were a teenager," Nik said, sitting down at my kitchen table Wednesday night after having helped himself to my last Dilly bar.

"It's a journal, not a diary," I informed him, wondering if I had the energy to give him crap for reading my diary when I was fourteen. I decided to rise above and let it go. "For my Group sessions."

"I can't believe you're really doing that. It was meant to be a joke, you know."

"You have a very misguided sense of humour."

"Maybe I should register you for online dating next."

"I'm not your sign up guinea pig, Nik."

"Did you write about lighting my curtains on fire on my birthday?" he asked while doing that annoying thing where he tried to eat all the hard chocolate off the frozen treat before eating the ice cream.

"No, and I already apologized and replaced them so I think it's time you let that go. Anyway, it has to be something current."

"I bet I could write millions of things about you. Remember that time we spent an hour looking for your car that you swore you'd parked in 4D and it turned out you'd parked in a totally different lot in D4?"

"Maybe you should also put that on your list of things to let go."

"Can I read it?"

"You mean like how you broke into and read my diary when I

was a teenager?"

"Maybe you need to put that on your list of things to let go."

"Very funny."

"So can I?"

"I don't know why you're asking, you're already halfway through it," I answered.

"To be polite."

"Right."

Journal Entry:

Date and Time: Saturday, April 8*th*, 2:00 p.m.

Weather: Dry fall day.

Food Consumed: Eggs Benedict for brunch at Milestones

Alcohol Consumed: One mimosa

Non-Alcoholic Beverages Consumed: One coffee in the morning and lots of water during my karate workout

Wearing: White Karate Gi, white belt, and two inch Black High Heels

Location: Intersection of Boundary Road and Rumble Street

Emotional state: Happy during karate, panicked during traffic accident

Situation leading to event: Two-hour karate workout. (I have been doing this for two weeks now, to improve my coordination and balance.)

Description:

- went to Saturday noon karate workout after brunch.

- discovered the showers had broken down (of course), and didn't feel like changing back into my brunch clothes so stepped into my heels and hit the road.

- reached the intersection at Boundary and Rumble. Knew I wouldn't make the left turn during the current light so was inspecting the bruise on my arm I'd gotten that morning during training. (My fault as I was supposed to step back and block a kick but got confused and stepped forward and punched instead.)

- heard the screech of tires and honking and looked up to see that one car had crossed the median and was in the wrong lane, a truck was in a ditch, and another car was pulling over to inspect its dragging bumper.

- looked across the intersection to see a guy in biking gear collapse to the ground with his bike lying beside him, askew, with its front tire still spinning.

- screeched across the intersection, pulled over, and ran towards him.

- he was lying on his back, eyes closed, chest heaving up and down as if he was going into shock.

- ran and straddled his chest and shook him by the shoulders screaming "NO, STAY WITH ME! DON'T GO TOWARDS THE LIGHT!"

"You know, Dr. Masterson, if someone loses consciousness it's not actually good medical practice to mount and shake them," Nik interrupted his reading to comment.

- his eyes opened and he tried to sit up. I pushed him back down.

- he looked at me in shock, asking, "What's going on? What are you doing?"

- answered "There's been an accident and you've been knocked off your bike. Help is on its way."

- *he stared at me for a while with his mouth open while I tried to get him to understand that he was in shock.*

- *he explained that he had seen the accident himself and hadn't been hit, he had just biked up the hill and wanted to lie down in the grass for a while and catch his breath.*

MATCHING PLATES AND ACCESSORIES

Score! I'd broken almost all my dishes in the move (or during what my neighbor Larry now fondly referred to as "The Terrorist Incident") so had ventured out to the mall and found the most fantastic set with a funky cow pattern on them. Ah, destiny.

Okay, so they were actually for children and were a little smaller than normal plates but the sales lady suggested that if I was really hungry, I could just use two dishes. And if it turned out the mugs were too small to hold my morning coffee, she added, I could just start drinking espresso like the Europeans did. And they just happened to be having an almost unheard of sale on a high quality Keurig coffee machine that day. What finally sold me was that because the dishes were designed for kids, they were harder to break. Surely this was the positive leg of my Even Steven Factor after the injured biker misunderstanding. I thanked the beaming employee for her help and loaded my arms up with my new treasures.

***

My new kitchenware was getting quite heavy and I wished I'd lugged it to my car in two trips. My arms were aching under the weight of the boxes I carried in front of me, a Gap bag with a skirt and pair of jeans hanging off one elbow and my purse (three pounds due to the first aid supplies and flare gun I always carried with me) hanging off the other. I got onto the escalator ahead of a teenage boys soccer team and their coach. My biceps were graduating from burning to shaking when I felt something funny going on around my waist. My remaining moving boxes still hadn't magically unpacked themselves so I was wearing a full length tattered and shredded black skirt that was actually part of an old witch costume. Uh oh. I couldn't feel the pressure of the elastic waistband anymore and the entire thing had started to slide down my waist. Widening my legs slowed down the sliding but was only a temporary solution. I couldn't risk bending forward to put the boxes down and I didn't have the strength to carry both with one arm while using the other to yank my clothing back up. The last thing I wanted to do was flash the group of excitable teenage boys crowded behind me.

"Here, hold these." I spun around in a flash of inspiration and shoved my dishes and espresso maker towards the dread-locked teenage boy behind me. He didn't have time to answer before I'd thrust the packages into his arms and went to yank the garment back up. It had slid down almost to the indecent exposure stage but I'd caught it in time.

What the…? My skirt wasn't coming back up because something was pulling it down. Crap. I'd always thought those escalator warnings were bogus. The bottom half of my witches outfit was ripped off, the alarm was ringing, and I was spat out the bottom of the escalator, standing in the middle of a group of teenage boys in my Expo 86 t-shirt and cow print underwear. There was a moment of shocked silence from the soccer team before they started howling and pointing.

Then, there was a piercing whistle.

"Boys. Eyes on the ceiling!" the coach barked and the team quickly obeyed. I was thankful they weren't staring at me anymore but that still left the rest of the mall. If anyone's attention hadn't been caught because of the escalator alarm, they would for sure be curious about the ear piercing whistle and a large group of teenage boys staring straight up at the ceiling. Thankfully, most people's eyes were diverted upwards as well, searching for the assumed object of interest.

"Now form a circle around this lady," the coach said. The boys moved.

"Can we escort you somewhere?" he asked.

"Uh, my car?" I answered.

"Okay boys, listen up. We are going to walk this lady to her car. Anyone who has wandering eyes or falls out of formation will not play in the tournament next week. And on my whistle." Beep beep beep! And off we all marched, in synch.

They delivered me to my car, deposited my dishes in the trunk, and the boys headed back to the mall. The coach took off his sweatshirt and, looking the other way, handed it to me to wear over my lap to hide my cow print undies.

"You sure must like cows," he commented as I settled into the drivers seat. His pleasant smile switched to embarrassment. "Errr...I mean...there was cow print on your box...I mean, not your box...on your dishes...your box of dishes..."

Hmm. That sounded like something I would say.

As he blushed, I took a good look at him. He was pleasant looking with big brown puppy dog eyes and a very fit body. What did I have to lose? Instead of just staring in disbelief at my Strangeness Attracter event, he'd rescued me. And even after witnessing my matching panties and plates he was still sweet enough to blush in front of me. I checked and didn't see a wedding ring. Plus I had the car started and was ready to peel out if my plan went disastrously wrong and he just pointed and laughed at me. (I always parked my car nose out in case I was in a hurry to get somewhere. Say for example, the emergency room.)

"So hey, could I buy you lunch some time, to thank you for your help?" I asked with a tone more casual than I felt.

"Really? That'd be great. Are you sure?" He asked, oddly disbelieving and a little overexcited but then again, maybe not many women asked him out. I felt proud and very liberated.

"Yes, I really owe you. I'd still be standing half naked at the bottom of the escalator if you guys hadn't helped me out."

"Okay."

An awkward silence followed.

"So why don't you take my number and phone me?"

"Oh, oh yeah, of course."

CALL FROM THE COACH

The phone rang while I was washing the four cow print plates I'd eaten lunch on.

"Hello?"

"Hi. Um, Karly?"

"Yes?"

"Oh hi, it's Keith…Keith from the mall? Keith the soccer coach? Keith that you-"

"Yes, hi. How are you?" I was thrilled to hear from him. After I'd given him my new number in the parking lot, I'd worried that I'd transposed some of the numbers.

"Great. Hey, so is your lunch offer still good? You know you don't have to-"

"Yes, I definitely want to thank you for your help."

"Okay, how about after our tournament on Sunday? Say one o'clock at the Park Royal White Spot? I can make the reservations."

"White Spot…uh sure, great! See you there."

***

Excited, I called Nik to analyze the call. Well, mostly I analyzed and he probably alternated between rolling his eyes and shaking his head. I also suspected that he was working at the same time and perhaps not giving me one hundred percent of his undivided attention but I couldn't say that I didn't do the same thing when he got excited and went on about plate tectonics to me. We had a strong friendship based on mutual love and non understanding that seemed to work for both of us.

"White Spot, huh? Classy," he said.

Nik's sarcasm took a while to get used to. If you didn't know him, it was hard to tell if he was being serious. His tone of voice was the same monotone no matter what he said but I found if I followed the rule of assuming everything he said was meant to be mocking, I was right ninety-five percent of the time. In fact, it threw everything off if he was genuine. On the way out for chicken wings the week before he had commented on my new top and I went back and spent twenty minutes changing. In the end, it turned out his "nice outfit" had actually meant nice outfit.

"Okay it's not the best place for a date but maybe he didn't want to cost me a lot of money, especially after seeing how I was dressed. I mean, I was wearing a skirt that was so old it actually fell off."

"Uh huh."

"Anyway, don't you think it would have been obnoxious if I'd offered to take him for lunch and he'd picked a really expensive place?"

"True."

"And he was very polite on the phone and double checked that I still wanted to take him out."

"Uh huh."

"And then he'd said he'd make the reservation which shows he's a take-charge kind of guy."

"You need a reservation at White Spot? Gee, I was thinking of getting a Big Mac for dinner, maybe I should phone McDonalds and make sure they have room for me in their early seating."

"Okay, but don't you think that it shows his ability to plan ahead and a desire to make sure the date runs smoothly?"

"Sure."

"What do you think I should wear?"

He was silent for a while.

"Karly, I'm not gay. Don't you have any girlfriends who can answer these questions?"

"I'm just asking a guy's opinion."

"Okay then, the general consensus is that we like short skirts and low cut tops."

"Be serious."

"I am."

"…okay then, what do you think he'll be wearing?"

"Goodbye, Karly."

***

I called back five minutes later, "Hey Nik?"

"I swear to God if you ask me about makeup, I'll hang up."

"Funny boy. Are you really getting a Big Mac for dinner?"

He sighed, "I'll pick you up on the way home."

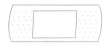

EARLY BIRDS

"Alex. How are you?" I'd looked forward to Group for the last two weeks.

"Karly! I'm great. How was your week?"

"Pretty standard. Standing in public in my underwear and stuff."

"Of course." He smiled. Not a judgmental, "you're crazy" smile, but an understanding one. "I was just about to run down to the coffee shop and grab a latte…if you wanted me to pick something up for you…or, you know…if you wanted to come with me, we probably have time."

"I'd love to, I'm dying for a 'TSL.'"

We walked to the coffee shop, making small talk about where we'd grown up (him in Vancouver, me in North Vancouver), common places we knew, where we'd gone to school (University of British Columbia for both of us), and where we lived now (North Vancouver, coincidentally twenty minutes away from each other).

He ordered for both of us when we got to the coffee shop.

"One espresso and one tall soy latte, please."

We grinned at each other.

***

Most of the group arrived by 7:15. Jeanette looked like a catholic school girl gone bad, with a short tartan skirt, white button shirt undone to allow an eyeful of ample cleavage struggling it's way out of a sexy red bra, four inch patent Mary Jane's, and her wild auburn hair somewhat tamed in two braids. Her sling was tartan patterned to match her skirt and Nelson looked jealous when he saw Kal carrying her purse into class for her. Only Kathleen was absent. She'd phoned earlier to say she couldn't make it because she'd driven the wrong way out of a parking lot and now had four flat tires.

We did some more tests and after break, during which I bought Alex and I GAs (ginger ales) from the vending machine, we talked about any events that had happened during the week that we hadn't put in our journals. I told everyone about the escalator/cow print underwear fiasco. It was very therapeutic. Nobody judged me. There was laughter, but it didn't offend me or make me feel like a freak, especially since everybody else had similar stories.

Earlier, I'd wrestled with whether or not I'd mention my upcoming date at White Spot. I still had a bit of a crush on Alex, plus it was kind of personal. But it supported my Even Steven theory and my honesty overruled.

Alex and I walked back to the parking lot together afterwards.

"That's too bad Kathleen didn't make it," I said. "Maybe one of us could have picked her up. I wonder where she lives."

"Hmmm," Alex answered.

"Ooof." I'd stepped into the only puddle (where was the water even from?) on campus and got a soaker. Alex didn't even notice. He looked like he was concentrating on something on the tip of his shoes.

"You know, we kind of live in the same area," he started off slowly, "If you ever needed a ride to group, I'd be happy to pick you up," he said.

"But aren't you usually here during the day? It wouldn't make sense for you to go all the way home in between."

"Oh, no, you're right. I mean, if you ever needed a ride home after class."

"Well, I'd probably have my car with me seeing as I'd have needed to drive out here first."

"Uh yeah, of course." He took a deep, uneasy breath and then refocused on his feet. "So, do you know if there are any good movies playing right now?"

"No."

He seemed stressed out and was really concentrating on the ground in front of him. Maybe he had some challenge with walking that he was self conscious about.

"Really? Oh." he said. God, he looked like he was going to fall over. He was absolutely mesmerized by his feet now. I felt so bad for him,

"Left, right, repeat…" I wanted to whisper encouragingly to him. His anxiety was making me tense.

"Well, how about…restaurants. Do you like restaurants? I mean, any particular ones?"

He wasn't making any sense. That was that way I got, randomly babbling about things, going off on tangents, heck – even my tangents had tangents, when I was nervous about something. Like when I first met Alex and was wondering if he was single and I went on that stupid soliloquy about his knee because-

Oh My God. Was he trying to ask me out? I did a quick rewind of the conversation. He was. At least, I think he was. Crap, and I'd unintentionally brushed him off. Idiot, Karly. Okay, don't panic. I could turn this around.

"I totally love restaurants and movies – all kinds!" I yelled out, maybe a little over zealous, startling him into standing still. Not my smoothest recovery ever. But I didn't care as long as it got the point across.

"Really?" He smiled at me. "Have you seen Pure Luck? It's replaying at the Dolphin."

Was he kidding? It was one of my favourite old movies. I wanted to play it cool but I had no control of the dippy smile that was taking over my face.

"Pure Luck?" someone repeated. I looked up and it was Jeanette, flanked by Kal and Nelson and followed by Patty, Matt and Warren, approaching us. "That's that comedy with Martin Short as a bumbling accountant, right? It's hilarious."

"It's playing at the Dolphin." Kal quickly informed her, "Do you want to go see it?"

"I could do that," Jeanette answered.

"Me too," Nelson said, glaring at Kal, "Let's all go."

"It's half price on Thursdays. We don't have Group next Thursday, right Doc? Because you have that conference to go to?" Patty asked.

"Uh, right." Alex answered, looking like he wasn't sure what just happened.

"Great, next Thursday, then. We'll have to let Kathleen know too." Everyone nodded in agreement and started to debate where to go for dinner beforehand. Crap, what just happened? My internal "What the heck?" was interrupted by Kal's real, very loud yell of "What the heck?" as a tow truck drove by.

I thought Alex might have tried to ask me out again but he didn't. Granted, he was soon occupied with chasing Kal who was running after the truck, then trying to reason with the driver to release the car, then yelling at Patty and Warren, who were dramatically lying down in front of the truck, and then dragging Jeanette out of the cab but not before she somehow convinced the driver to unhook Kal's car.

THE BIG DATE

It was time for my date with Keith. I knew it was only a casual lunch but still, I was pretty excited. It'd been a long time since I'd had a date to look forward to. And I was pretty sure Alex wanted to ask me out, too. I'd show the Ex. When we'd broken up he'd yelled some garbage about how lonely I'd be and how I wouldn't be able to live without him but look at me now, with two very nice men wanting to go out with me. What were people talking about, that it was hard to be single in Vancouver?

I didn't know Keith that well but he seemed nothing like the Ex, which was pretty much what I was aiming for these days. Keith wore sweats to actually run around in while the Ex…well, he seemed to think they were acceptable wedding attire.

Plus Keith had already seen me in the middle of a Strangeness Attracter moment and still wanted to go out with me.

It was a beautiful sunny day but I spent an enjoyable morning at home puttering around, getting ready. I shaved my legs, did my nails and put on nice underwear, making sure they were not the same cow print ones I'd worn during the escalator fiasco. Not because we'd be getting to whatever the panty-showing base was, but because statistically speaking, there was medium to high probability that I'd pull a Karly again. My skirt would get caught in a car door and ripped off as the vehicle pulled away or I'd walk out of the bathroom with it tucked into the back of my nylons. The only thing more embarrassing than Keith seeing my underwear again would be if I were wearing the same pair. I sighed after analysing the many potential scenarios and changed into my new Gap jeans. It was a waste of a pair of newly shaved legs but the risk just wasn't worth it.

At 1:10 I arrived at the restaurant and was surprised at the crowd and noise. I yelled to the hostess that I was meeting someone and that he had booked a table for one o'clock. We checked her sheet which took a mere glance because Nik had been right, nobody actually made reservations at White Spot.

"I don't have anything except a table for fifteen," she said.

Great. I'd been stood up. My first date in years. I'd been so excited that morning, dancing around the apartment, even pushing back my toenail cuticles, fantasizing about how great our date was going to be. Now I felt like the world's biggest loser.

"Why don't you take a look around?" she suggested, pityingly.

"Karly?" a familiar male voice asked from behind me. Oh thank God, he was just late. I turned around expecting Keith but it was Alex, looking cuter than I'd ever seen him in jeans and another one of his grandpa sweaters.

"Alex, what a surprise," I gushed.

"Oh that's right. You're on your date here."

"If he's actually here," I said. "I think I may have been stood up."

"Really?" he asked in a voice that sounded excited instead of pitying, "You're totally welcome to join me. I've been craving a Triple-O since a certain someone mentioned White Spot in group last week."

"That'd be great," I answered. Alex had a huge smile on his face as he asked the hostess for a table and I started to think it hadn't been a waste to have washed my hair when BEEEEEEEEEEEEP, a loud whistle blew and a familiar voice yelled, "Boys, sit down and be quiet or you'll all have ten extra laps at practice on Tuesday!"

I looked over and there he was, my date. And his entire soccer team. That was weird. One of the soccer players spotted me and yelled, "There she is, Coach!"

Keith ran over to me.

"Oh thank God you're here," he said as he led me to their table. "The boys were worried they'd have to pay for their own meals and most of them can't afford it."

What? I rewound to our initial conversation. I'd been sitting in my car with the motor running and had leaned out the window and said, "Could I buy you lunch some time, to thank you for your help?"

He thought I wanted to buy the whole team lunch? Crap. I considered clarifying. The bill was going to be huge and I'd never see these people again. Yes, I decided I'd quickly explain and then get the heck out of there when "For She's a Jolly Good Fellow" erupted from the team. Looking into their smiling faces, I knew I'd be staying.

"Your table's ready," the hostess said to Alex, who was standing behind me. I looked at him and he smiled back with sad eyes and told her,

"Change in plans. I'll just get a Triple O burger to go, please."

***

I was led to the head of the table. Keith was at the opposite end. Still recovering from the miscommunication, I half-listened to the conversation around me while wondering what my problem was. I mean, if a girl asks a guy out and he interprets it as not being a date, there must be something really wrong with that girl, right? And why had I let myself be guilted into joining them instead of having lunch with Alex?

I gave up analysing and made conversation with Martin, the boy with the dreadlocks who had carried my dishes.

"So what's the name of your team?"

"Brothers Unbeatable, cuz we're all little brothers."

I stared at him blankly.

"You know, from the Big Brother program."

"Oh, I get it. That's great. Your mom must be thankful for the help."

"Yeah. And it gives her someone else's life to butt into," he said and all the boys laughed.

"Watch out, Karly. My mom tries to set Keith up with every girl she meets. It's her new mission in life but I'm happy 'cuz she's directed all her energy into that and given up trying to get me to cut my hair." The guys laughed again.

"Um, Karly?"

"Yes, Martin?"

"Thanks for taking us out. We usually celebrate by eating cut up oranges in the parking lot. This was so awesome to go to a real restaurant."

I knew then it had been the right choice to stay. I mean, I'd treated the Ex to hundreds of meals and he was nowhere near as deserving or thankful as these boys.

Other than feeling like a complete failure as a woman, I did feel like a pretty good person as I picked up the tab. The genuine look of appreciation on each boy's face as they came up and expressed their gratitude was so moving. Their moms came to pick them up and they all thanked me as well. I knew which one was Martin's mom before she introduced herself. She was plump and dressed in bright floral print. In one breath she caught up with all the other moms, sent three boys to wash their hands, nagged Martin about his hair, and asked Keith to introduce her to the nice lady who'd treated the boys to lunch. She actually stopped talking, in shock, when Keith gestured in my direction. Her temporary silence seemed to unnerve everybody but she quickly recovered and returned to her hurricane-like conversing.

"Hi, I'm Gloria. Martin's mom. Well, I didn't expect you to be so young. When Keith said a lady was treating the boys to lunch because they helped her carry her packages to her car, I was expecting a little old lady-definitely not someone your age, dear. Keith, why didn't you tell me? How old are you? You must be around Keith's age. He's such a sweetheart." I got knowing looks from Martin and his friends.

"He's so good with the boys," she continued. "I don't know what a lot of us moms would do without this soccer team. They're a great group of kids but you know teenagers, if you give them too much time and not enough to do, they get themselves in trouble. Martin, you'd better use the bathroom before we get in the car. So, are you married?"

"Umm...no."

"Seeing anyone special?"

"Well, no, I-"

"Oh, really? Well, what a coincidence, neither is Keith. He'd be quite a catch for some lucky girl." She paused very briefly to give me a meaningful look.

"Now he's a bit shy," she continued as she grabbed my elbow and steered me out of the restaurant and out of earshot of the group, "and sometimes clueless about dating but he'd make a great boyfriend."

"You know, Karly," she whispered aggressively as she leaned her face in close to mine, "You should ask him out. I mean, nothing too direct, that might scare him off. Maybe just for coffee or a casual lunch somewhere."

My face was already blushing with embarrassment at where her monologue was going. Was it wrong to consider tripping myself and taking her down with me to create a diversion? I prayed for a Strangeness Attracter event to hit me. Why were there no runaway golf carts careening in my direction or rabid squirrels attacking me when I actually needed them to?

She kept talking, "It's too bad you already took the team for lunch, you could have said you wanted to take him for lunch to thank him for helping you at the mall-OH."

Damn. She'd come to a complete stop and I borrowed her arm steering technique and kept her moving.

"Oh Karly, you didn't mean to take the whole team out. You were asking him on a date and he didn't get it. Oh dear."

"Look, Gloria, I'd really appreciate it if you didn't say anything. It's no big deal really."

"But can you afford that?"

"Yes, it's fine." I lied. In actuality, the amount on the bill had made my stomach seize up. Especially since I wasn't sure what was going on with my career. But what was done was done and I'd just be careful with my money going forward. I led us to my car where I got in, waved one last good-bye, hit the gas, and escaped. But not before I noticed Gloria clamped onto Keith's elbow.

THE LATE EARLY BIRDS

I arrived at my next group session twenty minutes early so I could invite Alex to come get a TCSL. My non-date with Keith had been a disaster in a romantic sense but I still had Alex to hope for.

"Two tall chai soy lattes, please," he ordered at the coffee shop.

"You know, we're still pretty early," he continued looking at his watch. "Do you want to have our coffees here?"

We sat in the corner and had such an intense conversation about our social work experiences that we lost track of time and were ten minutes late getting to group.

During this session Alex tested our physical reaction time to various stimuli. Everyone had dressed in their most accident friendly clothes. Even Jeanette showed up in running shoes. Well, they were silver, two inch platform running shoes with a matching mini skirt that had Kal's and Nelson's eyes bugging out of their heads, but at least she wasn't in the four inch heels she'd been wearing last session and wiped out in.

After break, Jeanette defended her choice of shoes.

"You'd think I wouldn't wear heels, with the bad luck I have. My friends used to blame my accidents on them but the truth is, I'll fall down or bump into things regardless of what kind of shoes I'm wearing. And actually, it's less embarrassing if people are saying 'Oh, look at her high heels, no wonder she fell' instead of 'What is wrong with her? She's got running shoes on and there's nothing around she could have tripped on.'" Kal and Nelson nodded eagerly, demonstrating their unconditional support.

After class Alex and I both packed up our bags slowly and I just knew he was waiting for everyone to leave so he could ask me out again. The rest of the group left as his phone rang.

"Julia? Are you okay?" He answered with panic after looking at the number. I assumed this Julia was okay because he let out a loud sigh of relief after her response. "You had me worried. I'm leaving now. Do you want to go to a neighbor's while waiting?"

Upset, I walked out to catch up with the group while he was still on the phone. Who was this Julia? Obviously someone he really cared about. A wife? A girlfriend? Maybe it was one of his patients having a mini crisis. Someone who…had a phobia about entering her house. Yeah. And he was going to go to her place and counsel her through it. Sure, that might be it. Or not. Damn.

MY CALLING

After a bit of trial and error, I'd finally found it. My new calling. Volunteer work.

I dropped by the emergency room on the way home from the Burnaby Art Gallery to have them take a look my arm. One of my favorite interns, who I'd secretly nicknamed Dr. Blue Eyes, inspected the mild burn while I told him about my evening.

I'd gone to a board meeting at the gallery after responding to their ad in the paper looking for a treasurer while their current volunteer was on maternity leave. Within the first five minutes of the meeting there had been an unfortunate incident involving a large hot coffee, a loose lid, a scalded arm, and a donated watercolour that would never be hung on a wall again. At the end of the meeting, the curator had put forward a motion to function without a treasurer until the previous volunteer came back from maternity leave. I had raised my arm (the unburned one) when the time to vote came, sadly making the decision unanimous.

Dr. Blue Eyes laughed and said that they always needed volunteers at the hospital. I ended up there a lot anyway, he joked. Plus, if I injured myself during volunteering, I wouldn't have far to travel for help.

***

I showed up for my shift the following week. My assignment was to spend time with elderly patients in the recovery ward. The first patient I met was an octogenarian named Stella that the nurses referred to as "The Fireball."

"So, you're the new one. Good. I didn't like the look of the last one. She had those shifty eyes. Pass me that Jello then you sit here, dear, and tell me your story," she accosted me as I walked in with her snack tray.

"Oh, no story," I answered, taking a seat beside her bed, and thinking listening to my escapades might be too tiring for her. "Why don't you tell me about yourself?"

"I have three wonderful children, two girls and a boy, and seven grandchildren between the ages of eight and twenty."

"And your husband?"

She got a bitter look in her eyes. Oh come on, Karly. Why on earth was I asking an eighty-year-old about her husband when there was a fair chance he'd kicked the bucket?

"I'm so sorry. I wasn't thinking," I apologized.

"What are you talking about, dear?"

"Oh, I thought…that maybe he wasn't around anymore."

"He isn't and thank heavens for that, dear. That bastard used to use me as a punching bag. I got married when I was seventeen. Can you imagine that? Just a baby."

She paused to take a spoonful of Jello while I sat in shock.

"That little maggot would slap me around and then swear the next day that it would never happen again. What a fool I was, believing him time after time."

She'd angrily crushed her empty Jello cup while talking and was just glaring at it now, lost in her memories. I stayed silent, unsure of what to say.

"The turning point came when I saw my two little girls playing house," she continued, "I'll never forget it. The older one said that she would be Daddy and the younger one would be Mommy. 'You make meatloaf and I'll hit you because it tastes like cardboard,' the older one said. I let myself cry for two hours and then I decided that was it."

I was fighting back tears myself as she continued.

"Then and there I knew I had to make sure he wasn't in our lives. For my children. I tried to leave him but he wouldn't let us go. Things were much different back then, dear. People believed that it was part of a wife's duty to stay with her husband no matter what."

The nurse came in then to take some readings and I excused myself to get a coffee. What a nightmare Stella had been through. I couldn't believe she'd suffered under an abusive husband. She didn't seem like the type to put up with anything. When I got back, Stella told me it was my turn to tell her about myself. Something light, she instructed, the nurse had told her to keep her blood pressure down.

She howled when I told her how I'd botched things up at work. And then how I'd been let go from my volunteer position at the art gallery. Her false teeth almost fell out, she was laughing so hard. The nurse popped her head in to make sure everything was okay. Maybe it wasn't a good idea for me to be at a hospital. I mean, I'd destroyed a painting at my last volunteer position. What if I broke a senior citizen?

HOCKEY PRACTICE

"You know," Alex said as we headed down to the coffee shop before group the following Thursday, "I usually just eat a stale ham and cheese sandwich from the vending machine in my office on group nights. If you weren't doing anything...I mean if you could get here early enough...if you want...we could maybe, you know, eat dinner together."

"That'd be nice."

"Really? And you know, we wouldn't have to stay on campus. There's a nice Italian place close by."

"I'd like that," I answered. Bingo! I knew he liked me. Nik had told me that Julia definitely sounded like she was a girlfriend and that I was just in denial, thinking she was a patient, but it looked like I was right. Alex didn't get to set up an actual date yet before running into other members of the group again interrupted us but he was definitely interested.

***

After break, I asked if I could share something I thought would benefit the group. I announced proudly that I'd become quite good at falling.

"We all are, Karly," Kal said, confused. "That's why we're here."

"No," I explained, "what is mean is that when I do fall, I don't knock myself out anymore."

Nik, getting tired of driving me to the hospital all the time, had insisted on taking me out to public skate. He'd suited me up from head to toe in oversized protective hockey gear and instructed me to look at my belly button every time I fell backwards.

I hadn't planned on falling at all. Nope, I was going to walk along the edge, clinging to the railing for dear life, and head to the kids' area to get a cage to skate with. Maybe taking a hot chocolate detour on the way. But Nik had towed me against my will to the middle of the rink where I'd stood frozen and helpless, wondering what he was up to, until he'd skated towards me, full speed, with a devilish look in his eyes.

"Nik. Don't you dare!"

Boom!

As I'd sailed backwards through the air, I'd nodded my head forward and looked at my belly button and it had worked! We'd practiced until a grumpy employee had come over to tell us to skate clockwise like everyone else or leave.

After class, Kathleen dominated Alex's time on the walk to the parking lot but he kept looking in my direction. That's okay, I was patient. Just the knowledge that he had almost asked me out on a date was enough to get me so excited that I let out a little girly scream after I got into my car.

THE CRUSHED CRUSH

Giddy with the thought of seeing Dr. Weiss again, I tried to sit still in the waiting room at the University and concentrate on reading a 1993 Time magazine. Alex had sent me an email asking me to drop by and see him the next time I happened to be in the area. The message had popped into my inbox at eleven that morning and after a quick shower and change of clothes, I just "happened to be in the area" by twelve thirty. I wondered what he wanted. Was he going to ask me out? I was so rusty at this dating thing that I wasn't sure if I was reading signs that weren't there. Another person walked in the empty room while I daydreamed.

"Hi," she said to the receptionist. "I'm here to see Alex-I mean Dr. Weiss."

"Your name?"

"Julia Weiss."

What? My head whipped around. She was about my age, tall and skinny with long, dirty blonde hair, a supermodel face, and healthy, clear, tanned skin. Breathtakingly gorgeous. If you liked that kind of thing. She took a seat across the room from me.

Sad realization dawned on me. My wishful thinking had had me imagining signs from Alex. I felt like such a loser. He was married and she was absolutely stunning. Although, just because she was beautiful didn't mean they had a good marriage. Nobody that gorgeous could actually be nice. She was probably a stuck up cow.

"Hi," she called over to me, smiling "I like your purse."

Damn it. Did she have to talk to me? And was that a little bump? It's difficult to be gracious to someone whose husband you have a huge crush on, especially if that someone is carrying his baby, but I summoned the little bit of acting prowess I had and crossed the room and plopped into the seat beside her.

"Thank you, I'm Karly, from Alex's group study. Congratulations!" I sing-songed fakely and a little louder than I'd intended, gesturing at her belly. She looked at me in alarm. Oh crap. Was she not pregnant? I'd just pulled the biggest faux pas ever. Again. I should have learned my lesson the last time, after I made that heavy woman cry in the grocery store line up.

"Sorry," I tried to recover. "I thought you might be…it must just be the angle…and your shirt looked…well, that's just the fashion these days isn't it? Even runway models are-"

"Oh, yes, I am pregnant. Sorry, you just startled me. I haven't been sleeping well with the nausea and well, first pregnancy jitters. I'm just so emotional and scatterbrained right now. I don't know how Alex puts up with me." She was so honest and looked so vulnerable as she rubbed her hand on her belly. I could see how Alex had fallen in love with her.

"So how far along are you? Seven months? Eight months?" I asked, genuinely interested and resigned to the fact that I couldn't hate her. The receptionist looked up and gave me an alarmed look.

"Uhhh…no, just three months," she answered, looking uncomfortable and-oh God-why was she blinking so fast? Was she going to cry? Panic. What to say?

"You look great," I said quickly. "I just thought that you might have been further along because…" The light bulb went on, "because that's what I looked like when I was eight months pregnant with little Martha." Phew. I'd redeemed myself. Oh, hold on, did I get that backwards? Crap. She was doing that extra fast blinking thing again.

The receptionist cleared her throat and broke the uncomfortable silence. Alex had appeared out of nowhere. What was wrong with him? He'd gone a weird shade of puce and was just standing there with his mouth open.

"Oh Alex," Julia said, pulling in a dainty sniffle and wiping her tears away with her bare hands and somehow coming across as beautiful doing it. "I just came to get your keys. I locked mine in the house again."

"What?" He looked confused.

"I need your keys."

"Oh, right. Hold on."

He zombie-walked back to his office and came back with his keys. They looked like a TV commercial couple. Both tall, with the same shade of hair and skin, and beautiful green eyes.

"Will you be home in time for dinner? I'm making Mom's chicken casserole."

"Uh, yeah."

***

Alex led me to his office, still acting out of sorts. He bumped into his overloaded coat rack on the way in and we both ended up on the floor picking up his clothes.

"That was a surprise," I said, hoping to lighten the mood.

"Yeah. Sorry, what's what?"

"It was you instead of me that knocked over the coat rack."

"Oh, yes," he answered but seemed distracted.

"Dr. Weiss?" I asked.

"Yes?"

Something was definitely up. He hadn't corrected me and asked me to call him Alex.

"Are you okay?"

"Me? Yes, I'm fine. I'm sorry, I'm just…I'm acting so unprofessional here. I just received some news that…surprised me, but I'm fine now."

"Really? Because if you want to talk about anything, I'm a good listener." He just stared at me. And then smiled but not with his eyes.

"Karly, you're incredible."

"Thanks."

He was still staring at me.

"So, you asked me to come and see you?" I asked.

"Oh right, so I did. I wanted to uh…go over some of your journal entries."

50 WAYS TO MEET YOUR LOVER

He'd gone ahead and bloody well done it. After an hour long whine session by me about how hard it was to be single and how I'd been completely disillusioned about both Keith and Alex, Nik had signed me up on a dating website called 50 Ways to Meet your Lover. I'd received an email from him telling me to look at the profile he'd created and fill in the parts he'd left blank. Make sure you don't give your personal contact details out at first, he had written, you never know what kind of psychos are out there.

I'll show you psycho, I thought, as I plotted various ways of killing him. But then out of curiosity, I opened up my profile and was thrilled to see I'd been matched up.

Excited, I read how the website worked. Members chose characteristics from a long list, to describe both themselves and the kind of person they were looking for. A computer program suggested matches and if both members approved, they could view the other's in-depth profile and arrange to meet.

I looked over the online profile Nik had created for me, just to make sure he hadn't put anything odd in it like "enjoys rolling around naked in fruit salad."

First name: Karly

Age range: 25-35.

Heights: 5'4"

Body type: Average

I am:

Nik had checked off that I was honest and ethical and good-natured. There were so many other characteristics to choose from. I wondered if "bumbling" and "klutzy" were listed. If they were, was it unethical not to tick them off? I decided to leave that section as it was.

I am looking for someone who is:

To tell the truth, I wasn't sure what I wanted in a match. I knew I didn't want to be with someone who spent most of their time on the couch watching TV so chose "career oriented." There was quite a long list of characteristics to choose from but seeing as I wasn't entirely sure, I'd only picked that one.

Job/Career: In health care industry.

I guessed Nik thought it would be too complicated to explain the forced sabbatical I was taking from my accounting career and I was doing volunteer work at the hospital.

Looking for: friendship and romantic interest.

Hobbies:

Nik, trying to be funny, had put in that I "Spend countless hours trying to recover from loss of situational awareness" which I deleted.

***

Phil, a criminal lawyer, had asked me to meet him for lunch during the week. He looked like your stereotypical solicitor. Still, serious was not bad, especially since I'd been living with someone who quoted Homer Simpson as if he was a real person. I looked at the characteristics Phil was looking for: honesty and integrity. Well, I had those.

BAD SERVICE

I drove home fighting back tears. My lunch date with the lawyer from the website had been going along just fine. Well, maybe he was a bit serious and didn't laugh or even smile at any of my jokes but that was probably because he was in the middle of his workday. If we went out on the weekend, I was sure he'd be more relaxed. Not that I would ever find out. While we were waiting for dessert a man had appeared, given me an envelope, and announced "Karly Masterson, you have been served." I'd just stared at it until Phil had taken it out of my hands and asked,

"Do you mind?"

I'd shook my head and he'd opened the package.

"Divorce papers from the law office of Mr. Hasaar. You're being sued for alimony. You didn't say you were married," he'd said.

Alimony?

"'Potential future wages as a chartered accountant,'" he'd kept reading. "Didn't your profile say you worked in healthcare?"

I'd only stared stupidly at him. He'd continued,

"'for breaking the infidelity clause of the marriage contract by admittedly having an affair.'"

He handed the paper to me.

"I don't think we can continue seeing each other, Karly, if that's even your real name." He'd handed the envelope back to me and walked out.

***

"OhmyGod Nik. The Ex is divorcing me!" I cried from my

living room phone as I ripped open the Styrofoam container holding the two pieces of cheesecake I'd had the servers pack up.

"What?"

"I just got served the papers. How could he do this to me?" My hysterics continued as I stabbed at the dessert with my plastic fork.

"Stop yelling, Karly, I can hear you. Calm down. How can he divorce you? You weren't married."

"I don't know. I think if you live together for two years you're considered as good as married."

"Okay, so you were common law, but what's the point?"

"He's suing me for alimony."

"Son of a bitch. How does he think that would hold up in court?"

"Do you…do you think it would matter that I claimed him as a dependent on my tax return last year?" I cringed, waiting for Nik to explode.

"You what? Why would you do that?"

"Stop yelling, Nik. I can hear you. It seemed like a good idea at the time. He said it made sense because I was kind of supporting him. I didn't know he was going to break up with me a week after I mailed the return. Oh Nik, I can't believe I'll have to pay alimony."

"Karly! What the Hell are you talking about? There is no way that asshole is getting a penny from you. You need to fight this!"

"But…"

I didn't like the thought of confrontation. What if we ended up in court? There was usually a lot of confrontation there. I felt like puking. My stomach was so upset I didn't even want any cheesecake. I put my fork down. This was all happening so fast.

"Look, Nik, I just need some time-"

"No, Karly. This is one thing I won't watch you bugger up by sticking your head in the sand. I'll ask around and see if anyone can recommend a good divorce lawyer."

"But-"

Click.

CHEATER

I'd been staring at the TV, unable to focus. Was it even on? How long had I been sitting here? Were these the same pyjamas I'd gone to sleep in…how many nights ago was it? Had it only been two days since I'd holed myself up in my apartment and wandered aimlessly from room to room in between sitting comatose-like on the couch?

How had my life come to this? I'd gotten myself dumped, lost most of my friends, screwed up my career, discovered the man of my dreams was married, and now I was being divorced.

Nik showed up with sushi, made me eat, and sent me off to Group.

"It'll take your mind off things," he said.

Great, spending time with the perfect man knowing I could never be with him was supposed to distract me from the last man in my life divorcing me.

"That's like shooting me to take my mind off a knife wound," I told him, arms crossed in the foyer.

"Drama Queen doesn't suit you, Karly," he said, handing me my keys, turning me around, and shoving me out the front door.

***

This group session, Alex tested our physical coordination with a series of tests. As bad as I would have been normally, tonight I was deplorable. I tried but I just couldn't concentrate. Doubts about my entire relationship with the Ex plagued me.

At break, Alex pulled me to the side and asked if I was okay. I had made up a lie in the car on the way over, in case anyone questioned my bloodshot eyes and swollen lids, but one look at his sincere green eyes and I broke down, sobbing that I was getting divorced.

"You were married?" he asked, shocked.

"Apparently."

"And he's divorcing you? Why?" he asked.

"For cheating on him," I bawled. "I'm sorry. I have to go." I ran out of the building, away from Alex's questions and pained look.

THE REUNION

Wrapping myself up in the oversized, multi-coloured afghan my Gran had knitted me, I curled up on the couch watching High School Musical on the Disney channel. I had an appointment with a divorce lawyer in a couple hours and I didn't want to go. The thought of going to court made me nauseous. Of course, that may have been because I'd just wolfed down two large icing-loaded cinnamon buns for breakfast. Yes, I felt like throwing up. Good.

I phoned Nik and told him I was too sick to meet the lawyer. He showed up anyway, forced me to change out of my pyjamas and brush my teeth, and drove us to my appointment where we were led by an assistant to a plush corner office and announced.

"I believe we've met—Goddamn-yes, I believe we have," the lawyer said to me as he sprang up from his worn leather chair behind a desk full of coffee cups to vigorously pump my hand. His southern accent seemed familiar but I couldn't place him.

"Sam Schaeffer," he continued.

It was him. The hyper TV evangelist. If I hadn't parked in his place and then left his business card in my car, I wouldn't be in this predicament. I started crying. Not the beautiful, single-poetic-tear-down-the-face kind of crying that Alex's wife managed to pull off but the hysterical, snotty, messy, wailing like a banshee, needs-a-tranquilizer version.

"Goddamn," said Sam in shock as he took a step back. "You need a minute in the ladies room?"

I nodded.

"No," Nik interrupted, steering me into a chair. "She needs to start dealing with this now."

We quickly went over some basic facts about the divorce

process with Sam gulping down vast amounts of coffee and moving around his office the whole time, and then got started on my specifics.

"So basically you footed the bill for everything during your two years together?" Sam asked as he ran over to his bookshelf to squint at something.

"Well, we kept a ledger of how much he owed me and he said he'd pay me back when his book got published." It sounded weak as I said it.

I tried to keep up to Sam's movements as he picked up an invisible piece of lint from the floor, inspected it, and ran to the garbage with it.

"A ledger? That's great. That could end this all right here. You got a copy with you?" he asked, now intrigued with inspecting the contents of his garbage can.

"Um, no. He took it with him when he moved out."

"Goddamn, Goddamn, Goddamn." He put the trashcan down and perched on the side his desk, staring at a sailboat picture on the wall.

"Look," said Nik. "This guy was a mooch from the start. He got together with her the week after she received a large accident settlement and took off right after she…well after she had a little screw up at work."

"Just a little one? Not a big one?" Sam looked hopeful.

"I might be charged for trespassing and misrepresentation leading to invasion of privacy of a client. Or someone I thought was a client," I said.

"Excellent. When will you know for sure?"

"I don't know. I haven't talked to my firm recently." I left out the fact that I hadn't answered the cell phone that kept ringing from within one of my thirty unpacked moving boxes. Or that I just plain hadn't called them.

"Okay. Do not contact them. In fact, completely avoid them.

Do you understand? We don't want to hear any good news. It's better if we can work the angle that you probably don't have a career to speak of." He looked pleased.

"Oh." He was reading through the document again and saw something that made him frown. "You didn't really claim him as a dependent on your tax return, did you?"

I nodded while Nik crossed his arms and pressed his lips together beside me.

"Goddamnit, that is not good. Not good at all," said Sam as he crossed his office to the window and stared out of it, staying still for the longest length of time since we'd arrived. Nik and I exchanged worried glances.

He suddenly swivelled around to face us again and clapped his hands together, causing Nik and I to jump in our seats.

"Right," he said. "This is what I'm seeing." Then, like a movie director pitching his vision he continued, "You are a sad, pathetic, loser, living hand to mouth, barely affording food, and certainly not equipped to pay alimony."

"Uh, okay."

"You clip coupons. You survive on Ichiban noodles and Kraft dinner. On good nights, you are able to add wieners. You take public transit."

"But I have a car."

"Sell it. Do you have any illegitimate children?"

"What? No."

"Damn. Never mind, we'll work with what we have." He continued his artistic imagery, staring off into the distance and making bold gestures with his hands.

"You live in a poor area of town."

"I do?"

He consulted his notes. "Isn't this your address?"

"Yes, but-"

"Good. Do your parents have any organs that need replacing that you were saving up for?"

"No, and actually, I'm still getting a paycheque." I almost felt I should apologize.

"Goddamnit. Well, never mind. I guess there's nothing we can do about that. Okay. Let's stay focused. You should do some volunteer work. See if you can find some needy orphans or crippled animals or something," he said.

"I volunteer at the hospital," I said.

"Perfect. How did you know to do that?" Sam asked. I didn't know what to answer.

"And she's part of a group study at the University for people that attract unfortunate physical events," Nik added.

"A what? Never mind, group study, indicating mental unwellness. Goddamn, that's good. I like it." He looked pleased as he took notes.

My head pounded as we wrapped up the meeting.

THE GOOD LEG

The phone was ringing as I walked in from doing groceries. Struggling, I tried to answer it while carrying the two cases of Diet Pepsi I'd just bought on sale. I'd started to stock up on things because of the looming alimony situation. Normally I drank Diet Coke but one had to adapt in tough times. I might end up with no money for groceries, but at least I'd stockpiled two cases of soda, twenty-four packages of Stove Top stuffing, and twelve cans of mandarin orange pieces to survive on for a while.

"Hello?" I answered.

A man's voice spoke,

"Umm…hi. I'm phoning to say sorry…about lunch the other day? I don't know what to…how I even thought…"

Well he had a nice voice, whoever he was. Was it the lawyer I'd had lunch with when I was served my divorce papers?

"Phil?" I asked as the top case of Diet Pepsi toppled from my grip, bounced off the couch seat and hit the coffee table en route to the floor, knocking over a half full cup of mint tea I'd left there this morning.

"No."

Apparently I'd gone on a lot of embarrassing lunches.

"It's Keith, from the escalator? Or from White Spot?" he said.

"Oh, hi," I said as I quickly grabbed last week's papers and knelt down, trying to soak up the tea that was traveling to the edge of the table.

"I thought maybe I could take you out to dinner? To apologize? Like just the two of us?"

"Uh huh." I said, distracted by the buttered muffin bottom that I hadn't realized I'd also knocked off the table, and which was now ground into my right pant knee.

"To someplace other than White Spot," he added hastily.

Well, he was a bit of a bumpy conversationalist but he was probably nervous. I half wondered if Martin's mom was standing beside him with flashcards, coaching him on what to say. We made arrangements for him to pick me up the following Saturday. Smiling and hanging up the phone while scrubbing my pant knee with a grocery store flyer, I wondered if he was the upside of my Even Steven Factor after the news of my divorce.

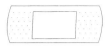

COACH DATE, TAKE TWO

Keith picked me up on Saturday night and took me to dinner. I hadn't finished unpacking but had borrowed some clothes from Desiree so I didn't look like I was on my way to a costume party or taking a time machine from another decade. It was so nice to have this date to look forward to. To keep my mind off…well, other things.

There were a lot of awkward silences in the conversation but I managed to fill them up, talking about myself. Keith was pretty quiet. It probably just took him a while to warm up to someone. Nik says I'm the opposite. That I just jump right in when I meet people, telling them all sorts of things about myself and asking them all kinds of personal questions.

Keith seemed a bit overwhelmed by the Strangeness Attracter stories I was telling him. I guess he'd never fallen, fully clothed, carrying his suitcase, into a hotel pool. Or got his arm caught in a sliding glass door at the grocery store.

I thought of the physical coordination tests that Alex had us do last session before I'd run out. He'd asked us to tap our heads and rub our bellies, and then we were supposed to switch to rubbing our heads and tapping our bellies. Maybe it was because I was so distracted by my divorce news or maybe this would have happened anyway, but I'd gotten so confused I'd stepped backwards and fallen over a chair. Luckily, Alex was right beside me and caught me before I hit the ground. He'd held me and looked into my eyes for a while until Jeanette had said, "God you two, get a room" and then he'd thrown me out of his arms like a hot potato. I'd catapulted forward and Kal had tried to catch me but stepped on Jeanette's ankle in the process. She'd screamed out bloody murder and stepped back onto Nelson's foot with her stiletto heel and Kal had just ended up falling on top of me. We'd all climbed off each other and Alex had decided to end that night's exercise.

Keith drove me home right after our meal, which was probably for the best. I'd run out of things to say and didn't have the energy to pretend that the big silent gaps weren't making me uncomfortable.

Plus, I was spending the silences fantasizing about Alex and what it had felt like being held in his arms.

What? Was Keith actually saying something to me?

"...tomorrow at one o'clock, if you're not busy."

"I'd love to," I answered automatically. Maybe I should have found out what I was committing to before answering but it was only the sixth thing he'd initiated saying the whole evening. How would he feel if I wasn't even paying attention?

"Great. Gloria keeps telling me I should invite you to one of our matches. It's at Ambleside." Oh good, it was just a soccer game and not some pagan ritual I'd just committed to.

Keith walked me through my apartment courtyard as I searched my purse for the foyer keys. I'd been so distracted thinking about Alex that I'd forgotten to get nervous about whether or not there'd be that awkward first date kiss. Keith was so shy, I doubted he'd even try.

Oh. I was wrong. He surprised me by very suddenly leaning in with his eyes closed and lips puckered. I was so startled that I stepped back and hit my head on a hanging planter, which then threw my head forward again.

"Owwwww!" We both yelped in pain.

My forehead had connected with Keith's face. Judging by the way he was holding his hands and the red trickle coming down his fingers, I'd given him a bloody nose.

"Oh my God Keith, I'm sorry! Do you want to come in? I'll get you an ice pack."

In fact, I had more ice packs than food in my freezer.

He declined, wished me "goobnighd" then dripped blood all over the patterned stone walkway on the way back to his car.

A GOOD MATCH, AND A GOOD MATCH

Gloria latched on to my arm as soon as I arrived at the game and introduced me to the rest of the "fans," mostly the boys' moms, proudly introducing me as "Keith's girlfriend" which made me a bit uncomfortable. We were all dressed in tracksuits or jeans and sweatshirts except for one overly bleached blonde mom, Chelsea. She had on high-heeled black boots, tight leather pants, and a long leopard print sweater under a leather coat with fringes. I had a similar outfit in my closet. Except mine was a costume.

We gathered around and congratulated the team after their win.

"Oh Keith," exclaimed Chelsea at his swollen nose and black eye. "What happened to your gorgeous face? Who did that to you?"

"It's nothing." Keith turned red.

"No it isn't, you poor boy," Chelsea insisted. "What happened?"

"Karly kind of bumped into my nose with her forehead."

Everyone turned to stare at me.

"It was an accident," I said defensively, wondering why I was stating the obvious.

"She head-butted you? Oh, you poor dear, let me take a look."

It ticked me off watching her fawn all over my boyfriend. I turned away and pretended to be watching the next teams warm up on the field.

"Hey, can you pass me that ball?" a man's voice called out.

"Sure," I called out as I stepped towards the stray ball that was headed my way, preparing to kick out some of my frustration. I'd better be careful not to launch it too far, I'd had a pretty lethal kick in high school. Let's see Chelsea do this in her stupid high heels that were totally inappropriate for standing in a field and kept sinking in the grass and bringing up divots. I wound up and leapt towards the ball but then somehow instead of kicking it, my foot ended up rolling on top of it, and I ended up flat on my back.

"Karly, are you okay?" screamed out Gloria and everyone ran over.

"I'm fine," I said as I attempted to get up. Oh, Ouch.

"Don't move, Karly," boomed an authoritative voice. A very masculine, deep, commanding male voice. Was it the player that had asked me to pass him his ball? No, he didn't know my name. There weren't any other men around, just young teenage boys whose voices hadn't dropped yet. And Keith.

"Look into my eyes, I want to see if your pupils are dilated." I stared into Keith's eyes. Beautiful, brown eyes that I hadn't fully appreciated the night before.

"You don't have a concussion but it looks like you've sprained your ankle. Hold on to my arm, I'm going to help you sit up."

I did what he said. It was so sexy, his taking charge and telling me what to do.

"Okay, I'm going to touch various parts of your ankle and foot and you tell me where it hurts so I can determine what kind of sprain it is."

God, he was so manly. I was so mesmerized by this new, take-charge Keith feeling my body that I forgot to tell him what parts hurt and he had to do it again. It turned out I only had a slight sprain and would be limping for a week at most.

He excused himself to run and get a first aid kit from his car. (I had a fully stocked one in my vehicle as well but his was closer.) As he ran to get it, Gloria commented that it was great that we had so much in common. That was true. We were a good match. I was good at falling down and he was good at picking me up.

CRUTCHES AND WHEELCHAIRS

I dropped by the hospital to get a second opinion on my ankle. Dr. Blue Eyes took a look and agreed with Keith's assessment. He also had one of the nurses get me a pair of crutches to borrow for the one or two days that it would be painful to walk.

I checked to see if Stella was in. She'd mentioned last visit that she had some more tests to do. It was so refreshing talking to her. Plus, I'd never found out how she'd gotten away from her husband. Limping from room to room, I finally found Stella in bed with her left knee bandaged up, watching an American Idol rerun that we'd seen together last week.

"I admire this one," she said without taking her eyes off a particularly awful but enthusiastic warbling teenager who admitted he'd only sung in the shower before.

"Really?" I asked.

"Well, not to listen to but look at the courage in him."

"But he's terrible."

"That's not the point."

"It isn't? But everybody's laughing at him."

"Karly, shame on you. Where would the world be if everybody played it safe?"

I thought about what she said while we watched Simon Cowell cruelly and creatively deny the boy's advancement.

"So what's going on with those crutches?" she asked during a commercial.

I told her how I'd started off watching Keith's game and ended up spraining my ankle because of Chelsea.

"Older woman, huh?"

"Yeah."

"I think I've got troubles with a younger woman."

"A what?"

"I think my boyfriend's been seeing a sixty year old on the sly."

"Your…boyfriend?"

"Yes dear. I never told you about him? We've been seeing each other three months, since he moved into the home I live in, just across the street. See? The pale yellow building there with the nice azaleas around it? Well, just as well I didn't waste my breath telling you about him. I'm pretty sure he's been sneaking around behind my back with one of the ladies from Bingo."

Wow, Stella was always surprising me. She asked what else I'd been up to and I told her about the Group study and eventually about my divorce.

"Divorce? But you-" Stella had lost her train of thought and was distracted by something she had seen out the window.

"Aha!" she screamed out. "I knew it. Ruth, you jezebel!"

"Stella? What's wrong? Should I get a nurse?"

"Quick, Karly, bring me a wheelchair!"

"What?"

"And do it without the nurses seeing you."

"But-"

"Go!"

I hopped next door and without knowing why, grabbed a wheelchair from beside the bed of a napping senior and made my way back to Stella.

"Come on, Karly," she told me, throwing her covers off.

"Stella, I don't think we should-"

"Look, I'm going with or without you and it would be very irresponsible for you to let an old woman wheel down the road by herself. Now grab those damned carnations and let's go."

"Carnations?"

"Come on, move!"

God, what was I getting myself into? The flowers were yanked out of their vase. Somehow we got her into the wheelchair and she held onto my crutches with one hand while using her other to help roll the wheels. I leaned on the handles for support and used my one good foot to push.

"Where are we going?" I huffed as we hop-push-wheeled through the hospital corridors and eventually down the road, but Stella was muttering to herself and didn't answer.

"You little weasel. Thought you'd get away with it, huh. Well I'll show you who you're dealing with. 'I'll miss you while you're in the hospital, Cookie.' Humph. The minute I'm gone you're catting around with that blue haired, over eye-shadowed, mini-skirt-wearing floozy. Trade me in for a younger model, huh? Well, this old girl isn't going to stand for it, no sir, and you can take these cheap weeds back."

Was I aiding her in some kind of dementia episode?

"Faster, Karly. Why are you slowing down?" she said.

My lungs were going to explode and my left calf muscle was on fire but I couldn't catch my breath enough to tell her that. I was sure someone was going to phone the hospital and report a hopping, red faced, sweaty girl pushing a mad looking senior in a flowing hospital robe and cap down the road in a wheelchair. Especially with Stella waving the bunch of carnations at any pedestrians in our way, screaming, "Move it, coming through, out of the way." If the flowers didn't get them moving she shook a crutch at them which seemed to do the trick.

We left a trail of red petals and confused pedestrians in our wake.

"Karly, turn here! Hop faster!" I turned us left and into a building labelled Beautiful Gardens Seniors Living Facilities and Stella used a crutch to ram the doors open. We could hear talking and moaning sounds as we approached the slightly ajar door at the very end of the hall.

"Oh Ruthie, I spent all afternoon fantasizing about all the things I wanted to do to you," a man's voice said.

"Yeah?" A woman's high-pitched nasally voice answered. "Well I kept thinking about that sexy chest you have hidden under your sweater vest."

"Ooh, you tigress."

Ruth meowed.

"You looked so hot at Bingo today, baby."

There was the sound of more moaning and clothing being removed and then Ruth's giggle.

"Ouch. Walter, you naughty boy, did you just bite my neck?"

"That's not the only thing I'm gonna bite, my sexy lady. I got my new dentures in."

"I have a surprise for you too, big Daddy."

There was a break in the moaning and we heard a rustling sound.

"What's this, doll?"

"I got the Princess Leia and Stormtrooper costumes, just like you wanted."

"Ooh."

There were more slurping and giggling noises.

I'd been so frozen in disgust by what was going on that I'd

temporarily forgotten why I was there. I stared at the back of Stella's head as I clutched the wheelchair handles. She hadn't moved. The poor dear probably didn't want me to see her crying. God, what a horrible thing to have happened to such a good person. Well, us scorned females would stick together. I'd stay with her tonight until she fell asleep, and drop by tomorrow, too. And the next day. And I'd bring her two boxes of the lotion Kleenex that I'd bought in bulk last week. I'd better tell the nurses what had happened, too, so they could keep a close eye on her.

"I'm so sorry, Stella. Come on, I'll take you back," I whispered and went to spin the wheelchair around.

"What?" Stella said loudly, putting one hand down and stopping the wheel. "Why should I be the one sneaking off like I've done something wrong? Hiiiya!"

She battered the door open with one of my crutches, wheeled into the room and started yelling.

"Ruth, you no good tramp! I knew it! Pretending to be my friend and all this time you were after my man."

"Cookie, it's not what it looks like-" The skinny eighty-year-old man wearing only tighty whities, a Stormtrooper helmet, a toy light sabre and orange lipstick marks all over his chest started.

"And you Walter, don't you dare to talk to me like you've done nothing wrong!" She threw what was left of the carnation stems at him.

"Cookie, calm down."

"Don't you tell me what to do!"

Stella was swinging the crutch back and forth like a maniac and knocking over everything within reach. Walter made an effort to defend himself with his lit-up, plastic sword but he was no match for my formidable friend. A saggy-bodied Ruth clad only in zebra print underwear and control top pantyhose screamed and ran and locked herself in the bathroom. When Stella broke Walter's plastic sword with a well-timed blow, he retreated with a high pitched yelp and begged Ruth to unlock the door. When she refused, he ran through his patio doors, dove over a small hedge, and ran screaming down the road. If the pedestrians Stella and I had forced off the sidewalk thought they'd encountered an unusual sight earlier, their minds were about to be blown by the scrawny, old man streaking down the street in fear for his life, screaming at the top of his lungs, clutching his broken light sabre to his chest, and clad only in underwear and a big white helmet.

COACH DATE, TAKE FOUR

Keith and I were going out for our second date. Or third if you counted the soccer game. Or even fourth if you counted the team lunch we had at White Spot. It was practically a relationship.

Last week, while Gloria and I had been waiting for Keith to return with the first aid kit, she had insisted I ask Keith to take me to a soccer club fundraiser at a bar downtown. She'd also told me about his jealous and controlling ex-girlfriend and how he was a little hesitant about dating again. Once bitten, twice shy kinda thing, which I understood completely. I personally had sworn off lazy jerks that mooched off me for two years and then sued me for alimony.

I'd found a go-go costume during my unpacking that could double as a nightclub outfit. Also, ready to test Jeanette's theory, I'd dug out my highest heels, and was teetering around in them, three inches taller.

A lot of the moms I'd met last week were at the party and we hung out on the dance floor together after Keith excused himself to talk to some of the other coaches. Chelsea was there too, again dressed very non-mom like. She was in a short, tiger-print dress with fish net stockings and ridiculous high heels that she could barely walk in. Well, whatever. She was entitled to dress however she wanted. She hung out with Keith most of the time. Not that it bothered me. All that much.

I couldn't tell if she was really drunk or just having problems with her stilettos but she sure looked off kilter. Not that I was much steadier in my shoes. It was great. Every time I lost my balance, people looked at them and nodded knowingly. I was totally buying into Jeanette's theory.

Gloria kept bringing me rum and cokes. I wasn't much of a drinker but it seemed rude not to accept them. Maybe she was getting me drunk so I'd make it to second base with Keith. Or even first base since we hadn't technically made it there yet. His first attempt to give me a little peck had gotten him a bloody nose. He was probably scared to try anything again. If anyone was going to instigate anything in the fooling around department, it would have to be me. I mean it was our fourth date. When I thought about it, it was embarrassing that we hadn't made out yet.

I'd never been much of a seductress but the more I drank, the more confident I became. Of course, I'd just make sure my first aid kit was fully stocked and that the phone was nearby to dial 911 if needed.

I looked around for my intended. My liquid courage was hitting its peak. It was time to head home and be the lean, mean, seducing machine that I was before I lost my momentum. Where was my man? I looked for Chelsea because it was easier to spot her tiger print. Hmm, no sign of her either.

"Do you know where Keith is?" I shouted over the loud music to one of the moms.

"With Chelsea!" she shouted back.

"Where?" I asked and then got a good look at her worried face. She started to say something to me but because of the loud music all I caught was,

"They need to cool it down!" as she looked up at the private balconies designed for the hoity toity champagne drinkers. What was going on? My imagination took off. Could Chelsea and Keith be...no, that just didn't seem right. I mean, Chelsea might be a bit of a cougar but Keith wasn't the type. Or was he? What did I know? I'd only had one date with him and it was hard to get to know someone if they never bloody said anything.

I followed the mom's worried gaze and saw Keith carrying Chelsea into one of the rooms similar to the way a groom would carry a bride across a thresh hold. Or the way a Neanderthal would take his mate back to his cave before throwing her on his woolly mammoth fur bed, pounding his chest and having his barbarian way with her. The way a two-faced jerk would carry a cougar soccer mom into a private room so they could stick their tongues down each other's throats. I was livid. Here I'd agonized over seducing him while he was sneaking off with another woman behind my back. And not even sneaking off very well-everyone in the club could see them.

I marched up the stairs and down the hall. As I approached, I could hear Chelsea,

"There, yes there, that's the spot." Of all the nerve. I flew into the room and saw that she had her leg up beside him and he had his hand running down it, caressing her while she made little "Oooh, oooh" sex moaning sounds.

Dismayed, I turned away and started to leave but then stopped and thought of Stella. She would never have wimped out and ran off. In fact, Keith and Chelsea were just lucky I didn't have any crutches handy.

Boiling mad now, I thought of all the things I'd never said to the Ex that I now wanted to, all the stuff throughout my life that I'd kept inside, and I turned around and stormed into the room.

"You little weasel!" I yelled at Keith. "How could you? And don't you dare look at me like you've done nothing wrong."

Chelsea looked at me like I was crazy so I let loose on her.

"And you! You no good tramp. You're embarrassing yourself! And…and…everyone can see your dark roots!"

They stared at me with their mouths hanging open. Well, I guess they thought I was just timid, passive, chump Karly that wouldn't stand up for herself. They wouldn't make that mistake again.

THE BEST PLACE IS HOME

I stormed out of the club. Well, until I collided into the red velvet rope outside. And then I fell and did a bit of macramé with it and my various limbs. A kind bouncer helped untangle me and get me back onto my feet.

Where were all the taxis? I waved at one half a block down but two guys that had exited the club with me jogged towards it and climbed in. So much for chivalry. Cursing them, I walked down the street towards Georgia Street, thinking there'd be more cabs there. Every once in a while I saw one with a light on, but these damn men with their stupid comfortable shoes and long legs always managed to run and get to it first. Even if I'd been wearing running shoes, I wouldn't have been able to compete with them. With my Jeanette-inspired three-inch heels on, I didn't stand a chance.

***

Crap. It was almost three in the morning. I'd been trying to get a cab for an hour. There were still a ton of other bar-goers out on the street, also looking for cabs, and they all had better shoes on than I did. What if I couldn't get home at all? Nik was back in Calgary for the weekend, Desiree and Bill were at their cabin in Whistler and I didn't have anyone else to phone for a ride. My pain-relieving alcoholic high was wearing off and the blisters on my feet were killing me. Desperate to relieve the pain, I tried taking turns limping on each side to give each foot a break.

Leaning against a building, I fantasized about a bubble bath and food. Cheesecake, sushi, pizza. Yes, if I ever got home, I was going to treat myself to a deluxe pizza with extra mushrooms. What was the name of that place the Ex always ordered from?

Ah, Tony's. Weren't they only a couple blocks away? A plan unfolded and I hobbled to the pizza place and asked Tony himself if I could order a small deluxe for delivery to the North Shore with an extra large tip if they could deliver me with it.

"Lady, we almost shut and the North Shore, it far away, not worth it for us."

"Please?"

"No, we shutting soon and my driver, he's on his a way home now. Here, you take a seat and I a bring you a slice of my famous pizza. This gonna be on the house cuz you looking a little rough."

"I am completely desperate for a ride home. What would make it worth it for you to deliver?"

"Lady, you order five extra large pizzas, I deliver you myself."

I calculated how much room I had left on my credit card, which I hadn't paid off the last two months. This was going to blow my budget, again, but I needed to get home.

"Fine."

"Really? What kind?"

"I don't care. I'm not going to be able to eat them."

***

I was delivered home to find Larry was having a party.

"Come on in, Karly. We're celebrating closing night."

"I'd love to," I said, "and I come bearing pizza."

***

Actors are so interesting, I thought later as I gazed up at Tyler, one of Larry's friends. I could totally picture Tyler reciting meaningful poetry in a dim coffee house, with his soulful eyes and neat goatee. He was telling me that to be truly free, one had to explore, embrace, and then completely rid themselves of their egos. I couldn't say that I totally related to, or even really understood, most of what he was talking about but at least he was talking, unlike Keith. He seemed very sensitive, not the kind of guy who would invite one girl to a party and then feel up someone else.

THE MORNING AFTER

Ring. Ring.

Oh, my aching head. Who was phoning so early in the morning? And why did my brain hurt? And my stomach? And oh my God, my feet. The answers clicked into place. Even if I had been in the mood to talk I don't think I could have made it to the phone. I let the machine get it.

"Hi Karly? Hello, dear. Oh, I have your answering service. How silly of me. It's Gloria, Martin's mom. Well, I just wanted to say good-bye since I didn't see you leave last night. But thank goodness you persuaded Keith to come out."

Why? So he could get jiggy with a trampy soccer mom?

"Chelsea twisted her ankle while dancing and Keith was the only one who had the presence of mind to get her off the dance floor and upstairs before she did any more damage. And what a coincidence, right after he helped you when you sprained yours. The poor thing went straight to emergency where she met the loveliest doctor. I asked Keith where you were and he just seemed confused so I do hope you got home okay. Anyway, you give me a call when you can."

MORE FISH ON THE WORLD WIDE WEB

The next morning, more or less recovered from my thirty-six hour hangover, I went to the hospital for my shift. Stella was there lecturing the doctor on his bedside manner—which was apparently totally lacking—and his treatment of his coworkers-which was apparently completely unacceptable. The nurses in the hallway fought to keep straight faces. I was happy to see her but concerned about her health. It was a bit embarrassing that I'd never asked Stella what she was in for but, well, what if it was bad news? Plus, I'd made the mistake of asking an elderly male patient what he was in for during my last shift and he'd pulled up his gown and shown me and I still hadn't quite recovered from the experience.

Surprisingly, Stella seemed fine after her dramatic break up. I even had to remind her what I was talking about when I asked if she was okay.

"More fish in the sea," she said and shrugged her shoulders happily. "Or in that world wide web. Maybe I'll try that dating thing you're doing with your computer. That sounds like a hoot." God, she was amazing.

I told her how I'd one-handedly ruined my relationship with Keith and she howled.

"Oh well. If it didn't work out, it wasn't meant to be. He wasn't the one for you anyway."

"How do you know? Maybe he was."

"He wasn't. You never got that ga-ga look in your eyes when you talked about him. Not like you do when you talk about your doctor friend."

My face fell as soon as she mentioned him.

"Karly dear, are you okay?"

She opened a floodgate with those words. I bawled while I told her how depressing it was being infatuated with a man that wasn't available. And about the divorce. And how I was thinking about settling so I didn't have to deal with fighting the Ex. Then I sobbed about how I'd wimped out and left a message with Dr. Weiss's receptionist last week saying I wasn't feeling well and wouldn't be at group because I didn't want to deal with him caring for me, or with answering his questions. It felt cathartic to get it out. Blowing my nose on a lotioned Kleenex, I waited for her sympathy.

"What in blazes is wrong with you?" she asked.

"What?"

"If you're upset thinking about your doctor, then get your mind off him. And this divorce business. How could you possibly think about settling?"

"I just can't stand the thought of going to court."

"So you're just going to give up? Reward his lies with your hard earned money?"

"It's not really hard earned. I have investments I could cash in from a settlement I got a while back."

"Karly Masterson. That is not the point. I do not believe this hogwash coming out of your mouth." The monitors at her bedside started to beep as her voice got increasingly louder. "You stop letting life push you around. You get your mind off your Doctor friend. Then you go back to your group sessions. And then you fight your Ex."

"Hey, finish telling me more about your life," I asked, trying to change the subject, noticing the nurses looking in concerned. "How did you escape from your husband?"

"I tried to leave with the kids but he said he'd hunt us down and kill me, that no good son of a bitch. Then he ordered me to go the store and get groceries. Can you imagine-threatens me and then tells me what he wants for dinner. All I could think of was that I had three children to be a role model for, that life couldn't go on the way it was." The monitors had started to flash double time and beep now. It was, perhaps, not my most brilliant topic change.

"Let's just say that his meatloaf might have had a very special ingredient in it that night," she whispered as a nurse came in and informed me that Stella needed to rest and I'd have to leave right away.

"I can be pretty determined if I have to be," she said as the nurse ushered me out of the room and tried to distract Stella by turning on American Idol. "Listen Karly, you don't have to care what people think but there's a difference between living your life trying to impress everyone, and standing up for yourself."

SPEED DATING

Nik the Signer-Upper had struck again.

We'd been at my place the weekend before entertaining ourselves, making fun of people's profiles on the dating website. Apparently when I'd gone to the bathroom, he'd signed me up for a speed-dating event. He'd even rifled through my purse and dug out my credit card to pay the twenty-dollar fee. I needed less obnoxious friends.

The money was non-refundable and Saturday night arrived and I didn't have any other plans so I went, thinking, what's the worst that could happen?

The event was being held at a hip restaurant, called "The Now" on their outside deck overlooking the inlet, at sunset. Alicia, one of the perky, cheerleader-like event hostesses, explained how the evening worked while myself and a cute, familiar looking guy with big dimples checked in. He smiled at me while Alicia told us that the women stay seated at their numbered tables and the men visited and then moved on to the next table every six minutes, when they played the song "There must be 50 ways to meet your lover."

Shortly after I'd gotten myself a virgin fruit punch from the bar, Alicia asked the ladies to sit down. In the jostling to find our numbered seats, someone bumped my elbow and I spilled my drink on my skirt. I raced to the bathroom to dab it out. Luckily, it had landed on my black skirt and not on my yellow shirt. I smiled at my reflection—I'd escaped a Strangeness Attracter happening. I could just tell it was going to be a great night.

Rushing back, I searched for my seat, which was now easy to find. It was the table for two with the khaki'd and button down shirted man sitting by himself and looking uncomfortable.

"Sorry I'm late, I'm Karly," I said as I slid into my chair, bumping the table and knocking his beer onto his lap in the process.

"Ohmygod, I'm so sorry." The music started playing and he glared at me as he wiped off the front of his pants and left and another man, this one smiling, replaced him.

Well, I could get used to this. I'd first thought six minutes wasn't long enough to get to know somebody. But the plus side was that there was a limit on the time you might spend enduring either their wrath or pity.

I talked about the weather and good restaurants with Darren who was in public relations. The music started to play and Darren was replaced by John. John was in between jobs and very impressed that I was an accountant.

It was a gorgeous summer evening in Vancouver. I met three more men and was enjoying myself. This was really taking my mind off all the crap I'd been through lately.

The only downer was a mosquito that had taken an interest in me. A Neanderthal type looking date sat down. Huge build, big, long arms, large forehead.

"James," he grunted.

"Nice to meet you, I'm Karly."

Zzzz.

"Huh," he said in a booming deep voice, looking for the source of the buzzing.

"So, is this your first time here?" I asked but he didn't answer, instead giving the insect his undivided attention.

"James?" I tried again.

He made brief eye contact, looking as if he'd just remembered that I was there, and then went back to focusing all his senses on the mosquito. Waiting, he'd poised for attack with his arms spread out, eyes darting back and forth, scanning for his prey. I tried again,

"So, this is my-"

"Shhhhh."

I gave up trying to engage him in conversation, wondering if he was able to use two words in a row anyway, and sat back to sip my juice and watch him in action.

"Sir, is everything okay?" One of the waiters, whose nametag identified him as Luke, had run over. Understandably, with his eyes now closed and upper body all tensed, James did look like he could be having some kind of attack.

"Mosquito," he slowly whispered this big three-syllable word as an explanation.

"Ahhh."

A female server would have winked at me and rolled her eyes but instead, Luke joined the hunting party, taking off his long serving apron and twirling it into a weapon. Alicia looked over, and then purposefully tick-tick-ticked towards us in her heels with a concerned expression on her face.

I heard a buzzing around my head and then–

"There!" yelled James and Luke. Two huge hands and a big flash of white shot towards me. I'm not sure what happened next but it resulted in me on the ground still in my upset chair with my legs dangling unladylike above me, clutching my now-empty fruit punch tumbler. I smiled, very pleased that I'd remembered to look at my belly button when flying backward and that I hadn't let go of my glass and broken it.

"Oh my God, what happened?" Alicia asked. Several male hands reached down and pulled me up, depositing me Raggedy Ann style in my now-righted chair.

"Bug," James said, proudly showing her a black and red smudge on his right palm. I half expected him to starting pounding his chest.

"You gave this poor girl a bloody lip trying to get a mosquito?"

I was bleeding?

"Are you okay?" Alicia asked me.

I took Injury Inventory. My lip felt tender and there was now fruit punch all over the front of my shirt. Or was that blood? It was hard to tell. The music started playing, Neanderthal walked on two feet to his next table, and the cute guy with the dimples from check in approached.

"Really, I'm fine," I insisted to the hostess.

"Are you sure? Do you want to go to the bathroom and tidy yourself up? Your shirt is covered—"

"No, please, I'm great," I tried to sound calm but I was panicking, wanting her to leave so I could have my full six minutes with Dimples.

"You really should go take a look—"

"Maybe you could get me a fruit punch," I interrupted, desperate to get rid of her.

She left and Dimples sat down.

"Hi, I'm Dirk. Bit of a commotion here, huh?"

Dimples Dirk, I nicknamed him.

"Yes, we had a bit of a Man versus Mosquito battle."

"Who won?"

"Man," I answered back in what I hoped was a flirty manner as Luke dropped off my fruit punch. Dirk and I had the standard conversation about what we did and where we were from. In the middle of his description of a recent audition (he was an aspiring actor and looked familiar because I'd seen him in a shaving gel commercial), my eyelid started to itch.

"Did you get your drink?" Alicia came over as Dirk left.

"Oh my God, what's wrong with your eye?" she asked as her perfect hostess-y smile was replaced with a look of horror.

"I guess the mosquito got me," I said as I prodded delicately around the itchy part. "I swell up sometimes. Do you have any antihistamines?"

"I'll find some."

My next date approached but stopped in his tracks as he took in my appearance.

"What the Hell happened to you?" he asked.

"Here's some Claritin," Alicia appeared and looked even more distraught by my appearance. "Oh, now your lip's swelling up."

I washed down two of the pills with the rest of my fruit punch, which Luke quickly replaced.

The next three men were a waste of time. Two were so distracted by my appearance that they couldn't complete their sentences and one suddenly remembered that he had to go to the bathroom. I thought they were being unfair. If I sat down in front of a guy with juice and blood all over his front, a fat lip, and an eye that was by now swollen shut, I'd…I'd…well, I'd probably fall in love with him because he'd be a male version of me. We could get matching crutches, his and hers blue and pink tensor bandages and have clumsy little babies together. God, that was the funniest thing I'd ever thought of. I laughed out loud while my next date stared at me like I had a monkey sitting on my head.

"Hey, I bet you jush realished you hafta pee." I managed to spit out while cracking up some more. God, I'd never been more hilarious. The magically appearing Alicia was frowning at me with Luke by her side.

"What's going on?" she asked.

"She's pissed," my date informed them as he left for the bathroom.

"Pished?" I howled. "But dish, dish is non alcoholic fruit punsh." God, that was so funny.

"No it's not," my very good friend and server Luke informed me. "Can't you taste the tequila?"

I tried my hardest to focus on the question. All I'd tasted was blood the first drink and I'd used the second to wash down the drugs, and the third and fourth…oh crap, I was drunk. I heard them whispering. Luke muttered something about Alicia not telling him I wanted a virgin fruit punch and Alicia hissed back did he really think she would have given me antihistamines and watched me wash them down with tequila. I got their attention back when my elbow slid off the table and I knocked over the plastic drink special listing with my resulting head bob.

They exchanged alarmed looks. Love and concern radiated from them. (Although, upon later reflection, I may have confused their "Oh no, another human being is in trouble" concern with "Can we be fired for getting her drunk and high" concern.)

It got a bit hazy after that but Alicia and Luke somehow got Nik's phone number from me. He picked me up and convinced me that it was not a good idea to go to a rave (never been, never wanted to, but seemed very important at the time). We drove home loudly singing "50 Ways to Meet your Lover" the whole way. Or maybe that was just me. And maybe I changed the lyrics to:

"Just shift the stick, Nik

You gotta be quick, Nik

You're an Albertan hick, Nik

But you're a good friend to me"

He let me know the next day that my "Please don't sue us Prize" was a gift certificate at The Now which he'd pocketed as payment for having to abandon his poker night to come get me.

THE OFFER

That was it. I was done being a coward and avoiding Alex. What did I think I going to do? Never go to Group again just because he might ask me about my divorce? Plus Stella wouldn't let it go.

I arrived early and unquestioningly, we walked down to the coffee shop together. God, he looked great.

"Are you okay?" he asked as soon as we settled at our regular table in the corner. "I wanted to phone and check up on you but wasn't sure if it was against University rules and...well, I didn't know if it was any of my business."

God, he really was the man of my dreams.

"I'm fine. I'm sorry about running out the other day."

"Is there anything I can do? Anything you want to talk about?"

"I'll be okay. It'll work out somehow."

"Really? I mean, I know it's none of my business but what about your daughter?"

Huh?

"Look, I want to help," he continued, fidgeting with his napkin, his eyes flitting back and forth from me to his coffee cup. "I'd have to ask you to leave the group because I can't be personally involved with someone that I'm studying at the same time, but I...I'd like to counsel you and Martha through the divorce."

"Martha?"

"Look, Karly, I just...you're an incredible woman and...I want to help you in any way I can. And maybe we can also explore your infidelity issues."

He looked at me with those intense, caring eyes and took my hand in his. I didn't understand what he was talking about but I did figure out one thing as electricity sizzled through my body. My feelings for him were way stronger than I had thought.

"Um, okay. Alex?"

"Yes?"

"I don't have a daughter named Martha. Or, any other daughter. And I've never cheated on anyone."

"But I overheard you telling Julia, when you were in the reception area…maybe I heard wrong…but I thought you said…"

Yes, Julia. His beautiful, pregnant wife. What was I doing holding hands with a married man with a child on the way? Even if his intentions were honourable, I knew now that I had too much of a crush on him to be able to spend any more time with him. I had to be strong.

"I don't need your help," I said firmly as I yanked my hand back, "It's time to go."

He looked devastated. I wanted to tell him he hadn't done anything wrong, that it was just me. That the only reason I couldn't accept his offer and his friendship was because I was too infatuated with him.

As soon as Group finished, I ran out so that I didn't have to walk with him to my car. It was better this way. That was my luck, of course. I'd finally met someone that I really, truly, wanted and he was married. With how horrible I felt and my Even Steven Factor, I should go out and buy a lottery ticket. The last one I'd bought was at Mr. Cho's and I had no idea where it was.

CHEAP BUT NOT CHEERFUL

John from Speed Dating asked me out and I suggested we meet for coffee. He was already seated when I arrived and was wearing the same clothes he'd worn the night I met him. I didn't have to worry about having to carry the conversation like I had with Keith, John had non-stop questions:

"So, where do you live?" "Yeah? Do you own or rent there?" "Just rent, huh, do you have other investment property then?" "No? So you're more of a stocks and bonds kind of girl?"

Eventually we got onto the topic of dating and I told him how I'd been served divorce papers when I'd gone to lunch with a lawyer.

"Divorce? Really?" He looked excited. "So, what does your Ex do? Will you get a large settlement?"

Aah, now I got it. What was it about me that attracted these cheap jerks?

"No actually, I may end up paying him alimony," I said and then waited for him to walk out.

"Really? Wow, you must really make a lot of money then. Chartered accountants do well, don't they? I read a survey in the Globe and Mail the other day right before I came to speed dating and it said-"

I interrupted him, "Actually, I'm not doing that anymore."

"You're not?"

"No, I'm at the hospital now, in the old folks ward."

"Oh. I would have thought that would pay less."

"Well, I just enjoy feeling like I'm making a difference in someone's life."

"Right." He drew the word out while he thought. "So how much less does it pay?"

"Actually," I said, going for the deal breaker, "I volunteer."

"What?" he said choking on his muffin.

"You know, I work without getting paid. And I enjoy it so much I'm not going to be looking for a paying job in the foreseeable future." I counted down in my head. 3…2…1…

"Uh, I have to…I just remembered I've got to go and…"

"Yeah. Whatever. You can leave your share, then."

"I can what?"

"Five dollars should cover your coffee and muffin."

He threw out a handful of change and stormed off. Proudly, I paid the bill and went to drive to the hospital to meet Stella for our American Idol watching date, excited to tell her how I'd stood up for myself.

Wait. Was that John standing at the bus stop? Was he hitchhiking? The loser must have used the last of his money to pay for his coffee and muffin. I was going to honk and wave obnoxiously as I drove by. I might even stick my tongue out. Maybe…maybe even my middle finger. He looked pathetic, standing there with his thumb stuck out. Slowing down, I unrolled down the passenger window so that he'd see me clearly.

But then I had second thoughts. Maybe he'd hit really hard times. Who was to say I wouldn't be in the same desperate position one day? Actually, I could end up in his exact situation if I ended up paying alimony and losing my job. Ugh, I was such a sucker. Maybe when I told Stella how tough I'd been I'd leave out the part where I pulled over and gave him money.

"Hi John, do you need some change for the bus?"

He looked surprised to see me but quickly recovered and flashed a dazzling smile at me as if all was forgiven. As he leaned into the car to take my change, he looked it over and took in the "For Sale" sign on the back.

"Hey, you're selling your car? Is it paid off? How much do you think you'll get for it?"

TWO HOT DATES

The next Thursday I arrived at campus and hung out in the bookstore so that I'd be five minutes late for Group. I was avoiding spending time with Alex. It just killed me to know that we could only ever be friends.

"You look nice. Did you get your hair done?" asked Alex as I handed in my journal.

"Uh, yes, thank you."

Alex had us read our journals out loud that night. He wanted to have the Group comment on each entry and relate any similar experiences.

Jeanette went first. Kal and Nelson turned red as she went into very detailed physical description about a date she had with a trucker named Dog she'd met at a bar. Alex stopped her when she started to describe what happened when they drove up to Lookout Point.

"So, Jeanette, um, where exactly is the accident part of your journal?"

"I'm getting to that. Where was I? Oh yeah 'I could feel his strong, forceful hand on the back of my head, his lips on mine, his tongue exploring my mouth, and the full weight of his body on mine. Finally, he-'"

"Jeanette," Alex interrupted. "I'm not sure if all that is relevant to the physical disaster part of your entry. Perhaps you could just skip to that part."

"Right. We were, ya know, going for it, and we somehow disengaged the emergency brake and ended up rolling into another car."

"Okay, thank you. Well, Karly, would you like to go next?"

I read mine:

Journal Entry:

Date and time: Saturday, August 3rd, 8:30

Weather: Warm, summer night.

Food consumed: goat cheese, caramelized pecan and endive salad, lobster ravioli

Alcohol Consumed: one glass of red wine.

Non-alcoholic Beverages consumed: Perrier

Wearing: Black dress, high heels.

Location: La Scala (crowded, upscale French restaurant).

Emotional States: Nervous, excited, hopeful, then disappointed.

Situation leading to event: First date with Dirk, an actor I met at Speed Dating.

Description of Event:

- was entertained by stories of various actors Dirk has met and auditions he has been on.
- Dirk was equally amused by my Strangeness Attracter stories and said I should write them into a screenplay.
- uneventful evening until he decided to surprise me with crepes suzette for dessert.
- unfortunate incident followed involving a larger patron who bumped into our waiter while trying to squeeze behind him, and our tablecloth lighting on fire.

- *waiter's quick reflexes saved us from catching on fire but not before the ends of my hair were singed.*

- *got our meal for free and gift certificates for future meals.*

- *although he wasn't hurt and Dirk said he really did enjoy my company, he also said he cannot risk breaking a limb or burning off his eyebrows while he is auditioning. Or after he lands a role.*

"Ahh…crepes Suzette." The group nodded knowingly.

***

Alex walked me to my car after Group. I'd originally planned on running out at the end of the session to avoid him but he'd quickly packed up and was waiting expectantly at the door for me. Okay, I told myself, I should be able to handle five minutes. If I walked fast, I could shave it down to four.

"So you tried speed dating?" he asked.

"Yes," I answered, thankful that I had my running shoes on as I picked up the pace.

"That's great that you're so willing to try new things. I bet you got a lot of numbers."

"Not really."

"What? How would you not have gotten a ton of numbers? You're so…I mean…You-Hey, are we in a speed walking competition here?"

"Sorry." I slowed down. "Thanks. Well, maybe I would have gotten more but I had a Strangeness Attracter event hit me after my first few dates."

I described the evening to him.

"You know, if your friend isn't able to pick you up next time, well, I live on the North Shore too and if you ever need a ride, I'd be happy to be your knight in shining armour."

God, he was so nice. If I could ever get over my crush on him, it would be great to have another friend.

"Sure. Then you could experience the tail end of one of my disasters firsthand. That would be great for the study."

"Yeah, right. For the study."

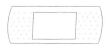

UPON REFLECTION…

I waited for my turn at the mirror in the crowded ladies room at the nightclub. The beautiful, trendy, scantily clad, unsmiling women there matched the beautiful, trendy, cold, minimalist décor. They scrutinized their faces, bodies, and hair while practicing their bored, unimpressed looks. I wished I'd practiced the same look earlier. Apparently I didn't know how to act in bars anymore.

I'd totally embarrassed my date Darren, yet again, by-God forbid-exclaiming aloud how amazing the opening night of Club Mantra was. Strings of glass baubles hung strategically throughout from the raised ceiling all the way down to the floor. Silver and white balloons filled the club while a bubble machine worked its magic. As we'd stepped in, gorgeous women in revealing toga-like outfits and glittery silver makeup had offered us champagne and told us to enjoy the many canapés that had been laid out. I'd started to squeal at how impressive it all was but quickly clammed up when Darren gave me the same look he had earlier when I'd picked up the fork I'd dropped on the floor at the five star restaurant he'd taken me out to. Halting his detailed description of his latest Hugo Boss purchases, he'd grabbed my arm and pulled me back up, mortified, whispering, "Karly, there are people here to do that. Do you want everyone to stare?"

Thank God he hadn't seen me accidentally using the men's' room right after that. I hadn't noticed until I walked out of my stall and shocked both myself and the older man there washing his hands. He'd kindly pointed out that I'd tucked the back of my skirt into the top of my panties which had saved me from flashing the whole restaurant so it was a blessing in disguise.

After dinner, the attendant got Darren's vehicle, which was some kind of showy sports car that I'm sure would have impressed Nik if I could have remembered the name of it, and we drove two blocks to the club. I spotted a parking place right across the street but Darren insisted we valet park again. Before we got out, he checked his reflection in the rear view mirror, turning his head to one side and then the other, practicing a serious look, a dazzling smile, and then the ever-popular indifferent look.

"On the back of your sun shade," he said when he caught me just watching him. "And there's gum in the glove compartment. I don't know why you ordered garlic shrimp if you knew we were going out after. You'd better have two pieces."

"Oh, right. Of course," I said and popped in three pieces to be on the safe side even though I had not, in fact, had any of the savoury seafood. Then I flipped the sunshade down and checked out my appearance as seemed to be expected of me. Feeling foolish, I half-heartedly made a couple of faces and even though I was confident there couldn't be anything in my teeth, checked anyway. Earlier, Darren had updated me on the status of my pearly whites after every single bite of spinach salad I'd had. It had been a bit unnerving. To the point where I declared myself done and had the server take my plate away. Then my over-sized, shell-on, garlic prawns had arrived and much to Darren's masked chagrin, in wrestling the first one off the bamboo skewer they'd come on, I'd sent it shooting off to another couple's table. I didn't think my technique would improve so I'd waited until he went to the men's room and then wrapped the whole second skewer in a napkin and dumped it in my purse. Now I was starving. I would have eaten my smuggled leftovers in the ladies' room but I'd checked and they'd fallen out of the napkin and were currently rolling around the bottom of my bag, covered in purse lint and hair.

I pretended to take a look at myself in the mirror once I finally got my turn in the bar bathroom but I was really there to think about my date. Okay, he was a little image conscious. Was that necessarily a bad thing? Maybe this was the norm and I just wasn't used to it. After all, I'd been exposed to the Ex for the last two years. I thought about the time I'd taken him out on a business dinner with a high profile client. We had been on the subject of fine wine and restaurants when he'd joined in, telling about the hilarious time he and his friends had done a dine and dash from Denny's after a night of drinking. The story had been not so well received. Really, my current date was a complete catch in comparison.

I took a deep breath to psych myself up. Okay, I would try harder to like Darren. Surely being immaculate about one's appearance and having impeccable restaurant manners wasn't a bad thing. Yes, if I applied myself, I'm sure I could find a way to enjoy his company. I'd go back to him and try hard to find something we had in common. Plus, there were snacks out there.

I marched myself back to the cocktail table where Darren was standing, excited about my new lease on this date but of course maintaining my composure deep underneath a suitably indifferent façade.

Awesome. I cheered internally. Someone had put a big plate of canapés on the table Darren was posing against.

"Oh, sorry," a guy passing by bumped into me as I was about to take a bite of a guacamole and smoked salmon covered melba square.

I inspected myself, assuming there was food on me somewhere.

"What the Hell!" Darren put his hand on the back of his hair and discovered something oozy and green there.

Uh oh.

"Christ. Get it out before someone sees me!" he hissed. Geesh. This guy needed to relax. A bit of mashed up avocado never hurt anyone. In fact, it was a main ingredient in the fancy conditioner that Desiree used. And it wasn't like I'd spilled bleach or acid on him. Or fruit juice at a family picnic near a bees' nest. I thought about my poor Uncle Paul.

"Karly!"

Oh yeah. My guacamole intolerant date was freaking out. I started wiping with the napkin I had in my hand.

"Ow. Stop pulling!"

I took a look. Oh crap.

"Hey Darren? I got most of it out."

"Thank God. Did anyone see?"

"I don't know. But there seems to be just a little bit of gum stuck in your hair now."

He stuck his hand up and discovered the large, bird nest-like tangle of hair I'd created with the wad I'd spat out into my napkin before trying to enjoy my appetizer.

"Shit. I knew I should have gotten rid of you after you kept embarrassing me at the restaurant."

What did that mean? Fair enough if he wanted to call it quits at this point, now that he'd have to shave his head because of me, but he would have ended it over some projectile shrimp and a rogue fork? And he didn't have to be so mean about it. My heart started beating and I thought about what Stella always said about standing up for myself. I swallowed the lump in my throat and made myself speak.

"Fine, then. You can apologize and give me cab fare home and I'll be on my way."

"You want me to say sorry to you? After what you did to me?"

"And cab fare. Or I'll…I'll throw my skirt over my head and do the can can while screaming out your name and pointing at you."

"Are you crazy?" His eyes darted back and forth as if imagining the horrible scene and all the stares from the rest of the partygoers.

I put my hand on my hip, grabbed the edge of my skirt and gave him my best "make my day" look.

"Okay, I'm sorry. Just leave me alone." He threw some bills towards me and I picked them off of the floor and walked out. Well, maybe it wasn't quite the altercation Stella would have hoped for, but damn, I was still pretty proud of myself.

ANOTHER NEW DO

"Hi Karly. You look nice. Is this another new hairstyle?" asked Alex as I handed in my journal at the start of Group.

"Uh, yes."

Journal Entry:

Date and Time: Saturday night, August 10, 8:00

Weather: Clear night, warm

Food Consumed: Macaroni and cheese dinner at home, Chips and dip at party.

Alcohol Consumed: two glasses of beer

Wearing: Black skirt, black T-shirt

Location: Date's friend's house

Emotional state: Nervous

Situation leading to event: First date with Tyler, a theatre actor

Description:

- had been asked out by my neighbor's friend, Tyler.
- thought he knew it was my birthday that day.
- went with him to friend's house and was hanging out with ten of his actor friends and fighting cat and dust allergies.

- assumed that cake brought to table was for me and was very touched by my date's thoughtfulness.
- stepped forward and went to blow out all candles but sneezed all over the cake instead.
- Then noticed it had someone else's name on it.

"Well at least you didn't burn your hair, like the time you dated that other actor," Nelson said.

I read out my second journal.

Journal Entry:

Date and Time: Saturday night, August 17, 7:30

Weather: Clear night, warm

Food Consumed: Take out Thai food

Alcohol Consumed: two glasses of red wine

Non-Alcoholic Beverages Consumed: one glass of water

Wearing: Jeans and T-shirt

Location: Anne Marie's house

Emotional state: Happy

Situation leading to event: Belated birthday celebration with friends from high school.

Description:

- *four of us gathered for take out and birthday cake.*
- *friends thought it was funny to order extra large cake and put thirty candles on it.*
- *closed eyes and took my time thinking out all my birthday wishes.*
- *Became aware of funny odor, very similar to last month's burning hair smell.*

OPERATION "FORGET ALEX"

Armed with an herbal tea and croissant, I sat at my computer, thinking. Turning thirty had made me reflect on my life and I wasn't where I thought I would be. Definitely, I needed to make some changes. But I'd start with baby steps. I wasn't quite ready to deal with my divorce or career but I could get out and have some fun, and get my mind off a certain unavailable doctor in the process. Operation "Forget Alex" was underway. It was up to me to bring myself out of this funk. I updated my website profile to show that I was looking for someone who:

- liked to have fun

- enjoyed life

***

Oh God, what was I going to do? Where did my fun night go? Yesterday I'd borrowed a short, Pucci-patterned dress from Desiree and had even pre-band-aided my feet and practiced walking in my high heels. Then earlier this evening I'd met my website date at happy hour, determined to be the new, fun, Karly. I'd spent two hours laughing my head off with charismatic Joel and all our new bar friends, dentists in town for a conference and a film crew that had just finished that week's shooting.

Now I was careening down Richards Street in my date's red convertible BMW, weaving dangerously in and out of traffic, with a newly found fear of death and dismemberment.

"What's wrong, doll? You don't look so good," Joel, a short, muscular Italian that sold photocopiers for a living had finally noticed my green face and death grip on the armrest.

Just this unshakeable feeling of impending doom, I thought as I begged him again to slow down.

"No can do, sweets," he answered, oblivious to my terror and patting my head like you would a puppy's. "I gotta get to an associate's house on Water Street in the Properties to pick some stuff up for those guys before we meet them at the club."

What stuff? He'd been discussing prices and inventory earlier with the group we'd been hanging out with and I'd assumed he'd been talking to them about photocopiers. I thought they'd been unusually interested but had put it down to good manners on behalf of the dentists and good acting on behalf of the actors. Why were we going to drive across a bridge and back in the middle of our date? I didn't have time to ask before having to scream, "Joel! Watch out!"

He'd gone right through a red light and narrowly missed hitting a mom in a mini van. The image of her terrified face would be on my guilty conscience for the rest of my life.

"Stop the car this instant," I demanded. "You almost hit that woman."

"Come on, we're fine."

"We are not!" I continued with my hysterics. "What's wrong with you? Let me out."

"You're starting to become a bit of a drag, babe. Come on, don't ruin the great time we're having."

Was he serious? Did he really think my crying and screaming in terror in between begging him to stop the car was a sign I was having fun?

"Joel! Red light again!"

He actually managed to stop at this one but not without jamming on the brakes and sending us flying against our seat belts. I bet I'd have a diagonal bruise across my upper body.

We rolled up beside a young guy and his overly made up girlfriend in a Porsche. The other driver looked over, sussed out Joel's car, and revved his engine. Joel revved back.

"Hold on tight, babe. I'm gonna drive fast now."

What the Hell were we doing before? No. I couldn't stand it. I wouldn't. My life wasn't great but I didn't want to die. Without thinking I ripped off my seatbelt, threw open the door, and jumped out. I made it to the sidewalk before I heard the peal of tires and turned around to see the two cars burning down the street. Oh Land, Sweet Land! If I hadn't been downtown on a street full of litter, I would have thrown myself down on the ground and kissed it.

Where was my purse? Damn, I hadn't thought to grab it during my escape. Crap, crap, crap. I was standing in a not-so-great area of town without a cell phone or any money. On the bright side, there was no reason for anyone to mug me.

"Excuse me," I asked a well-dressed older couple walking by me, "I was wondering-"

"Don't make eye contact," the woman hissed at the man and grabbed his arm tighter as they walked away.

"Disgusting," the man said back to her. "She's probably on hard drugs."

Were they talking about me? What was going on? I probably did look a bit of a mess with my hair blown every direction from the convertible death-mobile and my eye makeup streaked down my face from my tears but still, that was kind of harsh. Taking a deep breath, I tried to calm down. I just needed to phone someone to come get me. If I could get some change I could walk around and find a pay phone.

I wiped up my stray makeup from my face with the back of my hand and approached a forty-ish looking construction worker walking by.

"Hey Mister, can you spare a couple quarters?"

"I think you got the line wrong, honey, I think it's supposed to be a dime."

"Pardon?" I sniffed.

"Not that I'm saying I'm interested or nothing, but what is the going rate?"

"For the pay phone? I'm sure it's fifty cents."

"You a cop or something? That's freaking entrapment."

He stormed off. I felt like Alice in Wonderland. This was such a bizarre night.

"What the Hell are you doing?" a husky, female voice demanded from behind me.

I whirled around then took a step back after taking in the appearance of my very angry accoster. Her pale arms were folded over her well-displayed, ample chest and she was wearing thigh high, plastic, white boots, a tight mini skirt, and a sparkly gold and red bustier. She looked a little cheap. Like a…a hooker. Ahhk. I was on Richards Street, where the prostitutes worked, and those people had thought I was one!

"Oh my God," I said and burst into tears again.

"For Christ's Sakes. I'll assume that cute John of yours just dropped ya off in the wrong place so I'm givin' ya two minutes to clear out."

Great. Now a street tough hooker was threatening me. Maybe I'd been safer in the deathmobile. I wondered if Joel had even noticed I wasn't in the car with him anymore.

"Hey." It was the working girl again. "Someone's trying to get your attention."

"Pardon?"

"The lady in the mini van. I'm pretty sure she's not here to talk to me. And ya got one minute left," she said and then strutted off to talk to a car full of college boys. I looked over at the van. It was the woman Joel had almost crashed into.

"You okay, honey?" asked a motherly voice.

I nodded.

"You sure? You look a little lost."

"I uh, I left my purse in that guy's car."

"So he's not your boyfriend?"

"No, just a bad first date."

"Hmmmm," she sussed me out and then said, "Okay, jump in. Let's get you off the street first and then figure out what to do."

I hopped in. Nik would have a fit with me jumping into a complete stranger's car. But surely I'd be safer in this vehicle that had three cars seats in the back and Cheerios and juice containers on the floor than with my crazy, Mach-five, death-cruise date.

"Do you think you'll get your purse back?"

"I don't care if I ever see it again. It's just got lipstick and a bit of cash in it."

"You don't know where he's heading, do you? I was following him but turned around to come check on you."

I told her and she called the police and reported Joel for dangerous driving and stealing my purse. Okay, technically I'd left my bag in his car but I didn't want to interrupt. She insisted on driving me all the way home and I thanked her again as she dropped me off.

"No worries, honey. We've all made bad decisions when it comes to men. You just try and be more careful next time."

I took off what I would now refer to as my hooker outfit, removed my streaked makeup, wrote my Strangeness Attracter journal for Alex and called it a night.

EXTRA! EXTRA!

Pop Tarts and newspaper in hand, I sat down at my kitchen table in my faded pink terry cloth robe and fuzzy bunny slippers. I didn't regularly read the paper because there was so much bad news in it but I needed to take my mind off last night's drama. There was a sketch of someone who looked like Joel on the front page.

Mafia Cocaine Ring Busted

Friday evening was a good night for the Vancouver Narcotics Squad and a bad one for drug dealers. Police received a tip about a dangerous driver and purse thief from a concerned citizen and recognized the license plate as belonging to Joel Stefano, who has been a person of interest to them for some time. They tracked the offender to a house in the British Properties where they uncovered a major drug operation, reaching all the way to the top of the well-known "Mala Fide" gang. In a stroke of luck for the Police, all top gang members were gathered there for a meeting, complete with documented proof of their illegal activity.

Fifteen high profile arrests were made. Cocaine with an estimated street value of ten million dollars was discovered in the basement of the house. Unfortunately, Mr. Stefano escaped. Police believe he has fled the country but are circulating a sketch and asking the public to report anyone looking like him. Two years ago, Joel Stefano was charged with the violent murder of his ex-girlfriend who was set to testify against him on various charges.

```
He was released on a court technicality.

    Police were unable to ascertain the
identification of the purse owner but when
questioned later, the concerned citizen who
called in said she talked to the woman on
Richards Street, a location known for its
prostitutes. Police are urging the mystery
citizen to come forward.
```

I pushed my Pop Tarts away, my stomach now queasy. How on earth did these things happen to me? I scrapped the journal I'd written for Alex the night before, deleted my profile on the dating website, and thanked God for the mini van mom's discretion.

NANNY KARLY

"Aunty Karly, I want candy!"

"Okay, Siri honey, just hold on."

I stood at the open trunk of my car, sweating buckets in the guest parking lot of the snotty country club Bill and Desiree wanted to join. Desiree had phoned me the night before asking me to look after my niece and nephew at the club while Bill and Desiree were being interviewed, and then bring them the kids so they could be introduced to the panel.

"Bill's okay with me watching them?" I'd asked.

"It was his idea," Desiree had answered, not hiding that she was equally astonished.

This was real progress. My brother in law had been hesitant to leave the kids in my care after I misplaced Siri the last time I looked after her. Maybe the mall wasn't the best place to play hide-and-seek but in my defence, I didn't think she'd be such a good hider. The genius grandfatherly security man returned to the store I'd lost her in and announced that he had a chocolate bar for any four-year-olds that would come out of hiding and she'd popped out from the middle of a round clothes rack, two feet away from where we were.

Anyway, I was thrilled for the opportunity to get onto Bill's good side. It would make it easier later if my streak of back luck continued and I had to ask if I could move in and mooch off them for a while. Maybe they would even pay me to be their nanny. It wasn't the career I'd planned but what else would I do if I had charges pressed against me and my professional designation taken away?

I'd shown up at the country club to look after the kids and long story short, had accidentally fallen into the pool with Connor in my arms. We weren't hurt but we were soaked so I was trying to sew one of my spare T-shirts from my car into a onesie onto him. I'd thought I'd had it at one point until I realized I'd also attached him to his stroller.

Considering that I was sewing a garment directly onto a squirming baby, it didn't turn out too badly. I looked at my watch. Crap. Two minutes until family interview time.

After sprinting up the hill with one hand dragging Siri behind me and the other pushing the stroller in front of me, I arrived just in time. I was sweaty, out of breath, had squishy sandals and a clingy wet outfit on, but at least my niece and nephew looked presentable. I'd pass the kids off and get out of there before any questions were asked.

"There you are, my little angel!" Desiree sing-songed and picked up Siri for a big, twirling hug.

"That's my boy!" Bill bellowed out heartily to Connor and held out his hand enthusiastically for a high five. His son responded by staring blankly at him while wedging his middle finger up his nose.

Not that they weren't loving parents, but it was a little overboard. I guess it was a show for the elderly man that was with them. Desiree's eyes widened as she noticed my soaking wet outfit while Bill obliviously went on to the man, Teddy, about the importance of having good help that spoke English.

"Ah, you have an au pair, then? How wonderful," the man said in his nasal, aristocratic accent, "My daughter just had one imported from Surrey. Lovely thing. She once attended a birthday party for the six-year-old daughter to the hat maker to the Queen. Where did you get yours?"

"Pardon?"

"Your au pair? What agency did you get her from?"

Although I was the topic of the conversation, Teddy had barely given me a glance throughout this whole exchange.

"Oh, um, the Northern Windsor Royal Au Pair and uh, Governess Agency," Bill came up with.

Desiree shot him an alarmed look then looked at me pleadingly. That pretentious idiotic brother-in-law of mine was lucky I loved my sister so much. I grimaced but held my tongue.

"Mommy," said Siri, "I have candy."

"You do, honey?" Desiree looked at me and I shrugged.

"Siri," said Bill, "this is Mr. Hollyburn, can you say 'hello' please?"

"Hullo, would you like one of my candies?" she said dutifully and held out her hand and offered him one of the three colourfully wrapped packages she had in her hand.

Where did she get those? They looked familiar. Oh God, she'd gotten them out of my car. And they weren't candies. They were the condoms I'd stuffed in the glove compartment when I'd moved. Desiree, Bill and I all gasped in horror.

"Oh, no thank you," Mr. Hollyburn answered. "You keep those sweeties for yourself, little girl."

He wrapped her chubby little hand around them and then turned to admire Connor.

"Well, I'll be going if you don't need me anymore," I said and then, remembering I was supposed to be an English au pair, added in my best Mrs. Doubtfire accent, "Cheerio. And uh, toodles. And-"

"Yes, thank you," said Bill, cutting me off, finally breathing normally again. "I don't think we need any more help from you today."

"Righty-o, sir. Uh, very good." I did a quick, clumsy curtsy and scurried off leaving a trail of flip-flop shaped puddles behind me.

SAVE THE WHALES

Okay, so I'd had a minor setback with the whole dating-a-murderous-cocaine-dealer thing, but I wasn't going to give up. I started a new profile on the 50 Ways website, this time using the name Lyndsay, in case the mafia were trying to track me down. Shuddering at the memory of my date with Joel, I posted that I was looking for someone who was:

- Responsible
- Ethical
- Of high moral standing
- Caring
- Genuine

The following Thursday I was matched up with Artie, an environmental consultant with brown hair and soulful eyes, who wanted a match that was:

- Socially responsible
- Environmentally conscious
- Passionate

It seemed like a perfect match. He asked if I wanted to meet for dinner that night and because my group session had been cancelled due to Alex having the flu, my evening was free.

When I'd gotten the email about Alex being sick that morning, my first reaction had been to bring soup to his house. Not that I was a good cook and could have brought over homemade chicken noodle or anything. Although, I guess it would have looked odd to show up and hand over a can of Campbell's. What was I thinking? Showing up at his house would have just looked odd, period. His annoyingly beautiful Julia was probably busy dicing carrots and ginger for some nutritious home made dish for him right now. Or buying the ingredients for her mom's chicken casserole. He didn't need me. Determined to move on, I hit "send" on my message saying I would love to meet Artie for dinner.

He'd suggested a restaurant called "EraCeR" on Commercial Drive. I got there about fifteen minutes early having been lucky enough to have hit all the green lights, not gotten lost, and find parking right across the street.

The small eatery was dimly lit. One wall was completely covered with pictures, posters and newspaper clippings. The green-haired, multi-pierced hostess, who looked irritated at the thought of someone disturbing her reading, was impervious when I told her I'd just wait to be seated until my date arrived. I took a look at all the clippings covering the walls and discovered that the name 'EraCeR' was short for Environmentally Conscious Restaurant. That explained the articles papered all over the wall, "Greenpeace members arrested for surrounding fishing boats", "Government in denial about global warming", "Protest against the testing of nuclear weapons in France", and so on. Flyers urging people to buy locally or grow their own vegetable gardens were also posted.

After catching my reflection in the window, I felt like a bit of a slob. I wished I'd known I was going to get here so early. That extra fifteen minutes could have been spent getting more date-worthy. But that was Murphy's Law. If I'd left fifteen minutes later, I would have hit every red light, gotten lost, not been able to find parking and would have arrived half an hour late.

I'd lost track of the time and had had to fly out the door, without time to change. Consequently, I was in old, ripped, jeans and a comfy but very old and faded grey t-shirt that may have been black when I first bought it. Oh well, I was still unpacking unlabelled (well, technically they were labelled but with scribbled hieroglyphics) boxes and probably wouldn't have been able to find something much better anyway.

Artie had asked to meet for a casual bite but who knew what that meant? When Desiree and Bill went to 'casual' dinner parties, she had her hair professionally blow-dried and her personal shopper source her a new outfit. I continued to worry about my appearance while watching a homeless guy saunter towards the restaurant from the bus stop across the street, a holey, army green, canvas knapsack on his back. Funny, he looked familiar.

"Lyndsay? Nice to meet you," said the bum as he shook my hand after walking in. Well, good thing I hadn't dressed up. I would have felt like an idiot. My date was in tattered khakis that were held up not by a belt, but by an actual rope. And he had a similar "used to be black" grey t-shirt on but with obvious holes in the seams. Maybe this was some new fashion I wasn't familiar with.

Ooh, up close he was much cuter than his profile picture. He had messy brown hair that looked good on him, bushy eyebrows with a touch of gray, a bit of facial hair, and a nice smile with some crooked teeth that really just made him more endearing.

We sat down and looked at the menu. I'd hardly eaten all day, I'd been so determined to make a dent in my unpacking. I wanted a steak and potato with the works, something really filling. Should I have a T-bone? Or maybe a sirloin? I searched through the menu. Odd. I actually didn't recognize half the menu items. Was this in English?

"Are you ready to order?" asked the hostess who doubled as the server.

"Yes, what kind of steak do you have?" I asked.

They both looked horrified.

"We don't serve anything that has to be slaughtered," the server haughtily informed me.

"Oh of course not, I was just checking that you didn't. Uh, do you have any tuna?" I asked, praying they didn't think fishing was a form of slaughter.

"You're not looking for farmed fish or the kind caught illegally by Japanese overfishing off the coast of the Philippines that neither government is doing anything about?" she demanded, hand on jutted hip, her voice getting louder and more accusatory as she spoke.

"No, just regular tuna," I answered.

"We're out," she answered.

God.

"What do you recommend then?" I asked.

"That depends. I assume you're vegetarians?"

Artie nodded eagerly so I did too. Well, I wasn't technically a vegetarian but I was willing to try anything.

"What kind?" she asked.

Was she kidding? I looked at her stupidly.

"Lacto-vegetarian, vegan, ovo, pescatarian, raw foodist, frutarian, Ital, Buddhist…" she listed after letting out an exasperated sigh.

Artie was looking at me expectantly.

"Uh, the first one?" I said.

"Then the onion bhajia and brown rice tofu and sprouts bowl is good."

"Great, I'll have that."

"Me too," Artie said and smiled at me. I beamed back, happy to be done with ordering and eager to start getting to know him.

"And to drink?" evil tattoo waitress asked. Crap.

"A glass of red wine, please."

"What kind?" she asked with a look that said, "I'll get you yet."

Why was this so difficult? My mind blanked and there was complete silence except for the loud ticking of the wall clock that sounded like it was commanding "or-der, or-der, or-der." It was like I was on a game show and about to lose a million dollars. They were both looking expectantly at me. I'm not even good at ordering wine in a normal situation. Oh, hold on, what had I seen posted on the wall? Ha-

"Any kind that is not from France because I am boycotting their wine to protest the testing of nuclear weapons by the Government in the waters of French Polynesia!" I declared in one breath triumphantly, slamming my palm down on the table in excitement, as if I'd just come up with a brilliant answer on Family Feud.

"Hmmm. Good choice," she gave me begrudgingly.

My date gave me a little smile, "That's amazing that you're still boycotting French wine when they haven't tested there since the nineties."

"Well, it's something I was uh, quite passionate about at the time," I said to him proudly and then called after the server,

"Excuse me?"

"Yes?"

I went for bonus points.

"You'll make sure it's organic and locally produced, of course, won't you?"

Artie gave me a full smile.

Other than the food, which tasted like cardboard, dinner with Artie was nice. We talked about environmental issues, the evils of consumerism, and how greedy, bottom-line-oriented corporations were destroying our Mother Earth. Well, actually, Artie dominated most of the conversation and I nodded and threw in the occasional comment. Not that I didn't agree with him, but I was perhaps not quite as passionate as he was. But as he talked, I became more so. I mean, it was pretty upsetting that they were still slaughtering baby seals in Alaska and that there was no government-imposed punishment for illegal fishing in Asia, or that the authorities in parts of Africa turned a blind eye to the poaching of endangered species for their tusks and paws. Yes, I was becoming more zealous the more he spoke. Well, at the same time thinking what fast food I could pick up on the way home.

I pushed the odd-coloured spongy tofu around on my plate with my fork distastefully and hoped Artie couldn't hear my stomach rumbling. Even if I had the strength to go another round with the waitress and order dessert, there was no guarantee it would be edible. She'd probably serve me dandelion and wheat grass cake topped with organic recycled cardboard puree.

Burger King was my first choice. I would so kill for a Whopper but I didn't know if they'd still be open by the time I got out of here. McDonalds would have to be my backup plan. There was one that was open twenty-four hours even if they weren't on my direct route home. Were they still serving the McFlurry? I'd have to-

"Hey, I'm having a great time," Artie interrupted my fast food reverie. "But I've actually got to get going to a midnight rally for the homeless downtown. We're going to start at Pigeon Park and march all the way to City Hall and stage a sit in."

"That's great." Awesome. Burger King it was.

"You think so? Do you want to come with me?" he said.

"Huh? Tonight? Now?"

"Yes."

It was so sweet that he wanted to help the street people. Sure, I wanted to help them too. But it got a little chilly this time of night and I'd only brought a light sweater. Plus I had my Whopper plans. And I didn't want to be too tired when I went to the spa with Desiree for my belated birthday treat from her tomorrow.

"Oh, I totally would," I lied, "but I have to get started on some…volunteer work I do for…the whales."

"Really?" he said, "I've love to hear all about it next time."

Crap.

We walked out and he asked how I'd gotten there.

"How did *you* get here?" I asked back.

"It was too far to cycle so I took the bus. I felt sick when I saw the number of people driving alone in their cars. They could easily take public transit, or bike, or at least carpool. The amount of pollution caused by auto emissions just makes my blood boil."

"Uh, yeah."

"So how did you get here?"

"Um, I also took public transit," I said as I looked longingly at my beautiful car with its For Sale sign on it, three metres away.

"Hey," said Artie looking down the street, "aren't you from the North Shore?"

"Pardon?"

"Didn't you say you live just off Lonsdale when we were talking about the North Vancouver Bird Sanctuary?"

"Oh, yes, I did."

"What luck. Here's your bus."

The large vehicle pulled up in front of us.

"Great. Here it is. Right here."

"Well, mine won't be by for fifteen minutes so, um, thanks for having dinner with me. I uh, I have a fundraiser next weekend that I'd like you to be my date for if, if you want to see me again, that is."

"Um…" I was blanking out, perplexed about the transportation situation.

"Lady," called out the grumpy bus driver who'd opened the door and been listening to our conversation, "just say 'yes' and get on the bus. I got a schedule."

Artie laughed. I laughed. The bus passengers, who were all listening, laughed.

"Yes," I said and got on the bus to applause from the other travelers.

I smiled and waved to Artie as we pulled away.

OUT OF SIGHT

"Lady," the no-nonsense bus driver said as I took a seat.

"Yes?"

"Your fare."

"Oh, right. How much?" I stood back up and landed for a second on an older woman's lap as the bus lurched to it's next stop.

"How many zones you going?"

"I'm just going to get off as soon as we're, um, out of sight." I'd checked and could still see Artie.

"What?"

"It depends on how far apart your stops are. How many zones are two stops?"

He muttered to himself while shaking his head.

"Okay then," I tried negotiating, "how about three stops?"

"Lady, you never taken the bus before? We don't charge you based on number of stops."

"Okay, well, I'll get off at the next block, how much is that?"

"Three fifty."

"For that short distance? I could have walked that for free."

"Well maybe you could have, maybe you should have, but you didn't. Hand over the fare."

I dug in my purse.

"Do you take Visa?" I asked.

"That's it, get off." He pulled over and opened the doors. I looked down the street. We'd gone a surprising distance by this time so I was sure Artie wouldn't be able to see me get back off the bus. Perfect.

"Thank you so much," I called out happily as I stepped down onto the street.

The bus driver grumbled something undecipherable as he shut the door behind me and pulled away.

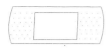

THE PINK FAIRY ARMADILLO

I mentioned the fundraiser to my sister and brother-in-law at dinner at their place after Desiree and I spent the day at the spa. Artie had sent me an email first thing that morning, giving me details for our date the following Saturday night. In honour of the pink fairy armadillo, there would be food, drinks, and an auction at the West Vancouver Sailing Club. It sounded fancy. I'd need to beg, borrow, or unpack something nice. Artie would look so handsome in a tux. He'd probably just dressed down for our first date seeing as we'd been at a casual restaurant and he was going to be hanging out with homeless people afterwards. I mean, he wouldn't have wanted to dress up and then be mugged by the very people he was rallying to support.

Desiree and Bill had never heard of the West Vancouver Sailing Club and thought I probably meant the Yacht Club where they'd attended the best fundraiser just last month. Neither of them could remember what it was for but Desiree was able to tell me what she'd worn and Bill remembered what business contacts he'd met and how impressed everyone had been when he'd won the bid on the main auction item, a trip for four to Hong Kong. Family dinner was less uncomfortable than I thought it would be after the Country Club incident, probably because they were accepted for membership in the end and managed to trade Siri an organic carob and granola bar for her "candy."

Bill was excited that I was dating someone who went to fundraisers and Desiree insisted on dragging me upstairs to her dressing room and lending me something to wear. She pulled out some dresses for me to try on.

"Well, they're all last years' styles and I've already been seen in them. It's not like I can wear them again," she reassured me when I double-checked if she wanted to risk lending them to me.

"I picked out red, navy, and black, so no one will notice if you spill red wine on them," she said, "or even blackberry coulis."

"I'm so sorry about your chaise lounge," I apologized again for an event that had happened two years ago.

THE FAMILY FARM

Saturday night, and my auction date with Artie, finally arrived. This time I made sure I allocated ample time to get ready and spent two hours showering, shampooing, conditioning, deodorizing, tweezing, up-doing, shaving, powdering, and finally, stepping into Desiree's full length, red, Prada dress and fur trimmed wrap. I arrived near the address for the Sailing Club but parked a block away, along the direction public transit route, just in case. My borrowed Kate Spade bag clinked with bus fare change. Last night I'd researched whales on the internet and had cheat notes in my purse so I could talk about them intelligently if it came up. I was ready.

As I approached the sailing club, I thought I saw someone who looked like Artie getting off a bus. Oh, it was him. And he wasn't in a tuxedo. In fact, I think he was wearing the same thing he wore for our first date, rope belt and all. What was going on? I ducked behind a tree and watched him walk across the empty parking lot. The couple greeting him while chaining their bikes up weren't dressed up at all either. They walked into a small, dilapidated, old building that was definitely not the yacht club Bill and Desiree had described.

Crap. I trekked back to my car, my feet killing me in my sisters' half-size smaller shoes. Sighing, I decided I'd make the best of the situation. It was a good thing I'd replenished my "emergency wardrobe" after sewing Connor into my T-shirt. I opened the trunk and looked up and down the street. Nobody was around and it was dark out so I jumped out of Desiree's beautiful designer dress and grabbed for my leather skirt.

Oh no. The hanging straps were caught on something in my trunk. Why hadn't I thought to get my change of clothes out before I took my dress off? Don't panic, I told myself, as I grabbed my pink t-shirt and wrestled it on. Now where did the skirt go? It was just here. I felt around for the leather in the dark with both hands. Okay, there it was. Were those footsteps I heard? Crap. There were at least two people approaching. My final piece of clothing was still caught on something. If I could just detach it from whatever it was caught on, I could quickly jump in it. Oh God, I was in high heels, nylons, and a shirt on a public street. Propping my right foot up on the rear bumper, I heaved with all my strength and still got nothing. Desperate, I tried pulling at different angles. First left, then right. Finally the skirt flew loose.

Unfortunately, I'd put all my weight into pulling it so when the strap snapped free, I went flying onto the sidewalk. Ouch. At least I had the presence of mind to cover my crotch area with the stubborn piece of clothing as I landed. Proudly, I noted I'd also remembered to look at my belly button while flying backwards, preventing yet another knock out. I was now three for three in concussion prevention.

"Are you okay, miss?" asked a man's voice. It was hard to see him in the dark. Maybe he couldn't see me either.

"Yes, thank you," I answered, still lying flat out on the sidewalk. "Just having wardrobe difficulty."

"Like you forgot to finish putting it on?" asked an unimpressed-sounding woman's voice.

Damn. I guess they could see me.

I lay still clutching the leather over my privates as they walked around me and continued down the street. As soon as the sound of their footsteps faded, I crawled up off the ground and jumped into my skirt. I grabbed Desiree's fur trimmed wrap and purse that were still fancy but at least most of my outfit was now a little less formal.

I hobbled to the sailing club and walked up the stairs to a small, dimly lit room. How much fundraising could they expect to do if they couldn't even fit twenty people in here?

"Karly, I'm glad you made it," Artie greeted me as I walked in. "This is Bear."

The tall man who put his hand out to shake mine had the lumbering physique of, indeed, a bear, complete with at least one rug worth of brown hair on his weatherworn face and body.

"Artie said you do some work for the whales," he said.

I nodded.

"What kind?"

"Uh, volunteer work." What did he think? Dental work? Massage?

"I mean what kind of whales?" Oh. That made more sense.

"All kinds, really. I try not to discriminate," I came up with, wishing I'd remembered to review the cheat notes in my purse on the walk over.

"That's great. What organization are you with?"

"Well, isn't that odd? I'm just blanking on the name."

"Earthtrust? Oceania? The Whale Rescue Team?"

"Uh, that last one."

"Really? I thought they were located in Hawaii."

"Yes, well, I'm starting up a movement here."

"Wow, that's so exciting. We'd love to help out if you need anything. Right, Artie?"

Artie smiled and nodded at me. There was something so attractive about these people. They were just so genuine.

Bear and Artie went to catch up with some people they knew and I wandered around looking for food. Giving up, I looked at the silent auction items instead. When I'd imagined the fundraiser, I'd pictured works of art, dates with local celebrities and gift certificates from locally owned boutiques. Hmmm, so what did we have here? Was that supposed to be a work of art? It looked like an ashtray some sailing members' preschooler had made. Nope, it had a silent auction sheet attached to it.

I went to the next item. Great, I loved gift certificates. What was it for? A one-hour intense chakra cleansing session. Well, I wasn't sure what part of my body my chakra was but I was fairly certain it didn't need any intense cleansing. The next auction item was a hypnosis session. Weird.

Handcuffs? That was a little odd. Surely that didn't belong in a fundraiser. I read the description. They were apparently the very pair that somebody named Aidan Bojangles had used to chain himself to the entrance of the Exxon head office with. Interesting.

Oooh, this looked promising. A one-hour massage with a value of eighty dollars and a starting bid of thirty dollars. I jotted my name down.

A heavy, grey-haired lady wearing a lumpy, oversized Cowichan sweater dress and granny eyeglasses hanging from twine around her neck smiled eagerly at me.

"Thank you so much," she said wringing her hands. "I wasn't sure if anyone would bid at all and I've just been worried sick about it."

She looked so thrilled that I decided to write my name down for some more items, just to get things going. People would start bidding, they were probably just waiting for someone to start. Yes, I'd do everyone a favor by getting the ball rolling on everything.

"This sculpture is nice," I said to the lady just to make conversation. "Where's the bid sheet for this piece?"

"Oh, no dear, that's the bowl I served the taro root soy chips in. Are they all gone already?"

"Lyndsay, can I introduce you to Spring?" Artie had appeared beside me.

I turned around expecting a sixties flower child look-alike complete with a daisy wreath in her long free-flowing hair and white, empress cut, cotton dress. Yikes, Spring's name didn't suit her. She was skeletally thin with a shaved head, multiple piercings, and a big scowl on her face. She was wearing a shapeless, floor length dress that resembled a potato sack, and had a matching purse that was close to de-threading.

"Nice to meet you," I said. She looked me up and down with her arms crossed as Artie excused himself to talk to someone else. Well, at least more people were arriving and would hopefully start bidding. Although, based on the way they were dressed, they didn't look like they had any money to spare on getting their chakras cleansed.

"Is that a Kate Spade bag?" Spring asked.

I'd totally misjudged her. Her outfit was probably the newest in Gucci's potato sack collection and I was too out of it to know.

"Yes." I smiled.

"How much does a bag like that cost?"

My sister, after five years of marriage to Bill, tended to describe her outfits and accessories by price point. So I knew that this was her six hundred and fifty dollar red Kate Spade bag that went with her twelve hundred dollar Prada evening dress (the one currently bunched up in my trunk), as opposed to her four hundred dollar navy blue and turquoise striped Michael Kors.

"About six hundred bucks," I answered. I waited for her to gush in awe.

"Don't you think you could have done something more productive with your money?" she said.

"Pardon?"

"Do you have any idea how many starving children in Ethiopia you could feed with that amount?"

"Uh, well, I didn't actually spend that much on it," I lied. "It's a knockoff."

"What?"

"It's just a replica."

"So you support an industry that exploits child labor? What kind of person are you? Are you proud that your little fashion accessory is made by five year olds forced to work in sweat shops?"

Why was I spending my evening being interrogated by a crabby bald stranger? I'd learned during one of my business networking courses that if you reached an uncomfortable pause in conversation (okay, perhaps this wasn't quite appropriate because by this point I was wishing for a moment of silence), you should get the person talking about themselves.

"So Spring, where did you get your potato s-I mean purse?"

"Well, I didn't waste good money on a new bag."

"Of course not. You probably got it second hand."

"I got this from the Third Hand store on Yew Street," she told me haughtily.

Good God, what was the world coming to? Was second hand not good enough anymore? Would there be fourth and fifth hand shops next?

"It's made from recycled hemp," she informed me.

I wouldn't say we were bonding but at least she had stopped interrogating me.

"Okay, everybody, five minutes left. Get your bids in now," the Cowichan sweater dress lady announced.

Really? I looked around. There were only fifteen or so people there. And nobody had approached the auction table at all. Except me. Crap. The grey haired lady repeated her announcement and everyone responded by looking at their feet.

I kept my fake smile up. Okay, I could re-budget. The new clothes I'd bought last Friday could be returned. That'd help a bit. And I'd figure out how to work my espresso machine. Plus, I was getting a great deal on all the items, even if I didn't know what half of them were. See, it all depended on how you looked at things. Even if I couldn't afford food next month, I could ask to be hypnotized into thinking I was full. And maybe I could get something for the handcuffs on Ebay.

"Okay, everyone, the auction is closed. First of all, I'd like to thank all of you who donated your goods and services. Second, I'm thrilled to announce that this year, we actually had a bid on every single item, a noted improvement from last year where we only had three."

"I thought that ashtray looked familiar," said Bear.

"Yeah, Pam, I remember that ugly thing from two years ago," said someone in the crowd.

Pam ignored them and continued,

"And I'd like to thank this young lady right here, who was the bidder on every single item."

A warm round of applause erupted. I smiled outwardly despite my panic at my downward spiralling financial situation. Pam tallied my auction items and I wrote out a check for the equivalent of two months worth of groceries.

"Okay, everyone. For the next step of our fundraiser, let's sit down in a circle," Pam instructed.

"That was fantastic," Artie whispered to me as we sat down beside Pam.

I grinned at him. He was so sweet.

"To begin, I'd like to thank all of you for showing up. This is almost double the attendance we had last year," Pam announced.

No wonder they were still fundraising. How could you accomplish anything with only fifteen people? Especially when fourteen of them didn't bid on anything.

"And next, I'd like to call for a moment of silence in memory of our dear friend and founder, the late Johann Crosstein."

There was complete quiet while we had our moment, except for my stomach, which was doing its imitation of the 1812 overture. I was just destined to be hungry when I went out with Artie. I'd have to remember to eat before we went out the next time. Or stock my purse with granola bars.

We opened our eyes at Pam's instruction. Everyone was giggling at my stomach noises.

"Sorry," I apologized, "I haven't eaten anything since breakfast at McDonalds this morning."

God, you would have thought I'd said I'd used the carcass of an endangered iguana to club a baby seal for sheer sport with the gasps of shock I got.

Spring rolled her eyes.

"You didn't," Artie said, his eyes pleading.

"Not the golden arches McDonalds," I lied.

There was a collective sigh of relief from the group.

"No, of course not," I continued. "I was at McDonalds, which is a new, organic Scottish restaurant, on Commercial Drive, that specializes in, um, hemp burgers and vegan foie gras, and they serve it on third hand plates, made from recycled tree bark, that they buy to support, uh, children's fine arts programs in Ethiopia." I waited for the response thinking I'd made the lie a little too far fetched.

Comments of "Oh, that's fantastic", "Great" and "Wow, we'll have to go there" came from the crowd. Everyone looked happy again. Well, except Spring.

"So the pink fairy armadillo is endangered because of damage to the environment," Pam said, "but instead of my normal lecturing about the problem, let's go around the circle and each say how we feel we contribute to the solution."

What kind of fundraiser was this with its hokey unpopular auction and forced participation? This was so different from my earlier visions of hob-nobbing with local celebrities and captains of industry.

"So I'll start, and we'll go clockwise from there," Pam announced, and then launched into sharing how last year she had started to cycle (looking at her physique, I wouldn't have believed it) from Vancouver to Ottawa, to demonstrate how people at any age could save the environment by using alternatives to driving. "And even though I only made it to Burnaby before I was run off the highway by an eighteen wheeler, I would like to think that my actions and subsequent letters to Ottawa have made a difference."

Everyone applauded.

"And also," she continued, "I'd like to let you all know that my hip replacement surgery went well."

There was more applause.

Why was everybody looking at me now? Oh, right, counter clock-wise. I had no idea what to say. Seconds were passing and people were looking at me expectantly, and then uncomfortably.

"Lyndsay, it's your turn," whispered Artie to me.

"Oh, of course, so many things to say," I said, while unable to think of even one thing to say. I wished I could remember the name of the whale saving organization I'd said I was involved in earlier.

"Well..." I said.

For once I actually wished my mouth would take off independent of my mind, which continued to draw a blank.

"Where to start..." I began, racking my brain.

Oh God. Still nothing. I couldn't stand the uncomfortable hush that had fallen. Aha!

"I'd like to have another moment of silence first," I said, happy with my stalling technique.

Everyone bowed their heads obediently. Well, almost everyone.

"And what's it for?" Stupid, detail-oriented, third-hand potato sack carrier Spring asked.

"Yes, I was just getting to that. It's for, I mean against, McDonalds. Not the organic Scottish restaurant, but the evil corporate mega monster."

"Moments of silence are for commemorating a death," Spring pointed out.

"I think it's brilliant, a moment of silence for the future death and destruction of McDonalds," Artie said, gazing at me with respect and unbeknownst to him, rescuing me for the time being.

Everybody's heads went down again.

Phew! I had more time to come up with something. Or, as it turned out, more time to whip myself up into a non-idea generating, internal frenzy. Absolutely nothing came to mind. I knew I'd come up with a ton of brilliant ideas later, as I was driving home, but that wasn't doing me any good right now.

"I think that's long enough," Spring said. "Lyndsay?"

"Yes, well, I contribute to the environment by…"

Spring had her arms folded across her chest again and was looking at me smugly. Damn her and her stupid ugly potato sack dress.

"I manufacture clothes out of recycled potato sacks," I heard come out of my mouth.

"Really?" Disbelief (granted, justified disbelief) emanated from Spring, "Is that what you made your leather skirt out of?"

Crap, was I really wearing dead animal to an environmental fundraiser?

"No, this skirt was made from a cow on our family farm that died of old age," I heard myself say, "Poor old Moo-Moo."

"Uh huh. And the fur trim on your wrap?"

Damn. I'd forgotten about that.

"Made in honour of our pet mink Mitzy that passed away of natural causes?"

"Right."

Everybody else looked confused. What a sweet group of people this was, so willing to believe me and not understanding Spring's scepticism. I felt ashamed for lying to them, especially to Artie. Any future dates we'd have would involve me constantly recovering from this web of lies I'd spun. We could never go to the vegan Commercial Drive McDonalds for dinner. I'd never be able to show him any of my recycled potato sack clothes. Or invite him over to the family farm.

When we left later, I told him that I really liked him but was moving to Ireland to educate them on how to make clothes out of their old potato sacks. He looked heartbroken, but understood that personal relationships often had to be sacrificed for love of Mother Earth.

GOBBLE GOBBLE

Well, there was no point crying over spilled milk or lost men. There were gift certificates to be used.

I made appointments at the "Granville Alternative Holistic Centre." The plan was to ask the hypnotist to make me less klutzy at ten o'clock and then have my Chakra cleansed (I was still too embarrassed to ask what that was but made sure I had a thorough shower before) at the same place at eleven. Then I was going to the evil, greedy, mega-corporation, McDonalds for a dollar ninety-nine cheeseburger.

I entered the Centre and felt instantly relaxed by the smell of incense and the sound of the mini waterfall.

"Have a seat," said the receptionist after I'd introduced myself, "Help yourself to some cucumber water and I'll let Spring know you're here."

"Who?"

"Spring, the owner of the Centre. She does fantastic hypnosis. You're in very good hands."

Sure, if I want to be hypnotized into thinking I was a rabid turkey or into taking my clothes off every time I heard a car horn.

"You know what?" I said. "I just remembered I have to be… somewhere else."

I quickly exited, leaving the confused receptionist staring after me.

ALICE IN WONDERLAND

I double-checked that my massage gift certificate was for a place other than Spring's and made an appointment for the next day.

"Ees unit 101," the lady with the heavy eastern European accent who answered the phone told me, "but you press number forty two on intercom and I buzz you in. Forty-two. You write it down."

"Okay," I told her, "but if I forget, I have the name of the spa right here on your business card."

"No. Just you write down."

***

I woke up the next morning and drove to the address. "False Creek Co-Op" it said on the building, which had graffiti on its walls and garbage and broken beer bottles strewn all over the front. Weird. Maybe I'd written the address down wrong. I buzzed number forty-two.

"Hello?"

"Hi, it's Karly? I mean Lyndsay? I'm here for a ten o'clock-"

"SHHHHHHHHH! Quick. You come up."

I was getting that Alice in Wonderland feeling again.

She was waiting for me in the hallway when I came out of the elevator, a heavy, dark-skinned lady in bare feet and a robe. And in bad need of a pedicure-or just a pair of industrial strength nail cutters-how did she wear shoes over those gnarled, yellow things? She also looked like she was also a stranger to the concept of a hairbrush.

Confusion enveloped me. Where was the cheery Barbie doll to greet me and offer a selection of soothing herbal teas while enquiring about my well being? Even tough-love Spring had a friendly receptionist and cucumber water. I tried to stay positive. Maybe this masseuse was in such high demand that she didn't have the time to find support staff. Or to dedicate to personal hygiene.

"Did any peoples see you?" she whispered as she grabbed me by the elbow, looked up and down the hallway and hauled me into her apartment. I cringed at her touch. Not a good start to the massage.

The apartment was a pigsty, crowded and dark with wallpaper peeling off the walls, a strong smell of boiling cabbage, two kids in front of the TV eating cereal out of the box, and laundry drying on a clothes line hung from the kitchen to the living room.

"This way, please."

I ducked under the discoloured, extra-large men's underwear hanging on the clothesline on the way to the "massage room." Well, at least she had a table set up and I wasn't expected to lie down on the bunk beds. I took a closer look at the rickety old desk with pillows on top of it. Good thing I wasn't a heavy person, it didn't look like it could hold much weight.

"Remove clothes and hop on table."

"Okay, I just need to use the ladies' room first."

"What?"

"The bathroom? I drank a whole coffee on the way over."

"Oh," she said, looking put off. She left, shutting the door behind her.

"Abner, get out of bathroom now!" I heard her yell. Abner shouted something back.

"I have client!" she continued. "And she needs to make pee!"

There were mutterings of protest from Abner and then a pounding on the door that caused the walls to shake.

"Abner, unlock door! Already you've been there fifteen minutes, I can't imagine what else you are needing to do. You put down newspaper and come out!"

I heard the toilet flush and the door open.

"What kind of mess have you made here? I tell you million times, you wash body in shower, not in sink. Sink is for hands. Quick, pass me towel so I can wipe up mess, disgusting man."

She came back in the room, all smiles.

"Go ahead, is next door on your left," she said.

I ran in and "made pee" quickly, careful not to touch anything. When I returned, one of her children followed me in to play truck along the desk.

"Out," she instructed. "Mamma is working."

"No!" The child threw himself down on the floor in a tantrum. "Play here! In my room!" He grabbed on to his bunk bed with both arms and she pried him off of by pulling his legs with him screaming and her berating him the whole time. She shoved him out the door and locked it but not before he hurled his truck at my leg. He was still on the other side of the locked door, screaming and throwing himself at it.

"You know, this doesn't seem like a good time for you," I said, rubbing the tender spot on my knee. "Maybe we should reschedule for a calmer time."

"No, is fine," she insisted, putting on her fake smiley face again, "You are looking so tense."

That was true. I was five times more stressed out now than when I'd left my apartment.

"You are badly needing massage. Just we get the paying business out of the way first. I am having special deal right now. You buy package of nine, you get tenth one free."

"Actually, I have this gift certificate."

"What?"

"I got it at a fundraiser. See?"

"Oh, this," she looked at it like it was fresh road kill. "You know, my son is so upset right now, is better if you come back at different time. Like you said, a calmer time."

"Yes," I agreed while gathering up my bag, eager to leave and never return.

THE BEST COFFEE EVER

I phoned Stella on the way home and dropped by her apartment where we watched American Idol re-runs. During commercials I told her how the masseuse had backed out of my treatment. Not that I wanted it by that point but still, it was the principle.

Stella laughed and told me how she'd clipped out a two-for-one coupon for a local restaurant and gone there with her son Adam. At the end of the meal, the owner said the coupon had been issued by the previous manager and refused to honour it.

"That's not right," I said.

"He just laughed and told me that if I wanted to hire a lawyer to fight for my nine dollar meal, I was welcome to. Of course, he assumed I was just an old woman that wouldn't stand up for myself."

"He must have been shocked to find out he figured wrong." I smiled, imagining what revenge Stella had exacted. "So what did you do?"

"Who said I did anything, dear?"

"Come on Stella, I know you. What did you put that poor man through?"

"I just told him that his coffee was the best I'd ever tasted, even better than what I'd had in Brazil. That's all."

"What?"

"I repeated it several times, so he'd remember."

"That's it?"

"Well, the thing is, Karly, I have a lot of friends. Including a number from my seniors drama club. And I told all those friends that this restaurant served the best coffee."

"Oh." That wasn't what I'd expected. Maybe Stella was getting mellow in her old age.

"Of course, you know us old people, sometimes we get confused. My friends would phone up and make reservations for eight people but then forget to invite anyone. So every Friday night, three weeks in a row, there was a large table with one lone senior citizen sitting at it, enjoying their single cup of coffee. That same man would bark at them to leave."

"He sounds like a real loser."

"Yes. Well, dear, you have to be careful around old people. Especially ones in drama class. Yelling at them might cause them to have a fake stroke, heart attack, or dementia episode where they think they're getting ready for the shower and start to take their clothes off, just for example," Stella said, fighting to keep a straight face.

"You're kidding." I cracked up. This was the Stella I knew.

"And when they recovered from whatever attack they were having, they would take a sip of their hot drink and say 'This is the best coffee I ever tasted, even better than the stuff I had in Brazil.'"

"Too funny."

"Well, that owner didn't seem to think so. That silly man had no sense of humour whatsoever. And on the fourth Friday, a senior citizen walked in and sat down and asked for a cup of coffee and he went absolutely ballistic on the poor dear and kicked her out. He pushed her out the door and she tripped and sprained her ankle."

"What a complete jerk. So what happened in the end?"

"The plan was that all four of us were going to go in together so he'd recognize us and see what he was up against. Then we were going to ask before ordering if he'd honour the coupon."

"Four?" I asked. The accountant in me had inventoried the senior citizens involved. "Weren't there five of you?"

"No dear. That last poor lady he threw out wasn't one of my

army. Turns out she's the Mayor's mother. A city inspector appeared the next day and shut the place down."

"Stella, you're a riot. I bet he regrets ever crossing you."

"Well yes, dear. I can be pretty determined if I need to be."

DRIVING MISS KARLY

I sat at my computer, eating cereal from two half-sized kids' bowls for lunch, and checked the dating website with my fingers crossed. So my first attempts at online dating hadn't worked out. I'd thought of what Stella said about being determined. Well, I could be determined to. I was going to meet someone and get my mind off Alex.

Last week I'd updated my website profile under the name "Stacey" to show that I was looking for someone who was:

- **nice, considerate**

- **sensitive**

and to make sure I didn't end up with another environmentally responsible date fighting to change the world, I added that I was looking for someone who was:

- **happy with the status quo**

***

Oh God, what was I going to do? Where did my fun afternoon go? An hour ago I'd been somewhat enjoying lunch at the hip Robson restaurant Nine-One-One with my date Sheldon, a chemistry research assistant at the university with brown hair, big sensitive eyes, a slight build, and a soft voice. Now I was stuck in his car, puttering back and forth across Granville Street at five kilometres under the speed limit.

I'd been hesitant when Sheldon first offered to drive me to the impound lot after we'd discovered my car had been towed. But he didn't seem like he'd be an aggressive driver like Joel. Especially based on the way he'd been too nervous to check with the hostess about our reservation or send back his fettuccine alfredo when what he'd ordered was a salad with no dairy on it. And there was certainly no danger he'd want to drag race his somewhat girly-looking beige Volkswagen Jetta. If anything, he might be a bit dizzy from lack of food but I could always feed him a granola bar from my purse.

But we'd been traversing the bridge for forty minutes now, with Sheldon refusing to pull over and ask for directions. When we'd discovered my car was gone, an elderly lady sitting on her balcony had yelled out that we'd need to drive to Captive Impound which was on a little side street off of Granville, east of the bridge.

"Very easy to find," she'd said. "It's on Jessica Street. Or is it Mary Street? Some girl's name, anyway. You can't miss it."

"We should pull over and ask at a gas station," I said to my date. "I don't think that woman knew what she was talking about."

"Oh," Sheldon gave me the same uncomfortable look as he had when I'd asked him why he didn't send back his lunch. "Why don't we try driving by one more time? Maybe we just missed it."

"I don't know how we could have."

"She probably meant west instead of east. Let's try looking on the other side."

We drove back and forth again and didn't see anything.

"Come on, Sheldon, let's pull over and ask somebody."

"Just one more time," he begged.

"But-"

"I bet she meant it was a boy's name, let's try looking for that." He looked desperate.

Urgh. This was annoying. The four-second-rule driving he was doing had been comforting when I first got in, but now it was just severely irritating. We'd driven up and down the same road six times, with cars honking and passing us the whole time.

We stopped at a red light and a taxi was in the other lane. Perfect.

"What are you doing?" Sheldon asked, looking unnerved as I

unrolled the window.

"Asking the cab driver for directions."

"Don't do that." Sheldon rolled my window back up from the automatic control on his side. Giving him a dirty look, I went to unroll it again.

"Sheldon. Stop it."

"Stacey, it's embarrassing, please don't."

"We keep driving up and down the same street. We'll run out of gas before we find Captive Towing."

"Hey!" I yelled over the noise of the traffic at the large, dark-skinned, taxi driver sporting a turban and mad-looking mono-brow as I rolled the glass down again. "Can you help me, I'm-"

Sheldon had shut the window again.

"Stacey, can you imagine what he's thinking? You look ridiculous, yelling at him-"

I'd gotten the window open again. I had limited time before the light turned green.

"HELP, PLEASE, I'M"

Sheldon rolled the pane back up, "looking for"

I got it open again – "CAPTIVE"

He closed it – "Towing."

Open – "I WAS"

Closed – "at lunch and my car was"

Open – "TAKEN"

Closed – "while I was parked in front of"

Open – "NINE-ONE-ONE."

Closed – "We just"

Open – "CAN'T"

Closed – "seem to"

Open – "GET"

Closed – "to the impound lot. We don't know the area"

Open – "OUT"

Closed – "here."

Sheldon pulled ahead so I couldn't hear what the cabbie was yelling back at me. He pulled up beside us again at the next red light and I was hoping he had an answer but he was looking over at me strangely and talking excitedly. I looked in the back seat to see who he was ranting to but there was nobody there.

The taxi cut us off at the next light. Well, I think it did. It's hard to define what "cutting off" is when the car you're in is only going twenty kilometres per hour. The driver kept looking at us in his rear view mirror and then turning around and waving his arms at us and yelling.

"Oh great, now you've done it. I hope he doesn't do anything crazy." Sheldon's voice had risen an octave.

The cabbie was acting very strangely. Fanatical, even. Raving like a lunatic to an imaginary person. What had I done? Had the Strangeness Attracter struck again? Only I would have the bad luck to ask a psychotic cab driver for directions. He turned right at the next light and Sheldon and I breathed a stereo sigh of relief as we lost sight of him. We continued driving at a snail's pace, with Sheldon still refusing to pull over and get directions.

That was it. I couldn't do this anymore. We'd be here all weekend at this rate.

"Sheldon, I am going to jump out of the car in the middle of the street if you don't pull over. I'm serious. I've done it before."

He pulled into an empty parking lot.

"I'm sorry, Stacey. I just...I don't handle a lot of situations with people very well. But I'm getting better. It was a big step to go out with you today."

"Look, I get that a first date makes you nervous. Everyone gets that way. But I don't understand what's wrong with asking for directions. Or checking on our reservation."

He grimaced.

"I don't know. I guess I'm just scared about what might happen. I have these awful nightmares about how everything could go wrong and it paralyses me."

"Look, Sheldon, this isn't going to work out between us. Weird and embarrassing things happen to me all the time. My life is your nightmare."

He didn't look like he believed me. True, he hadn't witnessed one of my Strangeness Attracters on this date, but he would eventually.

"Stacey, I'm sorry. Let me at least get you to the impound lot and we can talk about it later. I can't leave you out here by yourself."

Awww, he really was a nice guy. But no, I just couldn't stand traversing that bridge again. I jumped out. Oh good, there was a cab at the other side of the parking lot. Feeling like my luck had turned, I started off towards it.

Sheldon got out of the car,

"Please Stacey, don't –"

"Runnnnnnnn!" the cab driver yelled at me. He was leaning out his window and beckoning wildly with his arms.

That was weird. Had he already started the meter and wanted to save me money?

"Stacey!" Sheldon yelled louder than I'd thought possible from him while grabbing my arm and pulling me back across the lot. "It's him. Get in the car."

He tried to push me back into the Jetta.

Several police cars screamed into the parking lot. The taxi driver was still yelling and waving frantically at us. I took a better look at him. It was the cab driver with the mono-brow I'd asked directions from.

"Get down, everyone down!" the police shouted with their guns drawn.

Oh my God. What was going on? Sheldon hit the ground beside me and I followed his example. Soon after, strong hands pulled me up.

"Are you okay, miss?" a cop asked me as I was half-dragged, half-carried across the parking lot.

Were they after the cab driver? He had acted kind of weird, talking like a lunatic to the people in his head, cutting us off and following us to the parking lot, and then all that crazy yelling and waving his arms. He was probably a dangerous criminal. Thank God the police got here in time. Who knows what he would have done to us? What deranged plans he had? Just my luck that I chose to ask directions from a psycho. I felt sick.

"Are you okay?" the officer repeated.

"I think so."

"Did he harm you?"

"No, but I was scared, he was just driving so erratically. He had this freaky look in his eyes the whole time and he was talking to himself like a crazy person."

"Did he threaten you?"

"I couldn't understand everything he was yelling but he was just acting so psychotic that I felt scared."

I looked back at Sheldon. He was on the ground, face down, surrounded by five police officers, all with their weapons drawn, and now they were-oh God-putting him in handcuffs!

"What's going on?" I asked my rescuers.

"What do you mean?"

"Why are you cuffing, uh..." Why couldn't I remember my date's name? "That man?"

"Your kidnapper? Don't worry, miss, you're safe. He can't hurt you."

"My what? Kidnapper?"

My escorting officers gave me a look, then nodded at each other knowingly.

"In shock," one whispered to the other. I looked at the cabbie, standing free by his cab. One of the officers walked up and shook his hand. This wasn't right. The driver was the criminal. He was the crazy one that had cut us off and followed us while talking to himself...oh. Or maybe he'd been talking on his phone that I could now see hooked to one ear. I had to explain.

"Excuse me, there's been-"

"What's your name, miss?"

"Karly. Look, I-"

"Are you sure you don't need medical attention?"

"No, really-"

"Stay here, please. We'll be right back."

They put me in the back of a cruiser and went to talk to the other officers, who were dragging Sheldon (now I remembered his name) to another car. For someone who couldn't check on a reservation or send food back, he was sure objecting now, kicking and screaming and wiggling around.

"Staceyyyy! Tell them!" he yelled at me.

A female police officer opened the door, "You said your name was Karly?"

"Yes, but-"

"Thanks." She shut the door and told the other officers that

Sheldon was likely delusional and had probably fixated on me thinking I was an ex-girlfriend named Stacey. I wanted to explain but when I went to get out of the car she stopped me,

"Karly, stay in here. We'll take you to the station and get your statement. Just try to relax. You're totally safe."

She shut the door and another officer got in and started driving.

Okay, I'd fix this later. In the meantime, I could work on my apology. If Sheldon couldn't handle asking for directions, he'd definitely be a little put off after being taken down in a parking lot by the cops. On the bright side, I bet I didn't have to convince him further about things not working out between us.

TRADESIES

We arrived at the station and I was instructed to wait at one of the officer's desks. I'd never been in a police station before. It was just like I'd imagined from the detective shows on television, with a constant buzz of activity and conversation.

The whole station was excited about a recent apprehension. They'd caught the perp after a crazy three-hour car chase and he was now sleeping in the station holding cell. There was something familiar about him. A group of loud, colourfully dressed prostitutes were milling about the station, looking annoyed and bored.

A short man whose pleasant, round face and white hair reminded me of a young Santa Claus approached me.

"Hi, Karly, I'm Captain Travers. Sorry to have left you alone after your ordeal. Please, come this way. Can we get you a coffee?"

A skinny, bald man in a sweater vest followed us into the Captain's office.

"Karly, this is Dr. Crittenden, our resident psychologist. I thought it might help to have him in," Captain Travers said.

I took a look around the small, messy office. It had a one-way mirror looking out to the rest of the station. The working girls were flirting with one of the younger cops, who had turned red-faced to the amusement of the older officers around him. The lone captive man was still passed out on the bench in the cell. Captain Travers saw me looking and pulled a curtain over the mirror.

"So, Karly, you never answered my question about the coffee. A warm drink might calm you down."

"Thanks. Um, I'd like an EHCSL please."

Dr. Crittenden and Captain Travers exchanged a perplexed look.

"An extra hot chai soy latte," I explained.

The psychologist got up and whispered something to Captain Travers about me being in shock and needing something familiar to cling to. Captain Travers opened the door and ordered the young cop to go out to Starbucks.

"And while you're there, officer," he added, "I'd like an espresso."

"And a tall hot chocolate," Dr. Crittenden said.

"I didn't eat much lunch. I'll take a peach danish if they have them. But if they're out, don't get me raspberry. I'll take a lemon scone instead," the captain said, then looked at Dr. Crittenden who nodded.

"Make that two," Captain Travers added. "How about you, Karly?"

"No, thank you." I said, figuring the poor rookie had enough to deal with, with all the other officers now placing their orders as well.

Okay Karly, you can fix this, I assured myself. We'd bond over our warm drinks and then I'd explain the misunderstanding and we'd all have a good laugh. I was talking myself into this when a tall, aggressive-looking woman in severe black-rimmed glasses and a red suit walked in.

"Karly, this is district attorney Gina White. Geen, you want anything from Starbucks?"

"No thanks, Captain. Karly, I'm sorry to hear about your recent trauma. Let me assure you, we will nail this bastard to the maximum extent of the law."

Dr. Crittenden nodded,

"Now Karly, I know it's probably very difficult to talk about what happened but you're going to feel better once you're done. Just take it slow and tell us everything from the beginning. You can even close your eyes if it helps."

Oh God. This was going to be harder than I thought. All these caring, concerned people expecting me to rat on Sheldon for kidnapping me.

"I...I can't...I can't explain," I said. I wanted to tell them the truth but it just wasn't coming out.

Dr. Crittenden nodded and said,

"I know it's hard, Karly, but we really need you to tell us what happened."

"Can I wait until my chai latte arrives? I think that'll help."

"Sure. Of course. Whatever makes you comfortable."

D.A. White had been listening impatiently while pacing the small office in her high heels.

"Karly, maybe we can at least start with identifying the man who kidnapped you."

She went over to the one-way mirror and pulled the drapes open.

Sheldon had been deposited into the holding cell, looking very ill and more than a little psychologically damaged. He'd squished himself into a corner, warily eyeing his snoozing cellmate. God, I was about to look like the world's biggest idiot. There was no way this would end well. I felt ill at what I'd put poor Sheldon through and gripped the chair arm.

"Shut the drapes, Gina, look at what you're doing to her," Dr. Crittenden whispered. "She's not ready to see him."

"Look," I whispered. Okay, just breathe. And tell the truth. I closed my eyes and concentrated on forcing the confession out of my mouth. "He didn't kidnap me. It was a misunderstanding."

There. I did it.

I opened my eyes, expecting looks of disgust. Instead, they looked compassionate. Maybe they didn't understand me.

"So, you see," I spoke slowly to spell it out for them, "he's innocent so you can let him go."

"Karly," Dr. Crittenden sat in front of me and took my hands.

"You are in a safe place, he cannot hurt you, you do not have to protect him."

"But I'm not, I'm telling the truth."

"He didn't kidnap you and then drive around, keeping you captive in the car?"

"No? I mean no."

More looks of concern passed between my three interviewers.

"So why was he calling you Stacey when your name is Karly?" Dr. Crittenden asked.

"Because I told him my name was Stacey?"

"Right. And when you were yelling at the cab driver…?"

"I was asking for directions?"

"Uh huh. And this Sheldon fellow kept driving off and rolling the window back shut so that you couldn't ask for help, because…?"

"Because he really doesn't like to ask for directions?"

Why was everything I said coming out like a question?

The young officer returned, laden down with bags of baked goods and trays of hot drinks. I listened to the attorney, psychologist, and captain talk about me as if I wasn't sitting right there while I sipped my latte. The district attorney argued that the whole thing might be a mistake while Dr. Crittenden disagreed, saying it was classic Stockholm Syndrome.

"Did you see her reaction when she saw him? She looked like she was going to throw up," Dr. Crittenden argued.

"Maybe she looks ill because she's wasted our time," D.A. White countered.

"Okay, you two, enough," Captain Travers said. "Karly, do you mind if I open the curtains again and ask you to identify Sheldon as your, uh, date from earlier today?"

I nodded and then steeled myself, concentrating on not looking scared or confused, so that they'd believe me.

Captain Travers drew back the curtain and for all their sakes, I took an extra long look at Sheldon. I breathed deeply and was doing a good job looking extra calm. Meanwhile, the other man in the cell had got up to stretch and I got a good look at him too. You know, if he shaved and his hair was fixed up a bit, he'd look like…like…

Oh dear God, it was Joel! My drug dealer date who had been charged with murdering his ex girlfriend, whose date with me had led to a historic mafia arrest! In shock, I yelped and jumped back, sending my extra-hot latte flying all over District Attorney White, who also screamed. I knew it was a one-way mirror but it seemed like he was looking right at me. All the nightmare memories came back to me. It felt like I was still in the car and was being rocketed all over downtown at breakneck speeds. Oh God, I was going to be sick, I was going to be sick, I…oh gross, I'd just been sick. All over the poor lawyer.

"Satisfied now?" Dr. Crittenden asked her, gloating like a child.

"Fine. Book him," she answered, taking off her suit jacket and trying to wipe her skirt clean with a wad of Starbucks napkins.

I wanted to correct them. I did. But the truth would include explaining why I'd just freaked out and I just couldn't be connected to Joel. What could I do? Sheldon was going to be arrested. Dr. Crittenden shut the curtain again and I tried to concentrate on breathing without hyperventilating.

Captain Travers had the young officer escort me to the ladies room to clean myself up.

"I'll wait right here for you," he told me outside the bathroom door. Damn. I'd been planning on making a break for it. I swore again when I got inside and saw the bars on the windows.

The vomit had made a beeline for D.A. White and I only had a speck on my hoodie sweater that I dabbed out. I rinsed out my mouth and splashed water on my face.

"You again," the other woman in the bathroom said. I didn't think I knew her but she could have been anyone given her long crimped blonde wig and old seventies aviator style sunglasses. She pulled them off and after getting over the sight of her black eye and bruised cheek, I took a good look at her.

Crap. This was turning out to be a bad date reunion. It was the hooker who'd kicked me off her corner the night I was with Joel. What if she could identify me as the mystery purse woman who'd jumped out of his car and then been picked up by the mini van? What if the mafia came after me? Or my family? Bill would never go into the witness protection program after they'd finally got into their Country Club.

I ran to the toilet and threw up again.

"Bad day, huh," she said while touching up her bright blue eye shadow.

"Um, do you…"

"Yeah, I know what's going on. Asshole's been harassing all us girls, thinking we know something about you. Girl, I don't know what you did to piss that man off but he is one mad freak show. Look what that bastard did to my face."

"I have to get out of here. Please don't tell them who I am…my family…if he ever hurt them…" I couldn't stop crying.

"God, would ya shut up already?"

There was an awkward silence while I forced myself to stop blubbering and she put on several coats of the brightest shade of red lipstick I'd ever seen.

"It's always some bastard man ruining our lives, ain't it?" she said bitterly, more to her reflection than me. "On second thought, maybe I don't know you."

I held my breath.

"Yup. Never seen you before in my life. Tell ya what, though. Maybe you wanna trade outfits."

"Really?"

"I gotta do my one good deed a year, right?"

"Are you sure? I-"

"Shit girl, let's do this before I change my mind."

We exchanged clothes, me in her spandex dress, high heels, wig and sunglasses, and her in my jeans, T-shirt and sweater.

I was going to ask what the plan was when she gave me a wink, pulled my hood over her brown hair, and pushed her way out the door to the young officer who was waiting for me. She grabbed him by the hair, planted a huge kiss on his lips, then kicked him in the ankle and screamed and ran in the direction of the Captain's office. Ten seconds later, I followed out the same door in her five-inch heels, and was able to stumble out the front door unnoticed while she created havoc inside. I could hear Dr. Crittenden yelling,

"Give her room! She's very delicate. It's classic Stockholm Syndrome. Karly, calm down. How about another soy latte?"

***

Two nights later I went to delete my website profile and saw a posting from Sheldon there.

Dear Karly or Stacey,

You cannot imagine what Hell I have been through. Odd as this sounds, I am writing to thank you. The day I was arrested was the nightmare that I had lived my life frozen in terror of. And you know what? I survived. It made me wonder why I have wasted so much time being afraid.

I'm starting therapy with Dr. Crittenden next week and I am so hopeful about my future, all because of you.

My eternal gratitude,

Sheldon.

Here was the positive leg of my Even Steven Factor. Thrilled, I phoned and told Nik about it.

"You helped someone else get over their fear of confrontation?" Nik asked in his monotone voice.

"Yes."

"And you don't see the irony in that?"

"What do you mean?"

"Maybe I should have you thrown in jail and then see if you're still afraid of facing your Ex in court. Have you talked to Sam lately to see what's going on?"

"No. I've been busy."

"Karly-"

"Gotta go, lots of unpacking to do."

I hung up. Why did Nik have to be such a downer? It wasn't that I was avoiding conflict. I was just busy, doing…stuff.

CHEESE, TERIYAKI, AND CURRY...TOGETHER AT LAST

God, what was I going to do? Yet again, I was stuck in a date's car that I didn't want to be in. We weren't going at breakneck speeds. Or being passed by seniors in wheelchairs. No, my karate Sempai, who had asked me out to a Jackie Chan movie that Friday night, was driving at a very comfortable speed. The problem was that his body odour was killing me.

I'd noticed a bad smell when we trained but had assumed it was the old community centre gym we trained in. Or from the twenty or so sweaty bodies I worked out with. Or from the old yellowed sparring gloves and helmets we all took turns using. But no, it was apparently all Ryan.

Insisting that I was carsick and fresh air would help, I'd unrolled my window and was now freezing and wet from the typical Vancouver rain that was coming in sideways. Should I tell him? People didn't usually like to be told that they stunk. But I'd be doing him a favor, wouldn't I? He'd probably be a little shocked to begin with, but then he'd realize that I'd saved him from a lifetime of wondering why people couldn't stand to be around him. Yes, telling him was definitely the right thing to do. Stella would have blurted it out within two seconds or two yards of meeting him.

"What's on your mind?" Ryan asked from across his pick up truck.

Okay, yes, here it was. The perfect opportunity.

"Nothing," I lied.

We got to the movie theatre where I insisted on my own large popcorn, planning on burying my nose in it after I loaded it up with extra butter and all the extra seasoning toppings I could get my hands on-ranch, cheddar cheese, caramel, spicy jalapeno, honey, blue cheese, and even teriyaki sauce from a fast food stall. It gave off an odd odour with all those things mixed together but still, it was better than the odour that was going to be sitting beside me, trying to hold my hand or, God forbid, trying to put his arm around me. I cringed at the thought of having nothing but a thin layer of cotton between my shoulder and his armpit.

"You sure you want all those toppings together?" Ryan asked as I shook on a heap of curry powder I was overjoyed to find at an Indian food stall. "It's giving off a weird stink."

Really? I'd assumed he didn't possess a sense of smell.

We found seats in the middle of the theatre and settled in.

"Ewww, what reeks?" said one of the four giggly teenage girls sitting in front of us.

"Gross!"

"Yuck."

They got up and moved. As did the couple to our left. And the senior citizen on our right.

"Your popcorn is grossing people out," Ryan told me.

"What?"

"It's actually making my stomach turn, too. Do you think you could get rid of it?"

"Throw it out?"

"Yeah, it's really bad. Look, you've cleared the seats around us."

Unbelievable.

"That's your popcorn?" someone behind us asked.

"She's got a bunch of weird toppings on it," my date answered as he leaned away from me.

Gee thanks, Ryan. I'd been so concerned with hurting his feelings earlier but he obviously had no problems doing the same to me.

"That's pretty damn rude if you ask me," someone from a couple rows behind us said.

"Lady, what could you possibly have put on it that stinks like that?" someone a couple rows back asked.

"Cheese, honey, and teriyaki sauce," Ryan the traitor answered for me. "She even put curry powder on it."

"Eww," the crowd commented together.

"Fine, I'll throw it out," I said and got up.

"Make sure you use a garbage bin outside of the theatre!" Ryan yelled down at me as I got to the bottom of the stairs.

There was applause as I left.

I dumped the container and continued out of the theatre where I went to hail a cab. Steaming, I stood on the corner with my arm up. Here I'd spent the night wrestling with whether or not to tell Ryan he smelled and then he went and did it to me without a second thought. And in front of a cheering crowd. If I could go back in time, I would definitely tell him. Absolutely. I'd just come straight out with it, no holds barred. Yes, I would. Oh crap, why was he standing in front of me?

"Karly, where are you going?"

"Home. I didn't like the way you treated me in there."

"I was just being honest, Karly, I thought you'd want that."

Okay, here was the perfect opportunity. Again.

"Ryan, you're right. It is better to be honest so I have to tell you something."

"Yeah?"

Okay. This was it. I thought of how Stella would do it. To the point. And quick. Like ripping off a band-aid. I took a deep breath to summon the courage, nearly passed out from the smell, and told him.

"You stink."

"I know. You had your popcorn beside me for so long."

"No, Ryan. You smell. Of very strong, very bad, body odour. It was your stench that everybody was complaining about in the theatre, not my popcorn."

For once in my life, timing worked for my benefit. I was happy to be able to make my speech, jump in the cab that had stopped for me, and take off. And take off. Huh?

"Lady, what are you doing in my car?" the cab driver asked me. Or the middle-aged businessman on his way home in his four-door sedan asked.

"Oh. I thought you were a cab stopping to pick me up."

"I stopped because the light was red. Now it's green and although you look like a nice girl, I don't want to bring you home and explain you to my wife. Get out."

Crap. Ryan was still standing there, looking shocked.

"Do you think I could get out next block?" I asked. "I was on a date with my karate sempai and I just told him he has B.O. and he's standing right there."

He took a look out at Ryan who was still standing there, looking completely bewildered with his mouth wide open.

"That's crazy enough to be true," my unwilling chauffeur answered. "Okay, one block and then out."

AUNT KARLY TO THE RESCUE

Beaming, I checked out the made-up Karly in my bathroom mirror. In half an hour I was going out for dinner with my klutzy group!

It was Alex's idea to meet in the real world for tonight's session. I'd made some progress unpacking and had a sexy outfit on. Not that I was dressing up for Alex, of course. It was just a good idea to be attractive in general in case I ran into any eligible men while out. Yes, that was it. My feelings for Alex were totally under control. It had been a while since I'd seen him. I'd probably fantasized that he was greater than he was because I'd been on the rebound. After all, he was just an ordinary man.

I applied the new lipstick I'd had fun shopping for earlier that day. It was a little brighter than I normally wore but the lady at the cosmetics counter had told me it looked great. She'd teased that it must be a really hot date I was so excited about which I quickly denied. God, couldn't a girl buy makeup without everyone jumping to conclusions?

The phone rang.

"Karly, it's Desiree. You don't have plans for tonight, do you?" my sister asked with panic in her voice.

"I'm meeting some friends for dinner," I answered. "Why?"

"Our nanny just came down with the stomach flu and we have thousand dollar tickets for a charity dinner tonight."

I was thrilled. Were they really trusting me to look after their kids?

"Siri's sleeping at a friend's house and we'll put Connor to bed so we were wondering if you could come over and phone us if anything comes up."

Oh. Okay, so it wasn't both kids and the baby would be sleeping by the time I got there. Still, it showed they were warming back up to the idea of my looking after their kids. I really did want to go out for dinner with Alex and the group but this was important. My family needed me. Plus, it would be a great opportunity to get back into Bill's good books.

I left a message on Alex's phone that I wouldn't make dinner due to a family emergency and drove the fifteen minutes to my sister's mansion.

Connor was already ready for bed and half asleep in Desiree's arms when I got there.

"I'll put him down," I offered.

He was so cute and cuddly. There was something so beautiful about holding a sleepy baby. I covered him with a million kisses as I hummed and rocked him to sleep in my arms in his already-darkened room. Gently, I placed him in his crib on his back. He rolled over onto his tummy with his little bum in the air and stuck his thumb in his mouth. I made triple sure that I'd put the crib side back up, checked that the baby monitor was on, looked for any potential hazards, and went downstairs.

"He's down," I announced to a well coiffed, expensively clad, worried-looking Desiree and Bill. "There's nothing in his crib he can choke on, his monitor is on, and I will check on him every five minutes."

Desiree gave me a few more obvious care tips, double-checked that I had their cell numbers, and was giving me a run down on his potential food allergies while Bill dragged her out the door.

I made popcorn, with just salt and butter this time, and settled in to flick through the three hundred satellite channels in the media room. When a commercial for diapers came on, I remembered to run up and check on Connor. He was still sleeping but, oh my God, was something wrong with his face? Hoping my eyes were playing tricks on me, I flicked on the light. There was a bright red rash all over his cheeks and forehead. I screamed and grabbed him out of the crib and he started crying.

"You're going to be okay, Connor! Aunty Karly's going to take care of you!"

Quickly, I phoned Desiree and yelled over Connor's sobs for them to meet me at the hospital. Then I found the keys to the SUV, strapped Connor into the car seat, and roared off to Emergency in a panic.

I made it there in record time and ran in with my screaming nephew in my arms, barely able to get the words out, I was so terrified.

"Food allergies-bad reaction," I managed to say. One of the nurses recognized me and came over.

"Hi Karly, can I see him?" she asked and I handed him over. "There you go, you poor thing, everything's fine, shhhhh."

She cooed her words out to him in such a gentle, soothing voice that it calmed me down as well. He stuck his thumb back in his mouth, put his head on her shoulder, and fell asleep. Or did he just pass out? Was he going into anaphylactic shock? Oh my God, he was. I told the nurse.

"Karly, babies don't suck their thumbs when they're going into shock," the nurse pointed out. "Now, tell me why you think he's having an allergic reaction."

Was she blind?

"He has welts all over his head."

She looked at the red marks and then took her finger and smudged one on his forehead.

"It looks like lipstick, actually."

"It does?" I was so relieved I started to bawl more. "Oh, thank God, I thought-"

"Connor! Oh my baby. What happened? Is he all right?" I heard my sister's voice screech as she ran towards us and yanked her son from the nurse.

"You must be the mother," the nurse responded coolly to

almost having her arms ripped out of their sockets.

My nephew awoke briefly, took a look at his mom, yawned, and went back to sleep.

"He's fine. It was a false alarm," the nurse continued.

"Oh, thank God," Desiree cried and then kept repeating as she held Connor close and rocked him back and forth.

"What kind of false alarm?" Bill asked me.

Damn, I'd been hoping this wouldn't come up.

I looked at him sheepishly. "I thought he had an allergic rash on his face."

Bill and Desiree looked at Connor.

"Oh my God!" Desiree cried. "He is having a reaction. Did you feed him something, Karly? You didn't give him peanuts, did you? Bill, go get a doctor!"

"Desiree, calm down," I said. "It's just…uh…my lipstick."

"It's what?"

"I guess I was kissing him a lot before I put him to bed and I'd just put on my new lipstick, see, and it's kind of the same color as a rash would look. In fact, I think that's what this shade is called, 'Rash Red,'" I tried to joke.

They just stared at me until Bill took a look at Connor, wiped some of the lipstick off with his finger, and then held his finger up beside my mouth to verify that it was, indeed, the same color. Bill's face turned a similar shade. Maybe it wasn't the right time for humor.

"Jesus Christ," Bill said angrily. "Come on Desiree, we're going home. Karly, I assume that's my seventy thousand dollar Lexus you've abandoned at the entrance with the keys in the ignition and doors wide open?"

"Uh, yes?"

Jaw tightened and forehead vein throbbing, he turned around without another word and Desiree followed him with Connor in her arms. As they went out the front door, she turned around and mouthed, "I'll phone you later." Bill put Connor into the Lexus, which was conveniently right outside the door, and I assumed Desiree was going to drive the Mercedes home, which left me with no transportation. Not that I wanted to point that out right then. On the bright side, I only lived a couple of blocks away. I could walk home and get my car after Bill calmed down, tomorrow. Or maybe next week.

"Karly."

I turned around and thought I was imagining Alex standing in the waiting room, beaming at me, dressed up and smelling good. Until my fantasy Alex asked me if I was okay, likely wondering why I was just standing there, staring at him.

"Yes, I'm fine, just surprised to see you here."

"I got your message about the family emergency and was hoping I'd run into you here. Not hoping, uh, I mean thinking I might run into you here. No wait. I don't mean I came here just because you might be here. I mean…" He took a deep breath and started over. "Kal discovered he's allergic to seafood."

"What a coincidence. I'm here too because of food allergies. Well, not exactly, I mean…it doesn't matter. Is the rest of the group still at the restaurant?"

"I doubt it. As I was running out the door with Kal, I heard Jeanette scream 'fire' so I'd assume dinner was over."

"Hey, you know that ride home you offered me before? I left my car at my sister's place. I was wondering-"

"Of course I'll give you a ride. I'm just waiting for Kal's family to get here."

"Thanks," I said as I took a seat beside him.

"Hey Karly, how's it going?" one of the ambulance drivers called out as he wheeled a stretcher by.

"Fine, Hank, how are you?"

"Busy, as usual."

"Hey Karly, thanks for the doughnuts last week," called out one of my favorite cleaners as he pushed his cart by.

"Wow, you know everyone here," laughed Alex.

"Hey Karly," called out Dr. Blue Eyes. "There's a group of us going out to celebrate the end of our internship tomorrow night. Why don't you join us? We did most of our practicum on you anyway."

The staff within earshot laughed.

***

"Looks like someone has a crush on you," Alex commented as he drove me home later.

"Really? Who?"

"That doctor."

"Why do you say that?"

"Well," he looked like he was concentrating hard while explaining, "if a guy wants to ask a girl out and isn't sure if a) it's appropriate or b) he'll get shot down and will then have to continue seeing her which could get very awkward, he might start with asking her out in a group situation."

"Hmm." I tried to picture Dr. Blue Eyes and I as a couple, running towards each other in a meadow, symphony playing, arms outstretched. Now in reality, I'd be sneezing and my eyes would be bloodshot and watering and I'd be scratching the allergic welts on my neck and forearms and then my ankle would discover the only gopher hole in the meadow and I'd trip and give Dr. Blue Eyes a concussion in the process.

Anyway, all I could picture was the top of his head as he was doing my internal pelvic exam last time I was in with severe abdominal pains. I grimaced.

"No, I wouldn't want to date a doctor, especially one that's already seen my-I mean one that already knows so much about me. It would be kind of creepy."

"Really?"

I thought about it. How could I possibly be intimate with someone who'd poked around my private bits in such a non-intimate setting and then told me I had gas?

"Yeah. There's something just wrong about it."

"Oh." He was unusually quiet for the rest of the ride.

"Alex, are you okay?" I asked him as he dropped me off at my car. He hadn't even reacted to Bill and Desiree's mansion. In fact, he hadn't even seemed to notice it.

"Um, yeah. I just remembered Julia's near her due date so I should probably get home."

And he drove off. Well, rightly so. He should be with his wife, so near this next phase of their lives together. I hoped he was okay. He'd looked a little green. Poor guy, he was probably nervous about becoming a dad.

PLAYING CHECKERS

"I don't know what's wrong with me," I said on the phone to Nik.

There was silence.

"Hello?" I checked.

"I'm holding in so many sarcastic comments I think my head is going to explode."

"Ha. Ha. Focus, please."

"Okay, wrong with you in what capacity?"

"Huh?"

"Well, physically, mentally, spiritually, structurally, physiologically..."

Why was I having this conversation with a male engineering nerd? I needed more girlfriends.

"Dating-wise," I explained. "No matter what I do, I end up meeting guys I'm completely incompatible with."

"You're playing checkers."

"Huh?"

"Checkers," he explained. "When it doesn't work out with someone, whatever characteristic you most define them by, you go for the opposite next time."

"I do?"

"Sure. What did you hate most about your Ex?"

"Did or do? I hate the fact that he's divorcing me and suing me for alimony."

"Ha Ha. Focus, please. You hated that he was lazy and cheap and unmotivated and happy to mooch off you."

"Yeah…"

"So you wanted the next guy to be career oriented and serious."

"Oh, yeah, that was the lawyer."

"And after him you dated that guy who freaked out when you dumped guacamole on him."

"Yeah, that was Darren. The guy who was totally image conscious."

"Right. And after him you went out with that actor because you thought he'd be above caring about other people's opinions."

"Hmm…"

"But he also wasn't that fun."

"Nope. Don't you think a normal person would have laughed at me blowing out the candles on that other girl's birthday cake?"

"Well, I would have as long as you didn't light my curtains on fire. So after that you thought you'd look for someone fun and ended up with the mafia thug."

I shuddered.

"So then you posted that you wanted a man that was responsible and ended up with the tree hugger," Nik continued.

"He was nice."

"Yeah, but he wasn't for you. So then you looked for someone that didn't want to dedicate his life to changing the world and ended up with that guy who couldn't deal with confrontation."

"Okay, but what about Ryan from karate? How does he fit into your theory?"

"The guy that stunk? No idea what you were thinking there."

"Hmm...you might have something with this theory."

"I know, I'm brilliant. I'll send you my very expensive therapist's bill."

"But Nik, how does this help me?"

"It doesn't."

"You're exasperating. What was the point, then?"

"Just to showcase my brilliance," he answered. "We'll have to explore more in our next session. I gotta get some work done now."

"Nik?"

"Yeah?"

"What about Alex?"

"What about him? You never dated. By the way, you still don't seem like you're over your crush on him."

"I totally am."

"Methinks thou doth protest too much."

"Whatever. I don't want to talk about it."

"Thank God. I've spent so many hours hearing how wonderful he is, it was only a matter of time before I fell in love with him too." Then he went into what I guess he thought was a good Karly impression, complete with falsetto voice, "Oh Alex, my precious Alex. Wherefore are thou Alex? Where-"

"Ha ha." I cut him off. "Hey Nik?"

"Yeah?"

"Do you think I'll ever get over him?

"Sure. You got over your massive crush on me, didn't you?"

"I never had a crush on you, massive or otherwise," I answered. But as I said it, I remembered a time when I did. If he hadn't said anything, I wouldn't even have remembered. I'd been thirteen to his sixteen. Embarrassingly enough, I'd even spent a large number of hours kissing my pillow, pretending it was him. But I'd gotten over it and here we were, more than a decade later, good friends. Ecstatic, I thought about this revelation. I could get over my crush on Alex. It would just take time.

PROBABILITY TESTING

I got to group early and was happy to see Alex there too, especially now that I was armed with the knowledge that it would only take time to get over my crush on him.

"How have you been?" he asked as we walked to the coffee shop. "It seems like forever since I saw you last."

"Wasn't it just two weeks ago? At the hospital?"

"Well yes, but that was just for a short time."

"Yeah, it's too bad I didn't make it to dinner."

"It wasn't the same without you there."

"Because there weren't any Strangeness Attracter events?"

"No, we definitely had those. I just mean…"

He stopped mid-sentence and just looked at me for a while.

"I don't know," he finally said and checked his watch. "Oh, look at the time."

***

Alex walked me back to my car after Group.

"You were wrong, by the way," I said.

"About what?"

"About that doctor wanting to ask me out. I bumped into him and his boyfriend doing groceries last week."

"Ah. Well, you said you didn't want to go out with him, anyway."

"Only because he'd given me a…a personal examination the

week before and it seemed a little, I don't know."

"Wait." He stopped walking. "Is that why you said it would be creepy to date a doctor?"

"Yeah."

He was quiet for a while, with a funny, distracted smile on his face. Then he asked how my family was after the emergency room visit and I told him the full story.

"It must happen a lot," I said. "I mean, lots of women wear lipstick and it's only natural to want to kiss babies."

"God, you're adorable," he blurted out, completely out of character.

"What?"

We had stopped at my car and he was staring at me intensely, with the same kind of look that the soccer coach had when he went to kiss me on our first date. Maybe he didn't think about me as a friend. But that was wrong. He had a pregnant wife waiting at home for him. What was he doing? I panicked as he leaned in towards me.

"Julia!" I shouted out in order to stop him.

"What?"

He looked confused. Maybe he hadn't been about to kiss me. Crap, he'd probably been leaning in to get a closer look because I had lunch bits stuck in my hair or seagull poop on my shoulder. I felt like an idiot.

"Uh, you should tell Julia? About the lipstick? So she doesn't do the same thing. I mean, after the baby arrives," I explained.

"Oh. Yes. Right."

He looked bewildered as he turned and walked to his car.

HONEY POT GOLD

I ran for the ringing phone in the living room.

"Hello?" I answered.

"First of all, I want you to know I'm doing this against my better judgement."

"Hi Nik."

"And I will not be held responsible in any way, shape, or form if things don't work out."

"Okay…"

"And I don't ever want to hear any of the details, the good, the bad, or the ugly. Ever. E-ver."

"Uh huh."

"And I wouldn't normally do this but I know you're trying to get over your doctor friend and maybe getting out on a normal date will help."

"I give up. What are we talking about?" I waited. "Nik?"

"My buddy Jake, that you met last week when you barged in on my poker night, asked if you were single."

"He did? Really? What were his exact words? Wait. Which one was he? The tall guy that looked like a Swedish Keanu Reeves? Or the one with the dreamy eyes?"

"Karly, please. This is exactly what I don't want to get into."

"Okay then, describe him in your words so I know which one he is."

"I don't know. He's a consultant at some mergers and acquisitions advisory company, he rambles on way too much about what a God he is at work, and he's crap at bluffing."

"Is this one of those 'Women are from Venus, Men are from Mars' moments? What does he look like?"

"I don't know. He looks like a guy."

"Exasperating, Nik. What colour is his hair?"

"Brownish. I think."

"Height?"

"I don't know. Not as tall as me?"

"Oh him," I said. Nik is six foot four so most guys aren't as tall as him. "What about his eyes?"

"He has two."

"Ha ha. What colour?"

"Christ. Dreamy sunshine chamomile brownish blue with flecks of honey pot gold in them – how the Hell would I know?"

I giggled.

"Don't you look at them?"

"Only to see if his left eyelid is twitching which means he's bluffing. I gotta go. I'll give him your number."

"Wait, one more question. What kind of body does he have?"

Click.

***

The phone rang on Sunday evening.

"Karly? Hi, it's Nik's friend Jake. I'd love to take you to my favorite steakhouse Tuesday if you're free. I work downtown at Harper Consultants and I'm closing a big deal in the morning, I thought we could celebrate at lunch afterwards."

"That'd be great."

"Yeah, I'm helping one of my clients sell off their financial division to Morgan Wilson Investments."

"Morgan Wilson? That's huge."

"You've heard of them?"

"I audited SGK, one of their competitors," I said without adding in "by accident."

"Pat Wilson has been a nightmare to deal with but in the end I negotiated about ten percent over market. I can't wait to get the final papers signed."

"That's great."

"Yeah, old Don Harper has to make me a partner after this. The company would have been in real trouble without this deal."

***

I arrived at Harper Consultants early for my date with Jake. The receptionist must have been in the ladies' room but there was another woman there, waiting. She looked like a well-preserved, fifty something trophy wife waiting for her husband, who I assumed was Mr. Harper, to take her for lunch. She was continually checking her watch and looking very unimpressed. On her hand was the biggest diamond wedding ring I'd ever seen. It matched her impressive earrings, necklace and strands of bracelets. Her makeup was perfect and her old fashioned updo looked like she'd just had it professionally done.

"Hi," I said as I smiled at her and took a seat. "Your ring is amazing."

"What?" she said as she noticed me for the first time. "Oh, thank you. My husband picked it out."

"Really?"

"And my necklace and earrings as well." I finally got a smile out of her. "He says he likes to keep me in jewels."

"Aren't you lucky," I said, smiling but feeling sorry for her. Mr. Harper obviously treated her as a showpiece for his wealth.

She smiled and scanned me, looking for some way to repay the compliment.

"Nice purse."

"Oh, thanks. I'm borrowing it from my sister, I don't really have the resources for something like this right now."

"Well, we all have financial troubles, don't we?" she said, a wrinkle line trying to work it's way through her Botox'd forehead.

I pitied her. Her husband had obviously been complaining that the business was having problems but hadn't told her the good news about the deal closing today. It must be a horrible feeling having things completely out of your control deciding your future. Not quite the same situation that Stella had been in, but still, not having any power over your life was so sad.

"Not after today," I said.

"Pardon?" she asked.

"The company's closing a huge deal. And making a huge commission. The buyer's paying top dollar."

"They are?" she said, confused.

I knew it. She didn't have a clue about her husband's business. Well, she should. I hated it when Desiree said things like "Oh I don't get involved in all that financial stuff. I leave that to Bill." She didn't even know what their joint worth was or how much they made or spent. Women could be doctors and lawyers and…and accountants! Like me. God, I'd been out of work so long I'd almost forgotten.

I was going to impress Mrs. Harper with my knowledge, lead by example. Then she'd see that women could be forces in the work place too. I sat up straighter, smoothed my skirt, and cleared my throat, readying my business voice.

"Yes, I'm not sure how they let themselves get duped into that," I said.

"Duped," she repeated, still staring blankly at me.

Operation "Girl Power" was about to go down. She'd have to concentrate to keep up with me. I only wished I had a projection screen and one of those cool pointy laser things to emphasize my points as I paced back and forth in front of her.

"You see, it's easy to present a higher value on the selling side by making certain aggressive assumptions like increasing the value of the receivables by not accounting for potential bad debt. You can also place a value on intangible assets or play with the depreciation policy. What people don't understand is that book value and market value are two totally different concepts. It's like comparing apples and oranges. If I were the acquiring company I'd hire an independent accounting firm to audit the selling company's financials. It's kind of idiocy not to."

"Independent." She stared at me like I was speaking Japanese.

"Well, yes. If the buyer's existing accountants are helping them, it's not really independent, is it? Because they know if the sale goes through, they'll get extra business out of it. Actually, I'm not even sure why Morgan Wilson wants this particular piece of business."

"Well, maybe they want to get into that market."

Good for her. She was attempting to converse with me.

"Well, it just seems a slow, expensive way of doing it. If it were me, I'd be looking to purchase an existing M&A company that already specialized in acquiring financial companies," I explained then figured I'd take it down to her level. "You see, it's kind of like wanting to have a great purse collection. You could either buy one at a time, which is expensive and takes time to collect…"

I stopped and checked to see if she was able to follow what I was saying.

"Yes."

"Or, you could check the internet sites, like EBay or Craig's List, and see if anyone is selling their entire collection."

"What if nobody is selling any of their, uh, purse collections and purchasing them individually is the only option? Especially given financing costs in the current credit market."

Well, I had to hand it to her. She was really making an effort to understand me and was even using big business words she'd probably heard from her husband. And actually, she had a valid argument.

"That is a good point," I said. "But, in the world of high finance, hopefully you'd have some business connections that would know what was going on. For example, being a successful businesswoman myself, I happen to know that SKG–I mean, SGK would consider a sale. And that they'd be willing to help with financing at pretty competitive rates. That's confidential knowledge of course."

She looked shocked, obviously having assumed I was just another pretty face and not the important businessperson I had just presented her with.

"SGK?"

"Yes, they're probably the biggest competitor in the local market. In fact, twice last year they swooped in at the last minute and acquired companies that Morgan Wilson was in the process of buying. If Morgan Wilson bought them, they'd have the companies they wanted in the first place and be the biggest players in that industry. On a local platform, anyway."

She looked like she was soaking it all in.

"Sorry, what's your name?"

"Karly."

"And what do you do, Karly?"

"I'm an auditor with KLDP. Well, actually-"

I wrestled with whether or not to tell her the long, embarrassing story about my non-working status. It would have the polar opposite effect of impressing her but I had problems not telling the truth. But right then I looked out the window and saw a meter maid take out her pad of paper in front of my car. I could not afford a ticket right now.

"Sorry, I'll be right back," I yelled back as I ran out of the office and passed a group of four men in suits getting off the elevator as I was getting on.

***

I walked back into the building and took the elevator back up, relieved. The meter maid had just been writing down the details from my For Sale sign on my car.

Mrs. Harper was gone by then but the receptionist was back and let Jake know I was there. He came looking stressed out.

"Hey Karly. Listen, I'm really sorry but I'm going to have to take a rain check. Something's popped up."

"Is everything okay?"

"Oh, sure. Fine," he answered while his left eyelid twitched uncontrollably. "The Morgan Wilson team is here and Pat Morgan just has some last minute concerns about the deal I put together for her."

"Her?"

"Yeah, she freaked out at her team for getting here late and for not having an independent auditor on the purchase and now she's saying something about wanting to check out other investment options. I don't know why she's changed directions all of a sudden. When she first arrived she was all ready to sign and just wanted to wait for her team."

***

I ran from the shower the next morning to grab the phone.

"Hello?"

"I knew I shouldn't have gotten involved in your love life."

"Hey Nik."

"Did you lose your situational awareness again and blow a huge deal for Jake?"

"I can explain."

"Of course you can."

"There was a misunderstanding."

"Of course there was."

"I might have mistaken someone for someone else."

"Of course you did."

"Why don't I buy you lunch and tell you the whole story?"

"How about you just buy me lunch and we never speak of it again."

DAYDREAMING

I was late for Group. On purpose.

Early this morning I had decided, again, to avoid Alex. Up until then I'd thought I was doing well thinking about him only as a friend but based on the dream I'd woken up from, was failing miserably. It wasn't that I wanted to cut him off completely, I just needed time to adjust. Everything was so confusing.

I'd intended to arrive ten minutes late so had stopped for a chocolate bar at a gas station. Unfortunately, I'd unwrapped my Kit Kat while waiting in line and then realized my purse was still on my kitchen counter. The clerk was pretty grumpy about it. He wasn't even appreciative after I searched my car for loose change and came up with about two-thirds of the cost. Then, he told me I wasn't allowed to try and sell my complete, albeit unwrapped chocolate bar, for a third of the price, to other customers. Thank God for the kind, gray-haired businessman who just handed me five dollars and, even though I insisted, told me to keep my Kit Kat. Anyway, I ended up being forty minutes late instead of my originally intended ten.

"Karly! Are you okay?" Alex asked, jumping up as I walked in. He grabbed me by the shoulders and quickly inspected my face and then the rest of my body. "What happened? Are you hurt?"

"I'm fine. I just got held up at the store."

"The store was held up? Oh my God! Were they armed?"

"No, the store wasn't held up. I just meant I was delayed."

"You're not hurt? Thank God. I was so worried. I mean, we were all worried," he said, finally letting go of my shoulders and looking embarrassed but relieved.

"Oh. Sorry, everyone. I'm fine," I said to the Group who just looked at me confused.

***

"He's being a total freak," Jeanette told me as we walked to the vending machines together at break.

"His wife is due to give birth any day now. He's probably just worried about her."

"No shit, I always thought…"

"What?"

"Honey, if it's one thing I know, it's men. And our doctor definitely has a thing for you. He was worried something had happened to you when you didn't show up on time."

I thought about what she said. Maybe she was right. But perhaps not. Nik would have been equally concerned and he was never anything more than a friend to me. And Alex wasn't the type to cheat on his wife or even entertain the thought of a crush on another woman.

After break Alex explained that night's exercise. We had thirty seconds to look at the contents of a tray. Then after he took it away, we were to write down everything we remembered being on it.

The tray was full of things he must have grabbed from his house. I pictured him using the shaving cream in the morning, and brushing his hair with the comb. Then I daydreamed about us sitting down for breakfast and him putting on his reading glasses, taking the pen and doing the crossword. Lovingly, I'd hand him the coffee cup and spoon. Then he'd pick up the book that we'd both have read and we'd talk about it over breakfast. For some reason the power would go out and we'd grab the flashlight. We'd find the matches and light the tea lights and he'd pull me closer and—

Was someone talking to me? Real Alex had just interrupted Dream Alex.

"Pardon?" I said.

"Are you okay, Karly? You haven't written anything."

I surprised everyone by scoring one hundred percent. Alex was impressed. But I wondered how he'd have felt if he'd known the only reason I'd done so well was because I was in love with him. Yes, I'd been fooling myself that I could grow out of my feelings for him. This wasn't a thirteen-year-old's crush.

After class, I took off before Alex could offer to walk me to my car. I needed to think. And without him around because his presence got me daydreaming about stupid things like the way he'd look at me and hold my hand as we sat on the veranda and watched our grandchildren play in the back yard.

TAKE TWO

That was it. No more fooling around. It was time to get serious about Operation "Forget Alex." Sipping at my coffee on Saturday morning, I sat at my computer and started yet another profile on the dating website, this time using the name Donna. I remembered what Nik said about playing checkers and decided to put some thought into creating my profile. This time I wouldn't just go for the polar opposite of the last date that didn't work out. Instead, I'd put some serious effort into figuring out exactly what I was looking for.

Okay. I took a bite of my Pop Tart. So I wanted someone who had a job but wasn't as serious as Phil, the lawyer I'd had lunch with. Chewing, I posted that I was looking for someone who was both:

- **Fun**

and

- **Career oriented**

Remembering my dates with image conscious Darren and then no-sense-of-humour Tyler, I ticked off that I was looking for someone who:

- **doesn't feel the need to conform to societal norms**

but was also

- **open minded**

Leaning back in my chair, I thought of how much I hated when the Ex sat around on the couch all the time and chose that I wanted someone who was:

- **Physically adventurous**

Not wanting a repeat of my date with Artie, who wanted to

spend all his time fighting the world, I checked off the category:

- **Comfortable being submissive**

Finally, to make sure I didn't end up with someone like Sheldon who would run the other way when a Strangeness Attracter event hit me, I posted that I wanted someone who was:

- **Not afraid of new things**

Two days later, I was matched with Patrick who asked me to dinner that Friday night.

HOT GOSSIP

Ring. Ring.

"Hello?" I croaked out, groggy from having been woken up from my afternoon nap.

"Your doctor's wife – what does she look like?"

"Hi Nik. Um, uber model beautiful and carrying the child of the man of my dreams. Why?"

"Is she tall and really good looking?"

"Yes, and with perfect skin, a killer body, and gorgeous blond hair. Why are you torturing me?"

"What's her name?"

"Julia."

"I have some news. One of the guys who's been at the mine the last six months got another one of the engineers to switch places with him."

"Fantastic, glad you woke me up for that," I grumbled. "Will you be phoning again at four a.m. to tell me what kind of salad your secretary had for lunch?"

"Listen, crabby, I'm not finished. He wanted to switch because he has a pregnant wife here and she's due any minute now."

"And?"

"Her name is Julia."

"Yeah?"

"And she's been staying with her brother while he's away."

I was speechless as my mind raced.

"She kept her maiden name," Nik continued.

"What is it?"

I could hear him yelling to his coworker,

"Caesar, what's Carl's wife's last name? No, that's his last name. What? Yes, women can keep their last names. Look, I don't have time for a debate right now."

"Hold on," he said to me. "I'll ask the receptionist."

I listened to the on-hold elevator music while my life, or at least my love life, hung on the line.

"You still there?" Nik asked.

"Yes."

"It's her."

Ecstatic, I let out a scream that had Larry from next door running over and knocking on the door to check that everything was okay.

I don't even remember hanging up the phone. In shock, I collapsed back on the bed, replaying every interaction, every conversation, every look that Alex and I had shared. It all took on such different meaning now. For hours, I danced around the apartment singing "He's not married" to the tune of whatever was playing on the radio. I couldn't wait to see him again so I could explain all the misunderstandings we'd had. Then we'd start our relationship the way it was meant to be.

TOTALLY NORMAL

I was so busy dancing around my apartment and having imaginary conversations with the love of my life that I almost forgot about my date that night. Now that I knew about Alex, I didn't want to go out with Patrick but it felt rude to cancel at the last minute. What harm could there be in one little dinner date, I thought as I put on my Rash Red lipstick.

We met downtown for dinner, then walked along Robson Street and chatted. Well, he talked and I pretended to be listening while daydreaming about Alex. At the end of the somewhat vanilla date, I let him drive me home. I'd sold my car to the meter maid I'd met outside Jake's office and didn't want to run into the cab driver that had rescued me from my "kidnapper."

Patrick asked to come in for a drink. I didn't usually let strangers into my apartment but he'd been a complete gentleman all evening, even joking about how he'd be happy being submissive to a woman that wanted to take charge. Also, Nik had asked me to phone him halfway through dinner to update him on the progress.

"He's totally normal, Nik," I'd reported while looking in the reflective part of the payphone and picking out peppercorn bits from my teeth.

"Sure, he is. And we'd know that because you're such a good judge of character."

"No really, Nik. I'm sure this time."

"Has he changed your mind about your precious Alex?"

"Nope," I'd answered quickly before Nik could launch into his stupid 'Oh Alex, my Alex, wherefore art thou Alex' falsetto Karly imitation which only he thought was entertaining.

"So what does this guy do?"

"He's an executive at Trinity Corporation."

"And his name?"

"Patrick. I don't know his last name."

"Does he have a long face, bushy eyebrows, and brown hair?"

"Are you spying on me?" I had looked up and down the hallway outside the restaurant bathrooms in a flash of illogical paranoia. "Where are you?"

"No, freak. I'm on his company website. I just want to have a full description for the police if you go missing."

"Awww, it's nice to know you care but don't worry your pretty little head about it. Like I said, he's totally normal."

***

Patrick asked to use my bathroom and I busied myself searching through the kitchen for appropriate beverages. My somewhat pathetic offering consisted of coconut juice, watermelon crystal lite, yogi lemon ginger tea, and two cases of Diet Pepsi. I was wondering which he'd like when I realized he'd been gone for quite some time.

I didn't want to rush him if he was doing something that uh, required time but I was starting to have just a sliver of doubt that inviting a man I didn't know into my apartment was a good idea.

Nervously, I looked down the hall. The bathroom door was open and the light was off. Crap. Had I lost track of the complete stranger I'd let into my apartment? I reinterpreted everything he'd done and said that night. The way he cut up his steak was just practice for severing my head from my body. When he said "nice shoes," what he really meant was "that one will be a nice addition to my collection of right legs."

"Donnaaaaa…" he called out in a playful sing-song voice from my room. What was he doing there? I couldn't decide if his voice was "look at this cute baby picture of you" playful, or "I have a machete and am lurking in your closet, ready to decapitate you after lulling you into a false sense of security with my sing-song voice" playful.

I panicked. What should I do? Get a weapon? I looked around the kitchen and grabbed a knife. Hold on. What if he wrestled it from me? I hid it in the back of my broom closet and grabbed a wooden spoon instead.

Taking a deep breath, I made myself peek around the corner.

OH!

Oh...

Apparently his tone was "I've handcuffed myself naked to your bed" kind of playful.

"What are you doing?" I demanded.

"I've been a naughty boy, Mistress, I should be punished."

"Uh, I think there's been some misunderstanding. You need to leave. Now."

"But I've been so very bad, Mistress," he said, winking lewdly at me, "You should paddle me with that wooden spoon."

Ewww.

"I'm serious, get out. I don't want any part of this." Ugh. I saw a whip, a paddle, and some other things I didn't recognize laid out on the bed. Were those clothespins? What were they for?

"Can you get the keys then, Mistress, and unlock the handcuffs?"

Good. He was finally listening to me. But why was he still using that tone of voice?

"Where are they?"

He gave me a big smile and suggestive look down his body and then clenched certain muscles and did a couple of pelvic thrusts, to give me a hint as to where they were.

Oh. Dear. God.

***

I'm not sure how long I stood there with my jaw dropped, wooden spoon in hand, not knowing what to do, but the ringing of the phone jolted me out of my frozen state. Nik's number was on the call display.

"Hey."

"How was Mr. Totally Normal? Did he compare to your precious Dr. Weiss?"

"Uh…"

"Hello?"

"Um…"

"Oh, is he there? Sorry. I didn't think you'd—never mind. Okay, pretend I'm a telemarketer. Say 'No thanks, I don't need my carpets cleaned' if you're in the middle of making out, and 'I don't need a new set of encyclopaedias' if he's a psycho and has you at knife point."

"Do you have bolt cutters?"

"…What's that code for?"

"No, really, could you come over with either that or um, surgical gloves."

"Oh Christ, I'm scared to ask. I'll be there in ten."

Nik arrived with his bolt cutters and almost used them on err… the wrong parts when Patrick excitedly asked him if he was the new Master. He liberated my date from the bed and threw him out the front door and out of my life.

"Only you…" Nik shook his head as he left.

I closed the door to my room, made myself comfortable on the couch, and watched TV until I fell asleep.

FURNITURE SHOPPING

Ring. Ring.

"Morning, Nik."

"Hey, what are you up to today?"

"Burning my sheets and buying a new wooden spoon."

"Cool, I need help picking out a new coffee table. Pick you up in twenty."

***

We were at our third crowded big box furniture store with all the other weekend shoppers. I was past bored and approaching annoyed. Who would have thought a man, a straight man, could be so picky about a coffee table? Mine had been purchased at a garage sale for twenty dollars and I couldn't even tell you what it looked like other than that I was pretty sure it had four legs. The latest table's shortcoming was that its leg design was too contemporary compared to the traditional wainscoting in Nik's Calgary apartment that he'd be returning to at the end of his contract.

"You sure you're not gay?" I asked as we headed to the front door.

"You sure you don't want to be after last night?" he shot back.

"Ha ha."

"Ooh, do you need a new bed, Mistress Karly? This one feels good," he teased, jumping on one of the display beds and miming that he was tied down. This was one of the good things and bad things about Nik. Absolutely nothing embarrassed him. Normally this was a required characteristic for a friend of mine. Right then, though, I wished he was a little more self-conscious.

People were staring and then moving away uncomfortably. My red face and hisses to Nik to "cut it out" were all the fuel he needed.

"Please Mistress, tell me your bidding. Your wish is my command," he called out theatrically.

"Nik, I swear to God—"

"Have I angered you, Mistress? Will I be punished for being naughty? Are you going to get the wooden spoon? Will you tell the new Master I've been bad? Please?"

I tried to stay looking mad, stifling a giggle.

Nik egged me on.

"Oh no, not the clothespins!" he hammed in a falsetto voice, then continued with his favourite "Oh Alex, my Alex, wherefore art thou Alex?"

I lost it. We laughed long and hard, more or less clearing the area. Only a handful of shoppers remained. Some that didn't look like they spoke English, and a couple of nosy ones that were pretending not to listen.

"Your face was priceless last night," Nik smiled as he finally crawled off the bed.

"So was yours. By the way, you left the handcuffs attached to the bed rails, and all the whips and paddles lying out-"

I was going to finish "people might get the wrong impression" but it was too late as I finally noticed that one of the listening shoppers was Alex. By the way he had grabbed and was intently studying the ugliest lamp in the world, I could tell he definitely had gotten the wrong impression.

"Alex," I said.

"Oh, Karly, I didn't see you there," he lied.

"Hi...I was just...we were just...shopping for a coffee table."

"Oh. Of course." He took a polite look around and we both

pretended not to notice that there weren't any in the immediate area.

"Is this your boyfriend?" he asked, looking at Nik. "We haven't met."

"Him? No, he's not my boyfriend, just a friend. This is Nik. And he's just my friend. Uh, Nik."

Why was I babbling like an idiot? This man knew all sorts of embarrassing things about me and I could easily explain this situation. And he'd totally get it because he knew me. We'd laugh about it and then I'd tell him about our other misunderstandings. Then he'd smile that beautiful, familiar smile of his and ask me out. All these good thoughts raced through the "logic" part of my brain while the "panicked moron" part kept blabbering on,

"And Nik, this is Alex."

"Ah, the infamous Dr. Weiss. Nice to finally meet you. The two of us were just talking about you last night."

Alex looked alarmed whereas oblivious Nik had spotted a potentially suitable coffee table on the other side of the store, excused himself, and taken off.

"He seems…nice," Alex said.

I'd never seen him like this. He was so uncomfortable. I guess he'd never figured me for the S&M, threesome type.

"He's just a friend," I said for what seemed like the tenth time.

"A friend that left his handcuffs at your house?" he asked slowly. Well, at least he was listening, I could still redeem myself.

"No, that was someone else I met, online," I explained. "Nik came over afterwards. Or actually while my date was still over. To help out?" Crap. That didn't come out right. It was happening again. Somebody had taken over my brain and was saying stupid things. Why couldn't I lie or at least explain things fully?

Alex gasped in shock and dropped the world's ugliest lamp, shattering it into a million pieces. The store staff came over to help clean it up and before I had the opportunity to calm down and explain myself, he'd thrown some bills at them and ran out.

What just happened? Yesterday I'd been dancing around my living room having imaginary conversations with him, dreaming of our future together. Twenty-four hours later I'd completely scared him off. Sometimes I really hated my life.

THE INVITATION

I sat in my living room, telephone in hand, and forced myself to dial, almost hyperventilating with nerves. It had taken all day for Nik to talk me into phoning Alex. I'd almost jotted down notes for myself to prep but then remembered I wasn't an insecure, socially awkward fourteen-year-old calling a guy I wanted to go around with. Nope. I was an insecure, socially awkward thirty-year-old calling a guy I wanted to go around with.

Ring. Ring.

Please be home, please be home, I prayed. Then-

Please don't be home, please don't be home.

"Hello?"

Crap.

"Hi, Dr. Weiss, I mean Alex. It's Karly, from your research study?"

"Oh. Hi."

"I'm so sorry about...well, that thing at the furniture store?"

"Oh. Well, I...I reacted badly, I suppose. I just had a different sort of image of you. Not that it's any of my business, of course."

"Look, this is hard for me to say, just in case I've totally misread you, but Nik told me I should phone. I wanted to finish the conversation we started at the furniture store and," I took a deep breath and forced myself to say what I wanted without thinking of the potential rejection, "I get a certain feeling from you and I..." This was so much more difficult than I'd imagined. Which was odd because I'd always found him so easy to talk to. Maybe it was because we'd always talked in person. Seeing him face-to-face would probably make it easier.

We could meet at our coffee shop. Except damn, I didn't have a car.

"Could you come over?" I asked.

"Now? To your house?"

Oh God, I hadn't really thought this through. It was nearing dinnertime. I guess I had some frozen shrimp in the freezer and could make some pasta. Or order take out. Probably a better idea. I also had my two cases of Diet Pepsi. I mean, he normally drank Diet Coke but I'm sure either would do.

"Yes. For dinner and if you keep an open mind, some DP after."

There was silence on the other line, and then

"Sorry Karly, you've got the wrong idea about me."

I was shocked.

"I do? But, but Nik said he thought you'd want to-"

"I have to go."

Click.

I was shattered.

THE REVEALING

I'd ignored Nik's four calls the night before and then two more early this morning but couldn't pretend I didn't hear him banging on the door at nine a.m..

"Karly," he called out. "Remove yourself from the tub of ice cream and let me in."

"You suck, go away."

"I'm not leaving."

"And I'm not opening the door so you can just rot out there."

"I have fresh bagels, salmon lox, and that tofu cream cheese crap you like."

I didn't answer.

"And I have your spare keys so I'm just going to let myself in anyway," he added.

Oh right. He had a point. And surely it was better to wallow in self-pity on a full stomach. I opened the door.

"You look like crap," he said, taking in my swollen eyelids and red nose.

"Is that what you barged in here to tell me?"

"Okay, I'm sorry. I'm not usually wrong about these things."

"Whatever, Superego, just hand over the food."

We made breakfast in silence. Well, except for arguing continually about the correct way to make a smoked salmon and cream cheese bagel.

"So how about I pretend to be the gay best friend you've always wanted and you tell me what happened?" Nik asked.

"How about we don't talk about it."

"I just don't get how-"

"Is this part of not talking about it?"

"Okay, I didn't want to do this but I may have a fresh fruit pavlova for you if you tell me what you're so upset about."

"No."

"Shit, that's bad."

We ate breakfast in silence. Well, except for arguing continually about the merits of the open-faced sandwich versus the closed.

God, I was so tired. I'd hardly slept last night. An espresso would do the trick. Except my espresso maker was on the blink, making odd clunky noises when I turned it on. Soda was kind of gross first thing in the morning, but it had more caffeine than tea and I was barely able to keep my eyes open.

"DP?" I offered. Like Alex and I, Nik was also pretty loyal to Diet Coke.

"What?" he said, choking on his sandwich.

"Do you want a DP to drink?" I held up the can.

"Oh. Diet Pepsi. No, thank you." He smirked.

"Don't be such a freak. There's nothing wrong with DP. I tried it last night."

Nik started to laugh really hard. He kept saying "Nothing wrong with DP!" and then convulsing again.

I gave him some time to finish, not in the mood for his antics.

"You done now?"

"Yeah, I'm good."

"So you think it's too early for some DP?"

"Well, I guess I could phone a friend," he barely managed to get out, his normally deep, masculine voice going up an octave at the end of the sentence. He was laughing so hard his doubled-over body was shaking and he had tears coming out of his eyes. It was starting to tick me off.

He was still going strong as I decided to give up on the Diet Pepsi and make tea. I had time to boil the kettle, steep the tea, put the milk and sugar in, and cool it down before Nik stopped.

"Are you done now?" I asked with the tone of a seasoned mother letting her kid finish a tantrum.

"Nope, just taking a smoke break, that was exhausting."

"Well maybe you could laugh at me for longer if you didn't poison your lungs with that crap," I called after him as he let himself out to the balcony where he'd set himself up a little smoking station. Larry, from next door, was out as well and I could hear them talking. I tried not to listen when they were out there. For some reason, they both got annoyingly macho and talked like surfers when they got together.

"Dude, was that you making all that noise?" Larry asked Nik.

"Yeah, man."

"Were you laughing?"

"Uh huh."

"Wow, man, didn't know you had it in you. What's so funny?"

And then they were whispering and giggling like twelve-year-old girls.

"Hey, Karly, can you offer us a refreshment?" Nik asked.

"Do the two of you want some DP now?"

They cracked up.

"Oh Karly," Larry managed to gasp out between peals of

laughter. "I didn't think you were that type. I totally had the wrong idea about you."

"Wrong idea," I repeated Larry's words out loud. Someone else had said that to me recently. "Wrong idea…wrong idea…"

Oh. My. God.

It was Alex. He'd said that when I asked him to come over last night. And, I think, right after I'd offered him some DP.

I threw the sliding door open so hard that it made the whole balcony shake. Nik and Larry stopped laughing and looked at me in shock.

"Nik. You have to tell me what DP is."

"What's wrong?"

"Just. Tell. Me. What. It. Is," I said through clenched teeth, wanting to grab him by the neck and choke the answer out of him.

"Uh…" he looked at Larry for support, but Larry just stubbed out his cigarette and ran inside to his apartment, muttering something about "Hell hath no fury…"

"Don't get mad, okay?" he said, no longer laughing, but looking a bit embarrassed. "Uh, do you ever watch porn?"

"Of course not," I answered, dreading the eventual explanation.

"DP might stand for uh, double penetration which is, well it's when there's, you know, two guys…and a girl, and well, they…"

If I hadn't been so mortified replaying my conversation with Alex last night, I might have enjoyed Nik's stuttering. He talked in circles for a minute without actually saying anything new.

"Nik. I get it. Stop torturing me trying to explain it any more."

"Okay."

"Is it a well known term?" I asked.

"Well, not to destroy your rose-tinted view of the world but sometimes, when a guy has a stag, there may be some adult-oriented entertainment on in the background."

"Stop sugar coating it, Nik. Hit me."

"Okay. I'd say ninety percent of males over the age of nineteen know what DP is."

"Oh God." I flopped down on the couch.

"So what?"

"I might have offered Alex some DP yesterday when I was asking him to come over and talk."

"You did?"

"I was trying to get him to come over so I could clear up the misunderstanding about you and the handcuffs and stuff."

"And in the process of that, you asked him if he'd be interested in a threesome?"

"Well, not to my knowledge at the time, but I guess I did."

"That is so…so…"

His look of concern was fading as he tried to finish his sentence with the appropriate response. To give him credit, he was trying pretty hard. I thought of it from Alex's point of view. He must think I was some sort of sex starved dominatrix freak. It was…well, it was a little funny, really.

"And when he said 'Sorry Karly, you've got the wrong idea about me,' I said something about you thinking he'd want to and he hung up before I could finish my sentence."

Then we were laughing so hard we were both snorting.

NAGGING FRIEND

Ring. Ring.

I rolled over from my comatose position in front of the TV where I'd been for three days and picked up the phone, surprised to see that it was afternoon already.

"Hello?"

"So?" asked Nik.

"So what?"

"Have you gotten a hold of him and explained yourself yet?"

"No, he'll just hang up on me."

"You always do that, Karly."

"Do what?"

"Avoid anything that might be unpleasant."

"Whatever, Nik. I think it's pretty reasonable that I don't want to harass the man I accidentally asked for a threesome last week."

"If he's the kind of guy you've said he is, I think he'd listen."

"Well he sure didn't want to last week, Nik."

"Fine. How about the other thing you've been avoiding?"

"Which one would that be?" I asked even though I knew.

"Have you talked to your lawyer about the divorce lately?"

"No, I've been busy," I lied. I'd cancelled my last two appointments with Sam at the last minute and hadn't returned his calls since.

"Whatever. Karly, you're going to completely screw yourself if you don't deal with this."

"Okay, I'll phone him."

"When?"

"Soon."

"How soon?"

"Next week."

"Monday morning?"

"Sure."

"By eleven a.m.?"

"What?"

"I'll phone you at twelve to make sure."

"Piss off, Nik."

"Or what? You won't talk to me?"

"Uh, yeah, that's right. I won't talk to you."

"Good. Your constant yapping drives me nuts when we're watching a movie. I'll pick you up after work and we'll go rent a DVD."

Click.

BABY STEPS

Sitting around watching soap operas was going to do my brain in. Even the shows I normally found slightly interesting were now just pissing me off. Whoever wrote this crap had no grip on reality. Nobody ever lost their lover to their stepmother's twin sister who was, in fact, actually just the stepmother pretending she was her own twin. Of course, I didn't see anyone scaring off their true loves by accidentally harassing them for threesomes either. I turned the set off and went to visit Stella.

After tracking her down at the hospital, I gave her an update of my recent tragedy. Maybe the X-rated nature of the DP story stunned her because she was unusually quiet at the end.

"Stella? Don't you have anything to say?"

"Like what?"

"I don't know. You usually have some advice for me."

"What's the point? It just goes in one ear and out the other." She used the remote control to turn the TV volume up.

"What are you talking about?" I asked, confused and hurt. It wasn't like Stella to get so snappy.

"You know what I mean. Have you done anything I've told you?"

I didn't answer.

"Karly. Listen to me." She muted the television, reached for my hand and looked at me intensely. "This is important. The longer you avoid things, the harder it'll get. One day you'll look up and wonder what happened to your life. You'll regret so many thing-lost opportunities, years wasted. You need to find that breaking point that makes you decide you're done being treated like a doormat."

"I got that guy to pay for my cab home."

"Yes dear, you did, but you're avoiding the bigger issues of your Ex and your career. How can you live with those things haunting you?"

"I have you to talk to if I feel down."

"Stop depending on other people to pick you up all the time, Karly. You need to deal with your problems. You. I won't be around forever."

"Don't talk like that. I know I have to start dealing with things and I'm getting there, okay? Baby steps."

"You need to start taking bigger steps!" Stella's harsh tone left me speechless. She saw the hurt in my face and closed her eyes and let out a big sigh, as if her outburst had drained her of all her energy.

"Oh, Karly," she said with a totally different demeanour when she opened her eyes again. "I'm sorry. I believe in you. You just need to believe in yourself too."

The nurse popped in to tell us that Stella needed to rest and that I'd have to leave right away.

"I thought I'd have more time," Stella said to nobody in particular while staring at the TV and then to me, "You know that I only want the best for you, Karly. You deserve it."

ACRONYM RESEARCH

The closest video store was five minutes away but Nik insisted on going to the slightly larger video store, which was twenty minutes away. Well, whatever. It was his gas. I was just the passive passenger that wasn't talking to him. Except to criticize his driving. He insisted on timing his new route there which involved speeding through back alleys, flying through residential areas and some hairy and somewhat illegal left turns.

"Shaved off ninety seconds," he reported as we Dukes of Hazzarded into the parking lot.

"Certainly worth risking our lives for," I muttered to myself.

We had given up long ago trying to pick out a movie together. Instead, we agreed that one chose and the other suffered. Nik liked movies with cyborgs and car chases and time travel while I liked chick flicks and Disney classics. We'd watched "Wacky Wednesday" last time so it was Nik's turn to choose. He headed for the Action section and I wandered around, checking out the Top Ten rentals. Between number four and number five, I noticed for the first time a short hallway with a discrete sign marked "Adult Section." I hovered there, wondering if what Nik had told me was true, if DP actually meant…well, what he said it did.

I walked down the hallway and took a deep breath at the entrance to the small, empty room before stepping inside. It was intimidating being surrounded by all this…depravity, just out in the open for all to see. Unfortunately, another customer arrived after me; a short, balding, middle-aged man. I froze with self-consciousness. What if he thought I was looking for porn? Not that he'd think I was shopping for flowers, but I wanted to explain to him that I was just doing research, that I wasn't the type of deviant who actually watched porn. Not that I was passing judgment on him, of course, I'd say. Okay, I was botching this conversation even in my own head; it definitely wasn't one I could have with a real person. I turned around to head for the exit.

But wait. I needed to find out if DP was a common term. If it wasn't, Alex wouldn't know it and that would mean he just wasn't into me. Toughen up Karly, I told myself, women have done much braver things in the name of love. Look at what Stella did for her children. Reading a couple porn covers didn't even compare to poisoning an abusive husband.

Determined to stay but still too self-conscious to actually look at any of the DVDs, I burned off my nervous energy lapping up and down the aisles looking either at my feet or at the ceiling. This completely unnerved the other customer who left empty-handed. Only then was I finally able to look porn in the eye.

Oh my God. One of the cover pictures in the Bondage section reminded me of my date from Friday night, handcuffed to my bed. I stopped and took a closer look. Oh, that's what he wanted done with the clothespins. Ouch.

Yippee! A Threesome section. I flipped through the cases, speed reading through the plot descriptions, looking frantically for DP references. It was the same excitement I felt when going through the shoe racks at Winners, searching for the pair I wanted in my size. I was desperate to find a DP reference, even more than I'd needed to find that cute pair of black patent wedges in size seven last year.

I read through a couple more and then-

"Score," I exclaimed out loud triumphantly, clutching a DVD to my chest and doing my standard celebratory Sound of Music twirl, after having read the back of "Nadia does her Time on the Couch."

"So you've found everything you're looking for?" asked the squat but stealth video store employee standing behind me that I'd almost wiped out when I'd twirled.

"Uh, yes?"

"Why don't I take that to the front for you, then, while you continue browsing. We do have many more films specializing in this genre if that's your particular area of interest."

"Um, thanks," I said, handing the DVD over just to get rid of him, "but I only need this one."

"You're sure? There's a new series here I could show you that seems to be very popular with our clientele. Where did it go?" He flipped through the titles with his pudgy fingers. "Oh, they're out now," he said as if he was a librarian helping me find a book on Mayan history.

"Oh how disappointing, maybe next time," I said.

He left and I breathed easier. Or breathed at all, I should say. I hadn't exhaled for the whole exchange. It was a miracle I hadn't passed out. That sounded like something I would do. I could just picture it now. Me fainting between the S&M and Threesomes section and the ambulance being called to come and revive me. Of course, I'd know the ambulance attendees, and I'd probably pass by my third grade teacher, Sister Mary, and the Channel Five news as they wheeled me out of the porn section.

I grabbed the bondage DVD on the way out, to show Nik. The guy there really did look like Patrick from Friday night. Nik would get a kick out of it. Plus he'd see what the clothespins were for.

He'd be losing it by now. When it was my turn to pick, I took twenty minutes to peruse all the DVDs, narrowed it down to three, tracked down the staff and asked them which ones they'd seen and how they liked them, and then took a general poll amongst the other customers in the store before finalising my choice. Nik just walked into the action section and grabbed the first movie he hadn't seen.

After checking for any nuns or camera crews, I walked out of the adult section, saw Nik in the five-person line up and ran up to him. He'd just finished talking to the guy in front of him, probably using my "poll the other customers" technique.

"Hey Nik, who does this remind you of?" I asked, waving the DVD in front of him.

"Huh?"

How could he be so dense? Did he liberate handcuffed men from bedposts with bolt cutters on a regular basis?

"Doesn't he look like Patrick from Friday night?"

He looked mortified.

"No, hey Karly-"

He was embarrassed? After what he pulled on me in the furniture store, he was self conscious about this? Nobody could even see what DVD I was showing him. I always suspected he could dish it out better than he could take it. Well, it was payback time, baby.

"Surely you remember Patrick that was over on Friday night?" I said loudly. "You know, the one in the handcuffs? The one who brought the clothespins? How could you forget him, Master? Or do all of your servants look the same to you?"

Nik winced.

"So Karly, look who I ran into," he said as he grabbed me by my shoulders and turned me around to face the other customer he had been talking to. Who bore a striking resemblance to Alex. Oh God. He was staring at the cover of the DVD I'd been waving in Nik's face.

"Why don't I put that back while you two catch up?" Nik said, taking the DVD from my hands and taking off.

There was silence. Long, uncomfortable silence.

Nik turned around and mouthed, "Talk to him." Oh, what the Hell. What did I have to lose? It's not like I could make things any worse.

"Look," I began, "I think you may have gotten the wrong idea about some things."

"Really?" Alex monotoned as he turned his head and watched Nik walk to the adult section.

"You know how my life works, how so many things that I do are misinterpreted."

"That's true."

"Well—"

"Next customer," one of the cashiers called out.

"She's free over there," pointed out one of the customers in the long line up that had accumulated behind us.

"Uh, I'd better…" and he gestured in the free cashier's direction.

Well, he'd started to listen and of all people, he should understand how Murphy's Law liked to make a prime example of a select few. I mean, he'd based a whole research study on it. He looked like he was thinking things over and had even looked back and given me a little smile. I started to hope.

"Next!"

I got called to the cashier beside his and arrived as he finished paying. He took a step over to me.

"So I've misunderstood some things?" he asked tentatively.

"Yes. I got some things wrong about you, too. I actually thought Julia was your wife until yesterday."

"Really?" he said and I could almost see his brain working as he thought about what that meant. "You mean you…is that why you… why you didn't…"

He stopped his babbling and a huge smile spread across his face.

"Are you renting a DVD?" the cashier asked me.

I stared at my empty hands.

"Oh, I've got it here," the employee who had taken the DVD from me in the back room said.

No. Please. Not now. I was so close.

"Here you go," he said to Alex and I. "You two will really enjoy this."

Alex took a look at "Nadia does her Time on the Couch" and

went green at the picture of a brunette in a compromising situation with two therapists.

"And I'll put the other DP DVDs we discussed on hold for you," the overly helpful employee whispered and winked at the two of us, unknowingly destroying any hope I had of reconciliation.

The object of my now-rendered-hopeless love life made a little choking sound and turned around to leave, but got trapped between Nik and I as Nik had run up to bring me his action DVD.

"Wait, please," I begged Alex, grabbing his arm in desperation, causing him to recoil in horror. What could I do? Every time I opened my mouth, I made things worse. I needed someone to translate for me. "Talk to Nik, he'll persuade you."

Alex looked at us both in fear, pulled his arm from my grasp, extracted himself from our Karly-Nik sandwich, and headed for the door. No, I just needed more time. Just a couple more minutes, to make this all right. This was the breaking point Stella had been talking about. I was ready to fight. I was ready to believe in myself. I deserved happiness. I deserved love. I deserved Alex.

"Stop him!" I screamed at Nik in my frenzy, with an aggression that shocked all three of us. "Don't let him get away!"

Alex made a weird, cornered-animal sound, broke into a sprint and ran out to the parking lot. Heart sinking, I watched him jump into his car and hit the gas, leaving both the parking lot and my realm of possibility.

THE DEAL

Ring. Ring.

"Hello?" I answered, late on Wednesday night.

"I've got it."

"Hey, Nik. Got what?"

"The solution to your problem."

"I don't know what you're talking about."

"Your ex is suing you for alimony, your precious doctor thinks the two of us are stalking him for a freaky role-playing threesome, you-"

"Okay, okay. So which one are you going to wave your magic wand at and solve?"

"Tell you what. You fight your Ex and I'll get your doctor friend talking to you again."

"I thought you swore not to get involved in my love life after the Jake disaster."

"True, but I'm getting tired of seeing you sitting around moping all the time. Plus I'll be moving back to Calgary soon and won't be here to look after you."

"What do you mean, you're moving back soon?"

"We're finished at the mine. I'm gone at the end of next month."

"But you were supposed to be here for a year and a half."

"It's been sixteen months."

"But-"

"I know, how will you survive without me around to rescue you with my bolt cutters or pick your drunk ass up from speed dating?"

I almost blurted out something sappy about not being able to survive without my best friend around but Nik would never have let me live that down.

"Hey Karly, when are your mom and dad coming back?"

"In six months. Why?"

"I don't know. I just thought, with me going, maybe you'd want to let them know you won't have anyone around to take care of you. Maybe they'd cut their trip short."

I laughed it off before making up an excuse to get off the phone. For the rest of the night, I tried to ignore what he'd said but it caught up to me while I was brushing my teeth.

What was he talking about? It wasn't like I was eight years old. I didn't need my mommy and daddy to look after me. Okay, maybe I had relied on Nik a lot recently to pick me up when I was down, and Stella as well, but that's what friends did for each other. That's what I did for them, too. I'd totally been there for Nik when he'd…Okay, maybe he'd never needed my support. That was just a man thing. But I was there for Stella when she…when she…crap. Neither of them had ever asked me for help. Well, unless you counted Stella ordering me to wheel her down the street to Walter's apartment so she could attack him with my crutches. I'd planned on taking care of her after the break up but she'd gotten over it without me.

What was it Stella had said at the hospital? That I needed to stop depending on other people all the time and deal with my problems myself? Surely I wasn't that pathetic. Okay, maybe I had been the past while but I'd just been dumped. Everyone needed a little more support right after a break up. It'd only been…no. Had it been ten months already? I looked at myself in the mirror in disgust, thinking about how I'd buried my head in the sand about so many things and burdened my friends and family to look after me. Okay so maybe I'd ruined my career and there wasn't anything I could do to recover but I could at least confirm this so that I could formulate and then move on to Plan

B. And had I really been considering not fighting the Ex? What if I ended up spending the rest of my life working to pay him alimony? Is that what I wanted? Did I really want to have to beg to move in with my sister and Bill? And was I really a good example to have around Siri and Connor? When did I become so pathetic? And how had I become this person? I didn't want to be.

I wouldn't be.

PAST DUE

I marched in, first thing the next morning, to find Stella still asleep in her hospital bed. With her eyes closed and without her lively voice and arm gestures, she looked older and weaker than I'd ever seen her. Or maybe I'd been so self absorbed, I hadn't noticed the change.

"Stella?"

She opened her eyes slowly.

"Karly, dear, how are you?" She sat up slowly and went to pull up the covers around her.

"I'm good and I wanted to tell you, I get it, what you were saying the other day, and I'm going to get there. Soon. And not with baby steps. With big, huge, leaping steps. And I'm sorry for being so needy. And so selfish," I said in one breath.

"My, that's a big revelation for first thing in the morning, dear," she said as she pressed the button that raised her to a sitting position. "Did you sneak me in a coffee?"

I checked in the direction of the door for any passing nurses and handed her the cup.

"Tall Mocha with extra whip," I whispered.

"Good girl," Stella said. "So what's brought this on?"

She sipped at her drink as I told her how I'd been up all night, at first completely disgusted as I saw how I'd been acting all my life. Then how I'd cried at all the regrets I had and time I'd wasted. And then how, at two a.m., unable to sleep and determined to change, I'd put pen to paper and made a list of all the things I was going to deal with head on and stop hiding from.

"What about your doctor friend?" she asked when I'd read my

list to her and he wasn't on it.

I told her about running into him at the video store.

"You should have seen the look of pure terror on his face as he sprinted away. Like he thought we were going to drag him out of the store and keep him handcuffed in the basement as our sex slave or something."

"Well, at least you're laughing about it," Stella said, wiping tears of laughter from her eyes as well.

"It's just funny. I finally got really aggressive about something and it just went all wrong."

"And you're not upset?"

"You know what? Part of me is but if it was meant to be, it'll work out. I have so many other things that I need to fix right now, I don't have time to deal with him."

"Well, good for you, dear."

"What are you going to do when I really toughen up? You'll miss my constant whining and asking for advice that I just ignore anyway."

She was silent and I asked the question that I'd been in denial about since I first met her.

"Stella? Are you dying?"

"Yes, sweetheart," she replied calmly.

I sat, fiddling with my empty coffee cup for a while, trying to control my tears.

"How much time do you have left?"

"Just under two weeks."

"What? That soon? But…can't they do something?"

"Maybe they can, dear, but I don't want them to."

"But-"

"Twelve more days," she said with her final tone of voice I'd heard many times before, "I've been hanging on way past my due date, dear."

"Because of me? Because you knew I still needed you?"

"Well...there's that, but I also want to see who wins American Idol before I go."

A small smile crept through the tears streaming down my face.

"It's my time, dear, don't cry," she said, "I'm not sad, why should you be? I've had a wonderful, full life."

"I'll miss you so much."

"I'll miss you too, dear. But I'll keep myself plenty busy up in Heaven. I have some ideas I want to talk to the Big Man about. So you don't worry about this old girl, she'll be just fine."

"Stella?"

"Yes, dear?"

"You don't need to worry about me either."

"I know that now, dear.

TRYING TO GIVE AN APOLOGY

Next on my list was to square things off with Nik for being such a supreme pain in the ass to him. I took him to his favorite restaurant and as soon as we were seated, started reading out my apologies for every time I'd selfishly relied on him. He interrupted when I got to 2004.

"Really, Karly, do we have to do this? I'm starving."

"Don't interrupt, Nik. This is important."

"To whom?"

"I'm trying to apologize to you here."

"Are you going to add in inviting me out for dinner and then not letting me eat?"

"Fine. Have some bread but I want to finish this before we order."

"How about this? I'll take these-" He grabbed my note cards. "And read them tonight when I'm home digesting my lobster."

"Really?"

"Yes."

"You promise?"

"Yes."

"Are you lying?"

"Yes," he said before calling the server over.

TRYING TO GET AN APOLOGY

I borrowed one of Desiree's cars and drove to the forwarding address the Ex had given me ten months ago. Dealing with him was the next thing on my list.

His new place surprised me. Maybe he'd found a new sugar mama to mooch off. It was afternoon so I tapped lightly on the door since he sometimes napped after lunch. Then I caught myself, thought about Stella, rang the doorbell six times in a row and kicked at the door with my boots. There was still no answer.

I wouldn't have put it past the bastard to be hiding from me. Cursing him, I crept around to the side of the building and peeked in through a window to see a humongous TV, fancy stereo, gaming components, large surround-sound speakers, and a wall full of DVDs and video games. How did he afford all this stuff? He even had a new leather couch. I squinted to see if he'd deformed it with his big ass yet.

Maybe I was at the wrong apartment. I peered through the dirty glass. There were dishes piled up in the sink, a box of Fruit Loops on the counter, an open container of Oreos on the kitchen table and three empty Root Beer cans on the coffee table. This was definitely his place. I rapped at the window but there was still no sign of him.

I was about to leave when I spotted cow print just under the window, on the kitchen table. It was partially buried under a pizza box but yes, there it was, my prized attaché. He had taken it, that jerk.

I couldn't think about anything else, I just wanted it back. It was less than two feet away. If not for the stupid window I could have touched it. And it was still in perfect condition. Well, okay, there was the pink stain from the strawberry shake I'd spilled on it the first week I'd gotten it, and the brown mark from when I'd bumped into that grumpy construction worker and his coffee, but it was in perfect condition by my standards. And the new, determined Karly was going to get it back.

Poking around the shrubs and tree trunks, I searched for a big rock to break the window with. Damn it. What was wrong with this place? Why were there only stupid little matching white pebbles on the ground? I picked up a handful and threw them as hard as I could against the window but they just bounced back towards me, some pranging off my head in the process. Okay, this new, determined Karly was feeling like a bit of a loser and needed to remember to stand further away when throwing things.

I stood on my tippy toes and pressed my face up against the window, looking inside longingly at my attaché. My left foot took that opportunity to get caught in a shrub and I went falling sideways. Ooff. Okay, it wasn't too bad of a fall. Probably not enough of a disaster to attract a positive Even Steven event. Although…

Was it my imagination or had the window slid a bit with my face as I'd fallen? I got up and wiped myself off. Yes, it had slid open a couple inches. What an idiot I was, trying to break through an unlatched window. I'd be a terribly inefficient thief. After I slid the window open (with my hands this time), I grabbed my attaché and hustled out of there. Woohooo! The new Karly, kickin' ass and takin' names. Or attachés. It felt good. I phoned my lawyer when I got home.

"Well Goddamn, Karly, I'd almost given up on you."

"Sam, sorry I haven't gotten back to you for so long, I was just…"

"Busy?"

"No, wimpy. Look, I was just at my Ex's and something doesn't seem right. He seems to have gotten hold of some money."

"Well, if you'd returned my calls I might have been able to explain that to you."

"I'm on my way over right now."

"Right now? But it's the end of the day. I'm about to head home."

"I'm pissed off, Sam. And I'm coming over. Right now."

"Well…Goddamn. Okay. I'll see you when you get here."

AND THE WINNER IS…

"Sorry I'm late," I said to Stella as I threw down my oversized purse on the side table and loudly dragged the heavy visitor's chair up to her bed. "Some jerk in a Hummer was taking up two parking places so I had him towed."

"You did?"

"Yup, it's on it's way to Captive Towing as we speak. I hope he has the same luck finding it that I did."

"Poor guy."

"Well I asked him nicely to move so other cars could fit in but he just lipped me off. I warned him not to cross me."

"But I thought you sold your car, dear."

"Oh I wasn't parking, I was just walking by. But it's the principle."

"The principle," she repeated.

"And I reported that masseuse to the strata for working out of her home without a license."

"Who are you?"

"Your protégé."

"You're a bit scary, dear."

"And?"

"And I like it. So what else is going on?"

I told her about the progress with my lawyer and that I was looking forward to demolishing the Ex in court, that I was three boxes away from finishing unpacking, and that next on my list was to find out what was going on with my job. Then I asked her every question I could think of about her life and family and the different places she'd travelled.

"My, this is a long visit, dear," she said after an hour and a half. The nurses had been in a couple times but hadn't enforced the visiting hours.

I took a deep breath.

"But I just…"

"I know, sweetheart. But just five more minutes then I'm going to take a little nap and you go home and finish that unpacking."

I finished my visit, gave Stella a really long hug, and held my tears in until I walked out of the hospital. Neither of us had acknowledged the ads running on her roommate's TV, announcing the finale of American Idol that night.

OPENING THE LAST BOX AND A CAN OF WORMS

How pathetic, I thought as I squeezed my arm through the little space between my bookshelf and the wall, using trial and error to try and plug in my phone recharger. I'd been such a wimp, avoiding finding out what was going on with my career. Foolishly, I'd been telling myself it was because Sam had told me to but I knew now it was just another thing I'd been hiding from. And the new and improved Karly wasn't going to do that any more.

Finally I'd unpacked my last boxes and in the process, had found my work cell phone. It was a sign. I'd also found the DVD the Ex had rented the night we broke up, a pair of sunglasses I thought I'd lost a year ago, and a big pile of papers that I put to the side to sort out when I had time.

After knocking the bookshelf over and then reassuring Larry, who'd ran over after hearing the crash, that I was okay, I plugged the phone in and looked at the call display. Shit. Nineteen missed calls from my office. I listened to the first five messages from Bryan, the office managing partner, getting progressively louder and angrier, then deleted them all and made an appointment through Darryl's secretary, saying I'd be in on Friday at four o'clock to talk about my career status.

After they fired me I planned to go out for Happy Hour with my ex-coworkers.

***

I arrived in the office and was taken into the boardroom where Bryan, Darryl and the regional managing partner all leapt up to shake my hand and exchange pleasantries. A nice assortment of pastries had been put out. It wasn't what I expected.

"So Karly, let me get right to the point," Bryan said, grinning like a wolf at it's prey. "We want you to come back to work. I apologize for any misunderstanding or for making you feel as if you had anything to worry about in terms of your career. While we don't want to pressure you, we do need an answer from you now in order to ensure we allocate our resources properly." He looked at the other men around the table and gave a slight nod as they all smiled at me.

What? Why would they want me to work for them? Even I would have fired me. I'd been looking forward to the look on the Ex's face when I told him I wouldn't be able to pay him alimony based on my future wages as a Chartered Accountant. Crap. Sam had told me not to find out anything about the future of my career. What had I been thinking? Why couldn't I have waited just one more week? I was brought back to reality by the sound of someone clearing their throat. It had been a while and I hadn't responded to Bryan's speech. He looked uncomfortable.

"Look, Karly, we admit we made some mistakes and I wish I could take back some of the messages I left you. I was very, uh, reactionary and could perhaps have dealt with things better."

I just stared at him in dismay.

"And in fact," he continued, "while looking through your personnel file, I realized that you're due for a promotion so of course, you'd come back as a manager."

What? I stared at him dismayed. Now they were promoting me? God, this was all going pear shaped. I felt lost for words as my mind raced through all the implications of this news. Even though I wanted my job back, it would have been better if I hadn't found out right now. That way I could answer that I honestly didn't know if the judge asked about my future prospects.

Bryan exchanged a hesitant look with the regional office managing partner who frowned at him and then nodded.

"We would also give you a two month signing bonus if you came back to work on Monday," Bryan added.

Damn it. Why had I come here? Now they were offering me even more money that I definitely did not want to end up sharing with the Ex. The thought of him spending even more of my money on his stupid video games pissed me off.

"Humph," I said out loud, also thinking of the new large screen TV and leather couch that he didn't deserve. The men around the table looked completely unnerved. Okay, I needed to focus. Monday wouldn't work. I had to be in court then. And I was busy on Tuesday afternoon as well.

"I can't," I said. I was about to add that I could come back on Wednesday when I noticed they were exchanging looks and nodding again. Bryan brought out a piece of paper.

"Well, Karly. You're a tougher negotiator than we gave you credit for. As you know, we have a fee share structure set up for any manager that brings in a new client so we are willing to pay you a percentage of both the SGK and Morgan Wilson profit for the first two years. Why don't you take a look at our calculations here? I'm pretty sure this will change your mind."

He slid a piece of paper covered with numbers towards me with an arrogant look that changed when he saw me looking at it like it was fresh road kill.

What was he talking about? SGK and Morgan Wilson? Why on earth should I get a fee share for them? Were they clients now? I didn't know what to say as they all looked expectantly at me. I needed time to think and didn't think a moment of silence would go over very well with this group.

"Um, I uh…need to use the ladies room."

***

I sat in the stall, confused. Surely SGK didn't want us as auditors after I'd broken into their private documents? And what on earth did Morgan Wilson have to do with anything?

"Was that Karly Masterson in the boardroom? Did she finally recover from her mono and strep throat and broken leg?" I heard a voice say. A man's voice. I peeked through the stall crack and saw Darryl and another male manager. Crap. Was I in the men's room again? They'd both unzipped and started their business in the urinals that I'd failed to notice on the way in. I crept up onto the toilet seat, crouched down and eavesdropped, curious about the ailments I'd apparently had.

Apparently Goldstein and Kramer had wanted to sell SKG and retire, especially because Smith was getting old and making a lot of mistakes. The incident where I'd broken into the highest level of security with the password "Muffy" was the straw that broke the camel's back and they were finally able to convince the third partner to sell. Morgan Wilson had just recently acquired the company and both sides were thrilled with the deal. Pat Wilson had told my company that she would give them the ongoing audit engagements, which was a huge contract, but only if I was on the job.

Holy crap, I thought as I almost lost my balance and sunk my left Size Seven pump into the toilet bowl.

"Yeah, Bryan's up the creek if he doesn't produce Karly in the next meeting with Pat," Darryl continued explaining. "He can't possibly say she's still on holidays or sick again. I think he's given her every illness in the book. The partners will do anything to have Karly back. They think she's in negotiations with one of the other firms and that they'll lose the contract to whoever hires her."

Wow. That was the best sequence of Strangeness Attracter events I'd ever pulled off. They would make a fortune. I'd do very well from it too. But there was no way I wanted to risk any of it going to the Ex. I waited until they'd left and then ran out of the office, telling the receptionist on the way,

"Can you tell Bryan I came down with a sudden relapse of strep throat and had to go but I'll phone on Wednesday."

MY DAY IN COURT

    I sat in the courtroom on Monday morning tapping my foot a mile a minute, wringing my paper napkin into shreds. Sam sat beside me, cool and collected, but actually still. I'd been worried his constant "up, down, turn around" antics would be distracting in the courtroom. So when I met him at his office to review earlier that morning, I'd insisted on picking up the coffees and may have secretly gotten him a jumbo decaf. Then, when he complained about being tired and needing another cup of java on the way over, I may have done the same thing.

    I took a deep breath. Sure, I was nervous but that was natural, and more than that, I was determined. The old Karly would have hoped the Ex wasn't going to show up. She would have done anything to avoid the confrontation. But this new and improved, tougher Karly was itching to have her day in court with him. Especially after what I'd found yesterday. I'd gotten out my beloved cow print attaché to carry in to court with me for good luck. For the first time since stealing it back, I'd opened it and found some papers that I phoned and told Sam about.

    I looked around the courtroom. My family and friends had all shown up to support me, including the friends I'd lost previously in the breakup.

    When I met with Sam three weeks ago, he'd shared all the information he'd gathered for me. We met for hours during which I got to levels of anger that I'd never reached before, that I never even knew I was capable of. It actually scared him into sitting still for a while. At one point, he asked me to go for a walk around the block to calm down. Sure, I knew the Ex was lazy but I hadn't imagined he was the conniving, cheating son of a bitch that Sam had revealed him to be. I'd been completely naïve. The Ex had just assumed that I wouldn't fight him. Well fair enough, he'd seen me putting up with so much crap that he assumed that I would bury my head in the sand as usual.

    "Most divorces are settled out of court unless they're contentious," Sam had told me during that meeting. "He'll probably try to get you to settle."

"I don't care if he offers to pay me alimony," I'd told Sam. "We're going to court. Everyone is going to see what a scumbag he is."

"Goddamn. That's what I like to hear."

***

There was a buzz and I turned around to see the Ex and his lawyer walking in. Folding my arms across my chest, I gave him my best New Karly glare. I couldn't believe I'd been afraid of him. Or romantically involved with him. He'd gained even more weight but had still stuffed himself into the blue sports jacket I'd bought him last year. In contrast, his oversized black dress pants were loose and practically falling off him save for the casual tweed belt he was wearing. His face was red, probably from the snug collared shirt he was wearing and the tie that might have been the right size and shape in the seventies. Worn runners completed the ensemble.

How had I ever found him attractive? I thought while I sighed. The sad truth was that I hadn't. I'd just been so impressed by the fact that he liked me that I had forgotten to check that I liked him back.

I finally made direct eye contact and his face registered confusion before he looked away. He halted to a stop, in shock, when he looked over and saw his friends there.

A stern-faced, elderly gentleman judge walked in, reminded Sam that he did not abide taking the name of the lord in vain in his courtroom, and we got started.

First, the judge read the affidavit from the Ex which included the names of all the men I'd allegedly cheated with. When Sam and I had reviewed the affidavit, my list of lovers had grown longer than just Nik and Bob. It contained names of men I'd never even heard of.

We started off calling Bob as a witness who told everyone that the two of us had been planning a surprise party for his wife and swore that we had never been intimate. Then we called on Nik who talked about how long we had been platonic friends for.

After a long yawn and full body stretch, Sam called three more witnesses, all high school friends of the Ex that we used to hang out with. Before Sam had contacted them, they hadn't known that the Ex had written in his affidavit that I'd slept with them. Pissed off, they'd said they'd be more than willing to come to court. They were even able to shed light on who my mystery lovers, Walker James and Theo Parker, were.

I could practically hear what the judge was thinking as every friend came forward.

After our last witness, Mr. Hasaar pointed out that there were two more men on the affidavit that were conveniently not present.

"No, they're not present," Sam agreed. "We had problems finding them. Anywhere on this earth, anyway."

Mr. Hasaar looked smug. Sam called the Ex up next.

"So," Sam said, "you have seven names here on this affidavit here that you have accused my client of cheating on you with."

"Yeah."

"And yet five of those men have just sworn that they did not sleep with my client."

"Yeah, well, I thought she slept with them."

"You did?"

"Uh-huh."

"And did you ever accuse her of sleeping with your three high school friends, other than in this written affidavit?"

"Yeah. I mean, no."

"So you never confronted her about these alleged lovers?"

"No."

"And did you ever confront these men?"

"No."

"I see. How often do you see these friends of yours?"

"Once a week. They come over and we game."

"So when did you last see them?"

"Thursday."

"And you never once thought to confront them about sleeping with your girlfriend?"

"Well, no, uh, we were busy playing Guitar Hero."

"Goddamn-Sorry your honour-So you're telling me you're divorcing my client because you believe she cheated on you with various men, including these friends of yours, but you never asked them about it because you were busy pretending to be a rock star?"

"Yeah."

"Really," Sam paused to look meaningfully around the courtroom, "Are there any other games you play with your friends?"

"Lots."

"Do you play World of Warcraft?"

"Like all the time. I'm on level 22."

"Well isn't that wonderful for you," Sam said sarcastically. "From what I've heard, you have two different Avatars you play as. Can you tell us their names?"

The Ex looked panicked.

"Do you not understand the question?" Sam asked.

"No, I mean yes, I get it."

"Then what's your answer?"

The Ex mumbled something.

"I'll need you to speak up so the rest of the court can hear you," Sam said smugly.

The Ex just looked down at his feet.

"Answer the question," snapped the judge. "We don't have all day."

"Walker James and Theo Parker."

Sam repeated him loudly, enunciating each syllable. "Aren't these the same names you had on your affidavit? Aren't these the two remaining men my client allegedly slept with?"

The Ex looked flustered and didn't answer. Mr. Hasaar looked confused and a bit anxious.

"So to clarify, these two men don't even exist. You made them up, and then falsely accused my client of sleeping with them."

"Well, yeah. But why does it matter?"

"Why does what matter?"

"Whether or not I was right about her sleeping around on me with those other guys. She said she slept with Bob so she has to pay me alimony. I lived with her over two years. Those are the rules, right?"

"In certain circumstances." Sam answered.

"She claimed me as a dependent on her tax return last year which proves that she was supporting me and now she has to keep me in the lifestyle I'm accustomed to. It's a federal offense to file a false claim, you know." He directed this last sentence threateningly towards me.

"My client didn't claim you as a dependent," Sam told him.

"Yes, she did. I saw the return."

"No, son. She hasn't filed her taxes yet."

"What?"

"Your honour, I'd like to submit a letter from Revenue Canada to my client stating that her tax return is overdue."

The Ex looked shocked and stood up yelling, "What? But she

told me she'd filed it. I checked with her!"

I smiled. Idiotically, I had claimed him as a dependent on my return. Luckily my second act of idiocy, forgetting to mail the return, had cancelled out the first. Sometimes two wrongs did make a right. When sorting through my recently unpacked pile of papers, I'd come across the unmailed return. Soon after I'd phoned and asked Sam what to do, I'd lit a celebratory bonfire in my fireplace, fuelled it with the return, and then phoned Nik with the latest development. Well, until the alarm had gone off and I'd run back to the living room and noticed the entire apartment was full of smoke. I'd opened the door trying to air the place out and set off the building alarm so the whole complex had to be evacuated. I'd never had a place with a wood burning fireplace before, how was I supposed to know what a flue was for?

"Haven't you heard of a goddamn shredder?" Sam had asked when I told him later what I'd been through trying to get rid of the evidence, "I didn't tell you to light your goddamn building on fire."

I reflected on how far I'd come since the last time I'd set off a fire alarm and smiled, listening to Sam now embarrassing the Ex.

"Yes, you checked that she'd filed the return and then broke up with her just one week later, if I'm not mistaken," Sam said. "Let's move on. Tell me, how did you afford such an expensive lawyer?"

"What?" The Ex sat down again.

"Your lawyer, Mr. Hasaar. He's one of the best in the business, present company excluded. I hear you don't have any source of income so how did you afford him?"

"I came into some cash."

"Really? Money that you could have used to help my client with the rent and bills when you were living with her?"

"No. I got it after we split up."

"From where?"

"None of your business."

"Really? I saw your name in the paper a spell ago. Seems you won a substantial amount in the lottery. How lucky was that?"

"Uh, really lucky?"

"Where did you get the ticket?"

"What do you mean?"

"Surely you remember where you bought your winning lottery ticket?"

"At the convenience store near my old apartment."

Lying bastard.

"Do you remember what the winning numbers were?"

"Winning numbers?" He looked confused. "Whatever the machine picked for me."

"Really?" Sam said. "The records show that the numbers on the winning lottery ticket were manually chosen."

"Oh yeah, I remember now."

"And how did you pick them?"

"What do you mean?"

"People usually choose numbers that have some sort of meaning to them."

"I don't remember. They were just, like, random numbers that I chose."

"So you're saying you went to the trouble of manually choosing random numbers that don't have any meaning to you?"

"Yes?"

"And you're saying that you bought this lottery ticket yourself? You didn't steal it from Miss Masterson's apartment when you were picking up some of your personal belongings?"

"That's right."

"I see." Sam's tone reeked of disbelief.

Next, Sam read group study notes from a Dr. Alexander Weiss that he'd submitted to the study sponsor detailing that I'd talked about buying a lottery ticket at a convenience store after I'd knocked over a shelf and spilled flour all over the store. Alex's notes included that I'd chosen two of the numbers from the telephone number for the hospital and my medical plan number.

Mr. Hasaar pointed out that Dr. Weiss's notes didn't prove anything. That it didn't necessarily mean that the lottery ticket I'd bought was the same one his client was being accused of taking. It didn't even prove that it was the same convenience store.

Sam called Mr. Cho up next.

The convenience store owner was thrilled to be up on the stand. I'd been worried he might have forgot me being at his store and buying the lottery ticket but he remembered everything. He told everyone how I'd come in and spilled flour all over the store. He was even able to give the exact date because I'd accidentally unplugged his freezer when I plugged in my vacuum cleaner. All the meat had gone bad overnight and smelled up the store so that he'd had to shut down for a week. His wife had finally got him to go on holiday, he added, smiling at me, so it wasn't all a lost cause.

After Sam called me, I sashayed up, wanting the Ex to get a good look at the new, bold, confident Karly. Unfortunately, my heel got caught in an invisible divot and I went tumbling down in front of the whole courtroom. Sam picked me up and helped me to the front.

I told the court how I'd lied to the Ex about having an affair with Bob, explaining that I'd done this because I didn't have the guts to initiate the break up myself. Sam had originally come up with that for me to say and I'd realized since that it was true. Next, I answered Sam's general questions showing what kind of person I was; how I'd paid for everything for the Ex for two years, believing that he was going to pay me back; that I volunteered at the hospital; and that I participated in studies that would help benefit others.

He asked me to talk about the purchase of the lottery ticket and I explained how I'd chosen the figures from six different disaster-related things in my life. Sam submitted documentation of all those numbers.

Mr. Hasaar didn't have any questions for me and the judge called a recess. Sam shot off muttering something about a "Goddamn triple espresso."

***

We assembled back in the courtroom after the break. Surprisingly, I didn't even care what the judge ruled in the end. I was just glad I was able to show everyone what a lying creep the Ex was. Even if the judge didn't believe me, I knew the rest of the courtroom did.

The Ex and his lawyer were arguing. I overheard the Ex saying that if he ended up with no money at all, he wouldn't be able to pay his legal bills.

"Your honour?" Mr. Hasaar asked.

"Yes?"

"Given the misunderstanding about the ownership of the lottery ticket, we would like to propose that it be split fifty-fifty as part of the marital assets." The judge stared at him for a moment, and then recovered.

"First your client steals the ticket from Miss Masterson and straight out lies in my courtroom about it. Then, when evidence is given to the contrary, you try to argue that it's common property that should be shared fifty-fifty? Mr. Hasaar, this is not a trial and error courtroom and I do not take kindly to you wasting all of our time."

He turned to the Ex, "As far as I can tell, this young lady supported you for two years during which you did not contribute at all financially."

"She said she was happy to pay for everything," the Ex interrupted.

"Really?" said the judge and then turned to me, "Did you say that?"

"No, your honour. He said he was going to pay me back. He even kept a ledger of the amounts he owed."

Mr. Hasaar hissed at the Ex, "What is she talking about?"

"It's nothing. Don't worry about it," he answered.

I smiled at the Ex and presented my cow print attaché, a la Vanna White, for him to see.

"No. She stole that from me!" the Ex jumped up and screamed. "I stole that from her apartment and she took it back!"

"Sit down," the judge ordered. "Are you saying that you stole from Miss Masterson?"

"No?"

The judge glared at the Ex.

"Your motion was for equitable division of the marital assets and alimony to keep you in the lifestyle in which you were accustomed. Given that you expressed your intent to pay Miss Masterson back, there will be no alimony. In fact, you owe her the amount that you have written down here, in this ledger.

"I can't pay all that," The Ex protested.

"You should have thought of that before you filed for divorce."

"Well, then, I want to unfile."

The judge rubbed his temples, looking like he had a migraine coming on.

"Unfile?"

"Yes, I want to drop the whole thing," the Ex answered.

"That's okay with me, your honour," I called out.

"Fine," the judge said and then addressed the Ex, "You will pay all the lawyer and court costs for Miss Masterson. She is also entitled to the entire lottery proceedings."

"What? But I've already spent over ten thousand dollars."

"Well, you should have thought of that before you spent money that wasn't yours. Sell what you can and find yourself a job. If you do not find gainful employment and start making payments-and I don't care if you have to take the graveyard shift as the janitor at McDonalds-I will lock you up and recommend that you be charged with theft and fraud. Do you understand?"

The Ex hung his head.

"Court dismissed."

There was a cheer in the courtroom. I thanked Sam, then accepted hugs and congratulations from my friends and family.

GOODBYE AND HELLO

As I walked through the main entrance of the seniors dance hall on Tuesday afternoon, I took in the rows of chairs, the tables of pictures, and the bouncy castle that had been set up to make a play area in the adjoining room. A clown was there making balloon animals for the kids and looking confused about how to act.

"Bouncy castle?" Nik asked.

I smiled. Stella was still very much in charge. I imagined her demanding the powers that be for this beautiful, unusually sunny December day.

After a while, a tall man with brown hair instructed us to take our seats.

"Hello?" demanded Stella's familiar voice after he hit play on a portable stereo. "Is this thing on? Adam, how do I know if it's recording? The green light? Where? Oh, okay, I found it."

"Did you want to rewind, mom?" A man's voice asked.

"No, I don't want to start over."

Me neither, I thought, smiling to myself through my tears.

"Hello everybody. I hope you're all sitting down now. Adam, you make sure you pause this if everyone isn't seated. I don't want any noise while I'm giving my speech."

Adam scrambled up to the podium to hit pause while the stragglers rushed to their seats.

"If you're listening to this, it means I've passed on. Now listen. I lived a good life. The kind of life I wanted. To my three wonderful children, I love you so much. I know I pushed you hard, but it was because I wanted you to be the best you could be. To my grandchildren,

I wish I could have been around longer to watch you grow but I already know you are amazing. To all my friends and family, don't waste your time mourning me. Instead, live your life in a way you can be proud of. Live in a way that I finally learned to, with no regrets. Adam, where did you go? How do I turn this thing off? What red button? Oh, there it-"

And that was it. The last words I would ever hear from my amazing friend.

I was fully immersed in the beauty of the event-the children playing in the bouncy castle, getting to know Stella's family, laughing with her senior's drama class, and catching up with the nurses who had come out to pay their respects. I comforted Walter who was sitting in the corner, sobbing uncontrollably about how wonderful his "Cookie" was.

It took me until the end to see Alex, standing alone, watching me. Surprised, I gave him a little smile and watched him quickly cross the room with those long legs of his until he stood in front of me. But then he didn't say anything, which threw me. I'd expected at least a simple apology if not a frantic throw-pride-out-the-door grovelling.

"So…" I finally said.

"Uh, I got a very technically-worded journal I think Nik wrote pretending to be you, explaining things, and telling me to come here today and not say anything until you had a chance to explain things."

I looked around for Nik, who waved and mouthed "good luck" on his way out the door.

"Karly?" Alex continued. "I'm so sorry. I never-"

"I know," I said and took his hand and led him out to the parking lot, "Hey, I want to tell you all about this amazing friend of mine."

"Okay. Where are we going?"

"For dinner."

He smiled, "Really? That's great."

"And after that, I'd like you to drive me home where I'm going to get very emotional watching a recording of American Idol."

"Oh. Can I stay and watch it with you?"

"No. But you can phone me tomorrow."

"I'd like that."

THE END.

about the author

Michelle Morgan was born in Vancouver, Canada. She has years of experience falling down for no reason and may have left a wrap-around skirt or two caught in a date's car door.

She currently lives in the Caribbean with her husband, Peter, and their three children, Kiara, Leilani and Kai. Oh - and a three year old goldfish named Angel, who her kids haven't noticed looks different every time they come back from visiting Nana and Grandpa in the summer.

Michelle is passionate about theatre — watching, writing for, and acting in. Although she enjoys it all, she favours comedy. She is a black belt in karate, a classical pianist, and is addicted to pilates and pad thai.

Check out Michelle's website and blog at www.mlmorgan.net.

acknowledgments

Thank you to Dianne who started this journey off by recommending I read The Artists Way, and who then thought better of it and brought me The Complete Idiot's Guide to Writing a Novel. I am also eternally grateful to Cea for her honesty and wisdom and whose own writing is truly an inspiration.

I am truly blessed to have in my life strong women from the trophy wives club who gave me support when I needed it - for my writing, acting and life. Thank you also to my various 'husbands' who encouraged me at the finish line.

Lastly and mostly, lifelong gratitude to my real husband who so truly believes that I can do anything I put my mind to, that it convinces me too.